The Girls from
On Tuesdays, They Played Mah Jongg **are back!**

Michael's Secrets

I0679136

Milton Stern

Herndon, VA

Published in the United States
STARbooks Press
PO Box 711612
Herndon VA 20171
Printed in the United States

Many thanks to graphic artist John Nail for the cover design. Mr. Nail may be reached at:
tojonail@bellsouth.net.

Other Titles
by Milton Stern

The Girls (1985)

America's Bachelor President
and the First Lady (2004)

Harriet Lane, America's First Lady
(2005)

On Tuesdays, They Played Mah Jongg
(2006)

Dedication

My life would not be complete without my sweet, toy parti-poodle, *Serena Rose Elizabeth Montgomery*, who keeps me company while I write.

To W. Maxwell Lawton, who supported me during a very rough, yet strange, time; may he rest in peace.

To Wade Brown, my editor and fellow author, for his support and constructive suggestions.

The characters and events in this book are purely fictional. None of this ever happened ... but it could have!

Chapter One

May 2005

Michael Bern looked himself over in the full-length mirror in the bedroom of his modest, three bedroom one-story, ranch-style home in Santa Monica and adjusted his tie. At six-foot-four with black hair, green eyes framed by long lashes and olive skin, he wondered if wearing a black suit with a black shirt and black tie made him look seven feet tall and "Lurch"-like. As he adjusted the white carnation in his lapel, he scanned his bedroom, which was decorated in shades of beige and green, to be sure everything was in its place and the bed clothes were wrinkle-free. Satisfied that all was in order, he walked across the hall to his office, where Aunt Clara, his sixteen-year-old pug, was sleeping in her favorite chair, and nudged her. He then picked her up and placed her gently on the floor, watching her stretch her tired, old body.

"Come on, Aunt Clara, let's go outside, so you can pee before the guests arrive," Michael said in vain as Aunt Clara had gone deaf over the last year.

She followed Michael down the hallway but was confused when he walked toward the front door instead of the kitchen, where a patio door led to the deck and back yard. Michael decided to take Aunt Clara out front in order to let the caterers finish their work. As he opened the door, Aunt Clara slowly walked outside, and Michael followed her, pulling his car keys out of his pocket. He waited as she found the perfect spot to relieve herself, then he walked over to his recently-restored, 1965 gold metallic Chevrolet Corvair 500 and sat down behind the wheel. Aunt Clara walked over to the car, excited to go for a ride as Michael hardly went anywhere without her. He reached down, picked her up and placed her on the passenger side of the bench seat and started the car.

"I'm just pulling into the garage, Aunt Clara, so don't get too excited," he told her as he eased the car into the garage. He then picked her up, exited the car and carried her back to the front yard as he pressed the button on his key chain to close the garage door.

He looked back to his house with its green shutters and light beige brick and scanned the yard to be sure it was free of debris and the hedges and other foliage was neatly trimmed. The gardener had just finished two hours before, and Michael was satisfied with his work. He then walked back into the house and made his way to his office with Aunt Clara right behind him. He was obviously looking for something in the light oak book case, and he adjusted his Emmys, Critic's Choice Awards, Golden Globes, and various other trophies and statuettes while he tried to find the one last thing he needed before the guests arrived.

He smiled as he spotted a script on the third shelf next to *The Girls*, the screenplay he finally completed only a year earlier.

"How did I possibly miss it here?" he said out loud. He took it out of the bookshelf and straightened what remained, so no one would notice anything was missing. He could have left the space open, but Michael never was one for the lived-in look, preferring his home to look picture perfect at all times.

He carried the script to his living room, which was decorated in shades of beige, yellow and green with contemporary fabrics, reflecting a casual California style the Reagans would have loved, and walked over to the oak casket that was situated in the middle of the room, where the coffee table stood before being temporarily moved to the garage to make way for the casket. He lifted the lid and looked inside.

As he stood there, one of the waiters walked into the living room and watched as Michael took the script and threw it into the casket, saying, "Good fucking riddance, you bastard!" Michael then looked at the waiter and smiled. The waiter returned a nervous grin as Michael walked toward him.

"You wouldn't happen to have a cigarette would you?" Michael asked him.

The waiter said nothing as he fished a pack from his pocket and handed it to Michael. He took a cigarette from the pack. The shocked waiter tried to light it for him, but his hands were shaking, so Michael placed his hands on the waiter's, lit the cigarette and thanked him as he once again walked out the front door with Aunt Clara close behind.

The waiter watched Michael, and once he was sure Michael was outside, he slowly walked over to the now open casket to see who was inside. He hesitantly leaned over, and what he saw was puzzling. The casket was filled with what appeared to be hundreds of scripts, and the one that Michael tossed on top had written across the front cover, "Los Angeles Live, Pilot, September 25, 1986. Michael Bern and Mark Greenberg."

Michael stood out front and smoked as he thought about what was next. For eighteen seasons, he had been the head writer of *Los Angeles Live,* a Thursday night, comedy-variety show that had won numerous awards and earned him a great living. He and Mark Greenberg wrote the pilot and worked together for the first three seasons until Mark left to produce a series of sitcoms for the network. Mark had returned at the beginning of the last season in an effort to increase the show's ratings, but it was to no avail, and *Los Angeles Live* was unceremoniously cancelled at the end of the season.

Since they never had a chance to air a farewell show, Michael decided to hold a wake for the entire cast and crew a week after the bad news was delivered.

Within an hour, the guests started to arrive, all of them stopping to greet Aunt Clara, who was a daily regular on the set, and then hugging Michael, saying how sorry they were the show was over. Many shed tears, but not Michael, who greeted everyone with a smile, enjoying their reactions as they spotted the casket in the living room.

Mark Greenberg arrived an hour into the party, and Michael smiled as he saw him across the living room, also wearing a black suit, but with a white shirt, a pink tie and carnation. At five-foot-nine with a medium build, Mark had aged more than Michael had, which Michael attributed to Mark's pursuing a career as a producer with all its headaches.

Mark walked over to Michael and after giving him a hug, said, "Michael, I did all I could; I'm sorry."

"Mark, don't worry about it; even you couldn't raise the dead," he said with the smile that had not left his face.

Mark then turned to the other guests who were gathered in the living room and asked one of the stage hands to get everyone inside from the deck. Once he was sure everyone was in the room, he turned to Michael and raised his glass, offering a toast.

"To Michael Bern, a real trouper who was there from the first day to the last. I know I speak for everyone when I tell you it was a pleasure and great fun working with you. But hey, *Birthright* is set to release in January, so you should be set for life from what I've heard around town."

Birthright was the screenplay Michael had written two years before, which had just completed filming and was now in editing, set for a January 2006 release. It was the story of twins, one black and one white, born in the South and separated at birth. It was far from the sketch comedy Michael was known for writing, but the initial and sustained reactions were positive.

"Hear, hear," everyone chimed in as they sipped their drinks. Then someone yelled from the back of the room, "Speech, speech."

Michael, never one to seek the spotlight, walked over to the casket and placed his hand on it as he smiled to the guests. He took a deep breath then said, "I don't know what to say. I wish I could say I was shocked, but I think we all saw the writing on the wall. More than anything, I worry about all you unemployed people standing in my living room, which is why I hid all the silver." A few chuckles were heard around the room. "You think I'm kidding?" Michael smiled again. "Seriously, we had a great run. Eighteen seasons are nothing to scoff at. I just wish we could have made it to twenty."

Michael then became quiet and started to cry. Most everyone in the room was shocked as they had never seen Michael show any real emotion. He never raised his voice to anyone, and no one could recall a time they ever saw him get emotional or choked up. He turned away from them, embarrassed at such a display, but he need not have been embarrassed because once he started crying, there was not a dry eye in the room.

"It's over," Michael said as he wiped his eyes with the black handkerchief he had arranged in his breast pocket. "It just hit me. I may never see many of you again."

"What's worse," Albert Hochman, another writer, said, "is that we will never be regaled with any of the stories of your mother's friends anymore." The guests laughed and nodded in agreement as Michael loved to tell of the crazy antics of Florence, Doreen, Rona, Arlene, and his mother, Hannah, to the writers when they were stumped for material. Many of the stories ended up on the show, and one recurring skit was the "The Tuesday Mah Jongg Group," which was about five menopausal Jewish women who played Mah Jongg and bickered and gossiped about everyone in town. It had become an audience favorite.

"Enough of this, tell a story," Mark yelled. "Tell us one we haven't heard before."

Michael looked over at Mark and pretended to scowl at him. Then, he took a sip of his drink and said, "OK, if you insist."

The guests applauded as they waited for Michael to begin.

"Did I ever tell you about my birth?" he asked.

The guests looked at each other, and some shook their heads no or said no out loud.

"All these years, and I never told you how I was born in a Catholic hospital on Thanksgiving Day? Well, I don't know how funny this will be, but here goes," Michael began. "Picture it, the Lower Peninsula of Virginia, home to Hampton and Newport News, Thanksgiving Day, November 22, 1962."

"Quick," someone shouted from the back of the room, "How old is he?"

"Forty-two," Michael said without hesitation. "I thought all of you knew that? Can I go on? ... Anyway ..." he began again as he told his story.

* * * * *

Florence Greenberg was standing in her kitchen in Hampton, Virginia, preparing the turkey for that afternoon's gathering. Dressed in black Capri pants and a purple turtleneck sweater, one would never guess from her four-foot-eleven-inch, ninety-seven pound frame that she was the mother of three children, twelve, ten and eight years old. Her children were in the den watching the parade with her first husband, Al Greenberg. Florence, wore her dark brown hair in a style similar to Jackie Kennedy's and was every bit as attractive as the day she was married in 1949. Known for her petite figure and large endowment, Florence never hesitated to have her picture taken in a bathing suit.

Florence had just slathered oil on her hands and was rubbing it on the turkey when the phone rang. It rang three more times before she yelled downstairs toward the den, "Would one of you pick that up?"

The ringing then stopped, followed by the familiar whine of her oldest, Sally, yelling from the den, "Mom, it's for you. It's Hannah."

Hannah Bern was Florence's best friend. They had met at a Rodef Sholom Temple Sisterhood induction of new members several years back when Hannah dropped a mini pizza in Arlene Feld's hat. Arlene, along with Rona Sapperstein and Doreen Weiner, played Mah Jongg with Florence and Hannah every Tuesday, a game they started in 1955 and rarely missed.

Florence reached for a towel to wipe the oil off her hands and got on her tiptoes to reach for the receiver from the lavender, rotary dial wall phone that hung in her kitchen. As she tried to bring the phone to her ear, she had difficulty as the cord was tangled, so she screamed into the phone from a distance of a couple of feet, "Hold on, Hannah, the goddamn cord is twisted." She held the cord as high as she could and let the receiver dangle, turn and unravel on its own. After gathering it up, she put it to her ear.

"Hannah, I thought you would be here by now, what's holding you up?" she asked with a bit of annoyance in her voice.

"I'm in labor," Hannah replied between puffs of her cigarette.

"Are you kidding? Billy Bernstein was actually right?"

Dr. Billy Bernstein, a friend of Hannah and Florence's, had begun his private OBGYN practice a few months before Hannah became pregnant. Some people in the synagogue thought it was scandalous for Hannah to go to a friend for her pelvic exams, let alone a twenty-eight-year-old doctor who was fresh out of medical school, but Hannah didn't care, which was unusual for someone who was always concerned not only with her physical appearance, but also her public persona. And, when he told Hannah in early November that the baby was due on Thanksgiving Day, she was skeptical as this was his first full-term pregnancy since beginning his private practice.

"When did the contractions begin?" Florence asked as she cradled the phone on her shoulder and reached for the salt and pepper to season the well-oiled turkey while the cord worked its way around her small frame.

"Around 6:00 am. I thought I was having indigestion," Hannah told her best friend.

Typical Hannah, Florence thought. This was her first child, and at thirty-five, she was about to join her four other friends in the wonderful world of motherhood. However, Hannah would face it alone because her husband, Adam Bern, died in August 1962, when Hannah was six months pregnant.

"How far apart are they?" Florence asked as she bent down to check to see if the oven was preheated.

"Every twenty or thirty minutes, I don't know," Hannah answered with a strange nonchalance in her voice.

Florence could hear Hannah lighting another cigarette while she talked. Doctors were just beginning to worry about the effects of smoking on pregnancy, and Dr. Bernstein never warned Hannah of the dangers. He also felt that a pregnant woman should not put on too much weight. Hannah, a constant dieter who fasted once a week, thrived on his advice and managed to only gain twenty pounds, mostly in her belly.

"I'm coming to get you," Florence said as she opened the oven door.

"I can drive myself; just meet me there," Hannah told her.

"Are you *meshugina*? I'll be there in fifteen minutes," Florence yelled as she stood up, shook her head and realized she was fully wrapped by the phone cord.

"Florence, you cannot drive me, I want to get there alive," Hannah told her.

Florence had a reputation for being a bad driver, but in her defense, she claimed all her accidents happened while going in reverse, so she rarely backed up.

Florence screamed again for Sally to come to the kitchen. Sally ambled up the stairs, sighed, and whined, "What, Mom?"

Poor Sally, Florence thought, the spitting image of Al and with his attitude, too. "Look, Hannah has gone into labor. I'm going to get her. Call Rona, Arlene and Doreen and tell them we will be at Mary Immaculate Hospital. Put the turkey in the oven in thirty minutes and baste it every hour. I will call you from the hospital," Florence ordered as she unwrapped herself from the phone cord and reached up to put it on the hook.

"Mom, why can't Shirley do it?" Sally whined again.

"Because, Sally, you're the oldest, and I depend on you. Have Shirley and Danny set the table and no fighting!" Florence told her as she walked out of the kitchen, then she yelled, "Al, I'm going to Hannah's. She's in labor." There was no answer. She didn't expect one from her husband who rarely spoke to her unless absolutely necessary.

Florence grabbed her purse and searched for her keys, reached into the closet for her purple jacket and ran to her baby blue, 1962 Valiant, courtesy of Al's Chrysler-Plymouth dealership. As she settled behind the wheel, she realized Al had driven it last, so she scooted the bench seat up as far as it would go. Even then, she could only reach the pedals with her tip toes. She started the car, adjusted the mirrors, pulled the park lever down and pushed the button for reverse. She was so happy to finally have a car with an automatic transmission as she went through clutches on a quarterly basis with her previous Plymouth station wagon and depressing the clutch with her tiptoes was never easy. She backed out the driveway quickly, taking a small hedge with her. Why Al had the landscapers plant a hedge so close to the driveway was beyond her. He should have known it would not survive a week.

Florence drove like a maniac, arriving at Hannah's house on Dresden Drive in fifteen minutes on the dot. Hannah and Adam bought the house only a month before he died, and the newly developed Ivy Farms neighborhood was still full of empty lots. It was amazing that this neighborhood was once the city dump. Arlene and William Feld were the first to buy a house on Teakwood Drive six months before Hannah moved in. All of the girls had lived in Stuart Gardens in downtown Newport News before Florence and Al were the first to move out in 1957, buying a home in Hampton that at the time seemed a like a cross-county trek whenever the girls played Mah Jongg at Florence's.

Florence pulled up in front of the house as Hannah's 1958 brown Country Squire Wagon was parked in the one-car driveway. Hannah was standing at the door, smoking a cigarette, and holding a suitcase. She was dressed in her best maternity dress – a black knit with a Peter Pan collar and pearl buttons. She was also in full make-up, false eye-lashes, Pond's "Peaches in the Snow" lipstick and all. At five-foot-ten with her black bouffant hair-do, she hardly looked pregnant as her figure, except for the bubble in front, had remained unchanged. Hannah stepped out, locked the door and made her way down the walkway to her car.

Florence took one look at her, grabbed the suitcase and said, "Vaysmir, Hannah, what the hell are you made up for? You're going to give birth, not audition!"

Hannah ignored her and proceeded to walk around the front of her station wagon, aiming her key for the driver's side door as Florence followed her.

"Hannah, I'm not driving your car. We'll go in mine," thinking that Hannah would actually let her drive her car for a change, for whenever Hannah went in Florence's car, she drove.

"Florence, I'm not letting you drive me. You can ride along. I'll drive," Hannah said as she sat down behind the wheel.

Florence would have none of it and pulled Hannah's key out of the ignition, which fortunately for Florence's short arms was left of the steering wheel in the Ford. Hannah stomped her cigarette in the ash tray and crossed her arms in front of her.

"Either get in my car, or give birth in yours," Florence said as she took the suitcase with her and walked to her own car. Florence put the suitcase in the trunk and opened the passenger-side door for Hannah, who resigned herself to riding with Florence and walked over to her Valiant. Hannah tried to get in on the passenger's side; however, the bench seat was so far up that she had no room for her legs, so she got out and settled herself into the back seat on the same side.

Florence shut the door, walked around the front of the car, got in, started the engine and pushed the button for drive, satisfied that she had won this battle. She looked at Hannah in the rear-view mirror and saw her wince in pain.

"Another one, Hannah?" she asked as she watched her friend squint and breathe heavily.

Hannah did not say anything, just waiting for the pain to subside. When it did, she reached for a cigarette in her purse and put it in her mouth just as Florence pulled out and made a speedy U-turn to head up Beech Drive, cutting off three cars in the process and throwing Hannah into the door. The cigarette didn't even fall out of her mouth.

"Florence, be careful. Pay attention, you're going to get us killed."

But, Florence was on a mission and ignored her as she sped up the street doing fifty, going through two stop signs and a red light. She leaned into the wheel as if making a getaway, and fortunately, she did manage to stop at the light at Jefferson Avenue, not wanting to risk crossing the busiest street in Newport News against a light. When she stopped, Hannah finally lit the cigarette that was dangling from her lips, all the while thinking that calling Florence was the craziest thing she could have done. At normal speeds, Florence's driving was frightening, but now it was downright insane, and Hannah could not remember the last time she actually rode in a car when Florence was behind the wheel. The light turned green, and Florence burned rubber – no small feat from the slant-six engine – as she headed down Jefferson Avenue. Once downtown, Florence pulled onto Chesapeake Avenue and looked in her review mirror, spotting a bus on the sidewalk.

"Hannah, look at that crazy bus driver. He's driving on the sidewalk," Florence said as she smiled.

"That's because you ran him off the road, Florence!" Hannah said, retaining the fearful look that was on her face during the entire trip to the hospital.

They reached their destination, Mary Immaculate Hospital at 245 Chesapeake Avenue, in an unheard of twenty minutes – and in one piece. Florence ignored the parking and lane restriction signs and pulled right up to the emergency room door. Two orderlies came out waving their arms and telling her she could not park there. Florence pushed the button for neutral, pulled up the park lever and hopped out of the car, running around the front to open the rear door for Hannah. Then, she said to the orderlies, "My friend in is in labor; get a wheel chair before she breaks her water in my new car."

Hannah stepped out of the car and said, "Too late."

As the orderlies wheeled Hannah inside, Florence got back into her car and parked it in the lot, retrieved the suitcase from the trunk and rushed in to join her friend. When Florence returned to the emergency room, she could not find Hannah and decided to take the elevator to the second floor to maternity. Once off the elevator, she looked down the hall, and she found Hannah sitting at the registration desk. Florence ran over to her just as the nun began taking down Hannah's information.

"Mrs. Bern, is your husband here?" the nun asked.

"My husband died three months ago. He was killed by a runaway golf cart."

The nun gave a look of incredulity as she raised her pen, so Florence interrupted with assurance, "That's the truth. I'm here with her."

"And, who are you?" asked the nun as she looked at Florence, who was a vision in purple.

"I'm Florence Greenberg. I am going to be the baby's godmother," she said with a smile patting Hannah on the shoulder.

Hannah started to say something, but another contraction came on, causing her to wince in pain. The nun, sensing her distress, stood up and yelled for two of the other nuns who were also nurses, to take Hannah immediately to her room. Within minutes, Hannah was in her room, and Dr. Billy Bernstein, who had arrived before Hannah, walked in to examine her. He was a youthfully handsome man with light-brown hair and a medium frame, who did not look old enough to be in college, let alone her doctor. He asked her if she wanted an epidural, and Hannah did not answer as the look on her face was enough to tell him yes.

"Oh and Sister," Dr. Bernstein said to one of the nuns, "Make sure you get all that make-up and those eye lashes off her. We cannot have that in delivery."

"You have got to be kidding me!" Hannah protested, raising her hands to protect her face. Florence just stood there shaking her head at Hannah. "Can I at least have a cigarette?" Hannah asked.

"Not here," the nun answered. "You can only smoke in the waiting room."

Dr. Bernstein lifted up Hannah's legs to check how much she had dilated and crouched down like a catcher. "You better get that make-up off quickly and get her in the delivery room as soon as you can!" he shouted to the nuns. "Hannah, you're ready," he said as he stood up.

Florence knew she would not be able to accompany Hannah, so she told her, "Good luck," and stepped out of the room just as Rona, Doreen and Arlene stepped off the elevator. The three girls spotted Florence and walked toward her.

Five-foot-nine-inch Rona was dressed in brown Capris and a brown and white striped sweater, with hair as orange as ever and styled in a reverse flip. She had pink lipstick on her large mouth, amber jewelry in her ears and around her neck and was the first to speak, "How did she get here? Who drove her?" she asked as she stood to Florence's left, looking down on her friend.

"I did," Florence answered, while looking up at Rona.

Doreen, standing as tall as Florence and on her right, wearing a peach silk shift, her then-brown hair cut in a page boy, and wearing her mink coat, looked at Florence and said with a frown, "And, she got here alive?"

"You girls. I've been driving for almost twenty years!" Florence shouted to the three of them.

Arlene, standing directly in front of Florence and whose figure at the time was more fifties buxom than sixties svelte, wearing a navy blue dress with white buttons and a matching coat and hat, said, "You call what you do driving?" As the owner of Feld's Department Store along with her husband William, Arlene was always the best dressed of the bunch. She was also the oldest.

Rona pulled out a cigarette and started to light it, and Florence, ignoring all their comments, told Rona she could only smoke in the waiting room as she broke the semicircle and made her way down the hall. The other three girls caught up with her. Walking side-by-side, the four of them, all experienced in the pain of childbirth – Florence, Rona and Doreen with three children and Arlene with two – sympathized with their friend, Hannah, who would spend Thanksgiving Day pushing another Jew into the world.

In the delivery room, Hannah looked down at the pink gown they had her wear, and shook her head, imagining how she looked with no make-up and wearing her least flattering color. She wanted the delivery to be over with as quickly as possible.

Dr. Bernstein was crouched at her feet and asked, "Hannah, you ready?"

"Yes, let's get this over with," Hannah answered.

Two nuns stood beside Hannah, holding her hands as two others were at the doctor's side.

"OK, Hannah, I can see the baby's head, so you're going to have to give me one good push," Dr. Bernstein instructed.

Hannah closed her eyes and tried to push with all her strength, but the baby would not budge. The doctor tried to reach in, but his eyes opened wide as he noticed the baby had very broad shoulders.

"Hannah, the baby has a big head and broad shoulders, so I am going to have to perform an episiotomy."

"Will it hurt?" Hannah asked.

"You'll feel a pinch," he assured her as he was handed a scalpel.

He began the incision, and his eyes opened wider. He then asked Hannah to push one more time. She closed her eyes and did as instructed, and the baby started to come out. And, it continued to come out, and continued to come out, and continued to come out.

The nuns gasped as the baby finally arrived, and Hannah was alarmed at their reaction.

"He's huge!" one of the nuns exclaimed as she put her hands up to her mask.

Dr. Bernstein's eyes were still wide open.

"And, we are going to have a *Bris*!" another of the nun's exclaimed, clapping her hands, knowing of all the good food that would be served in the hospital during that time when mothers remained for ten days after giving birth. The nuns loved a good *Bris* – and a good white fish.

Hannah was not quite sure what comment to register. "Is he all right?" she asked and then heard a loud cry like none she had ever heard before, as it sounded like a scream for help.

"It's a boy, Hannah, and a big boy at that!" Dr. Billy Bernstein exclaimed in the excitement of his first full-term delivery and his precise prediction of the baby being born on Thanksgiving Day. After Hannah expelled the placenta, the doctor sewed up the episiotomy with seventeen stitches.

"Do you want to see him?" one of the nuns asked as she swaddled the baby boy and walked toward Hannah.

"Thirty inches, eleven-point-six pounds," one of the other nuns announced to everyone in the delivery room. Gasps could be heard all over the room again. Her baby boy was brought over to her and placed on Hannah's chest. He looked at her with the greenest eyes she had ever seen and fell immediately to sleep. Hannah looked down at her first born not knowing how to react to finally holding the baby who had caused her to lose her figure, albeit temporarily, and left her with seventeen stitches.

"What will you name him?" one of the nuns asked, standing next to her with a clipboard.

"Michael ... Michael Adam Bern," Hannah answered as she looked at her son.

The nun then wrote the name down on a clipboard along with hair and eye color – black and green. Michael was then taken away from Hannah, but she didn't care. She was exhausted and just wanted a cigarette and her make-up bag.

At the *Bris*, while holding baby Michael, Florence decided she wanted another baby. On November 26, 1963, she gave birth to Scott. At Scott's *Bris*, Rona, while holding Florence's baby, decided she wanted another child, and on November 28, 1964, she gave birth to Neil. At Neil's *Bris*, Doreen, while holding Rona's baby, decided she wanted another child, and on November 5, 1965, she gave birth to Marci. At all three *Brisses* – and one baby naming, Arlene never gave a second thought to having another child.

On November 23, 1963, Michael's first birthday, President John F. Kennedy was assassinated in Dallas, and Michael's birthdays went downhill from there.

Chapter Two

Michael sat in the waiting room of his therapist Dr. Andrew Mikowsky's office, having arrived fifteen minutes early as usual. He was thumbing through a magazine when the door to the doctor's office opened and he said, "Come in, Michael."

Michael stood up, put the magazine away exactly as he found it and walked past the doctor, who closed the door behind them as Michael settled himself on the couch. He sat there with his hands clasped in his lap while Dr. Mikowsky picked up a legal pad and a pencil from his desk and sat opposite Michael in his leather chair. He was nerdy in a sexy kind of way, with dark brown hair and eyes and obvious Semitic features. He was around five-ten with a slender build and an engaging smile as well.

"So, Michael, how are you holding up since the show was cancelled?"

"I'm doing all right," Michael said. "I have the opening of *Birthright* to worry about now."

"Why are you worried?" the doctor asked.

"Well, I'm not exactly worried," Michael said. "I call Stanley King, the director, every week, and he says everything is on schedule. He also told me not to worry as the writer has little to do with the film once it's in the can and ready for release. It's the actors who have to make all the appearances to promote it. I just feel kind of weird as if I have no control over it."

"Do you need to have control?" Dr. Mikowsky asked as he wrote on the pad without taking his eyes off Michael.

"I don't know. I guess I'm used to television where I was there from beginning to end. In film, once you write the script, you pretty much fade into the background once it goes into editing," Michael said as he leaned back. "But, no need to talk about that."

"OK, what do you want to talk about?" Dr. Mikowsky asked.

Michael shook his head, "I don't know."

"Well, are you seeing anyone?"

"You know I don't date anymore," Michael said as if the answer was obvious.

The doctor put the pencil to his chin and said, "Michael, how long has it been since you had a boyfriend?"

Michael stood up and walked over to the window, looking out at Sepulveda Boulevard. He turned around and leaned back on the sill and said, "I think about six years, ever since I broke up with Philip, but we've talked about all that."

"To be honest, Michael, we never really talked about that. You avoid the subject of relationships," he said as he gave him a knowing look.

Michael returned to the couch, straightened the pillows and sat down.

"Michael, what are you afraid of? Why do you not want to date?" he asked, knowing that his patient would either change the subject or avoid the question altogether, but he always hoped for a moment when Michael would open up. After all, it took almost two months for Michael to open up when he first came to therapy exactly one year before, right after his godmother, Florence, died, which he also failed to mention in the beginning.

Michael took a deep breath, exhaled slowly and said, "Because whenever I meet anyone, I lose my identity and end up miserable."

Dr. Mikowsky was surprised that he gave a reason. He then flipped the page on his legal pad and started sketching. "Michael, I want to show you

20

something." He then held up what he had drawn – a large circle with a small circle in its center. "This is what you describe as a relationship. You are the small circle in the big circle." He then pointed to the other drawing, which was two identical circles that were intertwined like a figure eight. "This is a healthy relationship. Each partner retains his identity while maintaining a healthy balance."

Michael looked at the drawings and said, "Yes, well that's all interesting, but the guys I meet are big circles, and I'm always the little circle." He then raised an eyebrow as if there was no further discussion needed.

"Michael, it's not the guys you meet, it's the guys you prefer to date." Michael was silent. "You have probably met men who are capable of healthy relationships, but you choose not to be with them, and what we need to understand is why," Dr. Mikowsky said. "Do you have any theories as to why?"

Michael looked at the ceiling and thought for a moment. He then looked at the doctor and said, "Probably because I never saw a healthy relationship when I was growing up. How Freudian is that?"

* * * * *

It was October 1969, Michael's mother, Hannah, and her new boyfriend, Bart Shimmer, went away for the weekend and left Michael with his Grandma Rose, his late-father Adam's mother. That Monday, after school, he was given strict instructions to go home from school, put on his football uniform and return to football practice at South Morrison Elementary School. But, when he arrived home to an empty house, he did not feel well and missed his mother, so he decided to stay and wait for her to come home.

They pulled up to the house around six o'clock, and he ran out to greet them. His mother opened the passenger side door and yelled at him, "What the hell are you doing home? Why aren't you at football practice?"

"I had a stomach ache, and I missed you," he said, upset with his mother's reaction after she had not seen him for three days.

"If you're so goddamn sick, go upstairs instead of prancing out here like some queer sissy telling me you missed me. NOW!" Hannah yelled as she stepped out of the car.

Michael went back into the house and into his bedroom, closing the door. He lay there on the bed, staring at the ceiling. An hour later, he was called down to dinner by Bart.

"Do you still have a sissy stomach ache or can you eat? We got some Chinese," his mother said as she put the food on the table.

Michael sat at the table and looked at Bart. He was a tall man with brown hair and a mustache. Michael never liked him, and Bart, who was no charmer, never liked Michael, either.

"Maybe he missed football practice because he would rather be a girl," Bart said laughing, and his mother sat down laughing at Bart's remark.

Michael started to cry, and his mother slapped him.

"We will have none of that. You hear me!" she said, staring at him with her cold eyes and holding his chin. Michael shook his head yes between sobs.

They ate silently for most of the meal. When they were done, Hannah told him to look at her as she had something to tell him.

"Michael, Bart is going to live here now. We were married this weekend. He's your new father," she told him as if she were discussing the weather.

"But, I don't want a new father," he replied.

"Get out of my sight! Go to your room and think about what you just said you selfish little brat!" Hannah yelled at Michael as he left the table and returned to his bedroom for the night.

* * * * *

"Michael, what are you thinking about?" Dr. Mikowsky asked, breaking his silence.

"Oh nothing," he replied. "So, Doc, you think I choose to be in lousy relationships?"

"To be frank, Michael, yes," he replied. "We cannot be forced into a relationship. We choose whether to be in one, and I think you choose to be in relationships with distant men who use you and treat you poorly."

"How do I stop doing that?" Michael asked raising his eyebrows to the doctor.

Chapter Three

Two weeks later, Michael attended a birthday party in Beverly Hills for his good friend, Dr. Sylvia Rose. She had arranged for valet parking, and Michael always enjoyed the look on the valets' faces when he pulled up in his car. They spent most of their time parking Rolls Royces, Bentleys, and Mercedes, and the occasional Lincoln or Cadillac. He always worried they could not drive a stick shift and would always instruct them before handing over the keys.

As he pulled up to the front of Sylvia's home, one of the valets opened the car door as Michael shifted into neutral and pulled the parking lever located under the left-side of the dash of his 1965 Corvair.

"Welcome, sir, leave the keys in and the engine running, please," a rather handsome young man who looked to be in his late twenties or early thirties said to Michael. He was around six-feet tall, with dark hair, thick eyebrows, piercing dark brown eyes and full lips. Michael guessed him to be of Mediterranean descent and was positive the valet had at least a dozen headshots on his person waiting to hand them out to the first guest who looked like a producer.

He stepped out of his car and gave him a knowing look, wondering when he would be done for the night, but as he figured the valet was around ten years younger than he, Michael toned down his usual flirtiness. The valet handed Michael a ticket stub and sat down behind the wheel, closing the door with the window still rolled down. He eyed the floor shift and the dash and gave the usual look of confusion Michael encountered with young valets, as no shift pattern was etched on the knob.

"Do you know how to drive a stick shift?" Michael asked as he leaned on the door frame and smiled, bringing on the charm after all, as if the valet were a potential trick he met at a bar.

"Yes, sir," the valet said nervously as he put his hand on the gear shift.

"It's a three-speed," Michael said as he pointed to the valet's hand on the knob. "First is down and to the left, where second is found on a four-speed. Reverse is up from first. Second is up on the right, and third is down from second, lower right. Be careful, I don't know how many valets have gone backwards in my car thinking they were in first gear or took an hour to retrieve it unable to find reverse in the first place."

The valet still looked confused, so Michael walked around to the passenger side, opened the door, and sat down next to him on the bench seat. He told the valet to depress the clutch, and Michael put his left hand on the valet's right hand to guide him as he showed the valet the H-pattern of a three-speed, floor shift. "Here is first, then second, then third, and over here is reverse," Michael said as he guided the gear-shift through the shift pattern. Michael couldn't imagine him trying to drive a three on the tree, which was how he learned to drive a stick when he first came to Hollywood and dated a man with an old Ford truck. The valet's hand was sweating, but Michael was sure he would get it. Michael removed his hand from the valet's, once he mastered the pattern.

"The key is in the dash," Michael said pointing to the ignition. "And, the parking brake is over there under the left side of the dash – that large, black, curved and tubular handle. Just squeeze it and push it back to release it, and pull it when you park," Michael said with a wink. The valet smiled at Michael with a perfect set of gleaming white teeth. "Oh, and when you start it, give it some gas. This car has two carburetors instead of fuel injection, and the transmission is not fully synchronized."

"Synchronized?" the valet asked.

"You have to be at a complete stop to shift into first, or you'll grind the gears," Michael said as if it were obvious, while he opened the passenger side door.

"Are you an actor or something?" the valet asked before Michael stepped out of the car.

He walked around the front of the car and over to the driver's side window, looked right at him and said, "I'm not an actor, and frankly, I'm not sure I'm something anymore."

"Well, if you don't mind my saying so, you should be because you are really good looking," the valet said as he released the parking break and smiled seductively at Michael.

Michael smiled at him and said, "You, too, but I think I'm old enough to be your father, and so is my car."

"Sam!" Michael heard someone yell behind him, "Quit bugging the guests and park that damn car."

"OK, Sam, I don't want you to get fired, so go park my car and maybe I'll see you when I leave," he said with a wave.

He waved at Michael and struggled with the unsynchronized clutch before lurching down the driveway to park his precious car. Michael turned around to walk into the house, and Sam's boss nodded to him.

"Be nice to Sam," he said. "With his looks and charm, some day, you'll be parking cars at his party." The boss huffed, and Michael thought about what Sam said about being an actor or something. With his looks, Michael often got that reaction when he said he had no desire to be in front of the camera.

* * * * *

Every year, the Rodef Sholom Sisterhood put on an annual fundraiser called "Cabaret," which was a variety show performed by synagogue members, followed by a dance and a midnight breakfast buffet. In 1980, Michael was helping with the lights, and Arlene was performing in the show with his mother, Rona, Doreen and Florence in a medley of songs about New York. They wore tuxedo tops, with large white ruffle shirts and black leotards, a la, Judy Garland in *Summer Stock*, one of Michael's favorite movies.

During one of the rehearsals, Arlene sat next to him. He liked Arlene as she looked like a heavy Lucille Ball, and she, like his mother's other friends, was always nice to Michael. She had also known both his grandmothers very well. Grandma Rose ran the men's department at Feld's Department Store for almost twenty years. When Arlene and William were first married, they lived above Michael's maternal grandmother, Nana Mary, in Stuart Gardens.

"Michael, how would you like to do a number with me?" she asked.

"Oh, I don't know, Aunt Arlene," Michael said, knowing what his mother's reaction would be.

"It'll be fun. They want me to do that 'Cuban Pete and Sally Sweet' number from *I Love Lucy*. You would be a great Ricky," she insisted. "They want Shlomo Katzenheiman to do it with me, but he's such a dry fart."

Michael laughed at her assessment of Shlomo, a nebishy accountant whom Doreen always referred to as 'Katzenfartsenheimen.'"

Doreen joined them, kissed Michael on the cheek and said, "Hi, Mr. Perfect."

"Hi, Mrs. Wonderful," he replied back.

"Doreen, tell Michael he should be in the number with me," Arlene insisted.

"I think that'd be great!" Doreen replied. "You should do it instead of Katzenfartsenheimen."

Rona then walked over, never wanting to miss a thing, and sat down in front of them lighting a More cigarette. "What's the big secret?" she asked as her bright pink lipstick coated the cigarette.

"Arlene is trying to convince Michael to be in the number with her instead of Katzenfartsenheimen," Doreen told her.

Michael knew he had to get out of this, and he could see his mother eyeing them as she was always nervous when Michael talked to her friends. She walked over with the usual frown on her face.

"What are you three girls up to?" Hannah asked.

"We're trying to talk Michael into doing that number with Arlene," Rona told her between drags of her cigarette.

"No," Hannah said.

"Oh, Hannah, let him do it. He'll be great," Doreen said.

"No," his mother said again.

"Hannah, why?" Arlene asked.

"I don't want him flitting on stage like some queer. He's too young to be in the 'Cabaret,' and my decision is final," Hannah answered.

"Too young?" Rona asked. "He's almost eighteen. Untie the apron stings, Hannah."

That remark really pissed his mother off, and everyone could see that on Hannah's face.

"Rona, I would appreciate it if you would mind your own business. Michael, I want to talk to you," his mother said as she walked away from the girls.

Michael got up and followed her, passing his godmother, Florence, who gave him a knowing look. Florence walked over to the other girls, and Michael could see they were whispering.

When Michael and Hannah were far enough away that they could not be heard, his mother said, "Michael, how dare you embarrass me in front of my friends."

"What are you talking about?" he asked.

"You know I don't want you on stage. I don't like that. Do you want people to think you're queer?"

"Arlene asked me," Michael said. "I never volunteered."

"I don't give a shit who asked you. You're not to be in the show. Is that understood?" He didn't answer as he looked at the floor. "Michael, did you hear me? You're not to be in the show!"

"Fine, I won't be in the show. I wouldn't want to embarrass you," he answered as he looked up at her and walked away.

* * * * *

Michael walked toward the front door to Sylvia's home, satisfied that if he didn't meet anyone there, he at least had a chance with the kid who was probably stripping the gears in his car. As he walked into the house, he also wondered if Sam was taking his car for a joy ride. If not, Michael would offer to take him for one after the party, if he was still in the mood.

The living room was crowded, and most of the guests at the party were over seventy, but Michael was perfectly comfortable in this setting having grown up an only child and a loner around his mother and her friends. Old Jewish women were his favorite people, and Michael often acted like one himself. There were a few A-list celebrities there and many of Dr. Sylvia Rose's colleagues from her days as Hollywood's leading psychiatrist, specializing in stage fright and panic attacks. Of the few people there who was Michael's age was Dr. Mikowsky, who was dressed in a blue suit with a blue oxford shirt and yellow tie. He was sexy in his own intellectual way, and after all this time Michael still had not met his partner, Brian, the attorney, who did not seem to appear in public with Andrew. Sylvia recommended him to Michael when he had sought out therapy a year earlier.

Sylvia looked elegant as usual. Still standing tall at six feet, with her gray hair perfectly coiffed, her large white framed glasses with the pink lenses, bright red lipstick and the endless Benson and Hedges dangling from her mouth, she was wearing a knee-length black sequined dress and her signature black stilettos.

"I hear your show has been cancelled, Michael," Sylvia said in her smoky voice as she walked up to him. "Chin up. You have a great future ahead of you. It's about time you did something other than write for television."

"Sylvia, this is your night. I'm just here to have a good time," Michael said as he kissed her on the cheek and handed her a present.

"Of course, darling. How often does one get to be eighty-five? I'm just beginning to live," she said as she kissed Michael, leaving a lip-print he knew would last a day or two.

He mingled around and talked to Stanley King. Michael had been calling him weekly, but promised to stop as Stanley assured him everything was right on schedule and reminded him again that the writer has nothing to worry about once filming has wrapped. As a matter of fact, they had not seen each other since filming ended in North Carolina the previous spring.

Michael also talked with a couple of older actors he had admired for years and always wanted the opportunity to write for, knowing that roles for them were almost nonexistent, and with each passing day, his chances at writing their lines were dimming.

At around eleven, they wheeled out an enormous cake from the kitchen. All of the guests were stunned not only by its size, but also the fact that there were actually eighty-five candles on it!

"I think they should dial nine-one," Michael said to Dr. Mikowsky, who had walked up to him. "Then once she blows out the candles, dial one." They laughed as they watched Sylvia. She snuffed out her cigarette in one of the many ash trays in the room and walked over to look at the cake.

"Oh my God!" Sylvia shouted. "How the fuck am I supposed to blow out all these candles?"

"Pretend it's a cigarette," someone shouted from the back, while the guests laughed and clapped.

Sylvia took in a deep breath, and with one try, she blew out every candle. She then looked up and smiled, while everyone applauded and began singing *Happy Birthday*. Michael smiled at her, and as she looked back at him and smiled, she brought her right hand up to her chest, rolled her eyes up and paused.

Sylvia then fell face first into the cake.

Everyone stopped singing. An older man, whom Michael knew to be a doctor, rushed over to her, pulled her off the cake and with the help of a couple of the waiters, who had just wheeled out the cake, placed her on the floor. Her face was still covered in frosting. After what seemed an eternity, but was only a couple of minutes, the doctor stood up and shouted, "Sylvia's dead."

What a way to go, Michael thought. *There goes my Wednesday night Mah Jongg game.*

Guests were crying, and a few of the more crass celebrities grabbed their gifts from the table in the foyer and left. After the hysteria died down, Sylvia's body was taken away, and most of the remaining guests had already left, not wanting to be there when the paparazzi arrived.

Michael was among the last to leave, and as he walked out, he noticed Sam was the only remaining valet. Michael handed him the ticket stub, not laying on the charm as he did when he arrived. Within a minute,

Michael could hear Sam destroying his clutch before delivering the car. Michael tipped him $100, making Sam's eyes light up as he thanked Michael profusely.

"Use that for driving lessons," Michael said, retaining a bit of his humor in light of his dear friend's death. Sam unfolded the $100 bill, and Michael's card dropped to the ground as he shut the car door. Sam was clearly embarrassed as he picked up the card, and Michael said to him before shifting into first and driving off, "If you want to make it in Hollywood, kid, you'll need to be a lot smoother than that."

Michael drove home, and after parking in his driveway, he checked the glove compartment, and as expected, he found Sam's headshot with his resume printed on the back. Some things in this town never change. *Poor kid probably thought I was an agent or a producer*, Michael thought.

He entered his house, but he did not see Aunt Clara sleeping by the front door as she often did on the rare occasion he left the house without her.

"Aunt Clara," he shouted, knowing she couldn't hear him. "Aunt Clara."

Michael walked into his study and found Aunt Clara sleeping in her favorite chair. It had been a while since she had been able to jump up on the chair by herself. Michael thought she must have really been determined. He also noticed she wasn't snoring as usual. Michael nudged her, but there was no response. "Aunt Clara, wake up." She didn't move. Michael leaned in to see if she was breathing.

Aunt Clara was dead.

Although it was after midnight, Michael went into the garage and grabbed a shovel and an empty box. He dug a grave in the back yard for Aunt Clara and buried her with her favorite stuffed rabbit and her blanket. After he covered the grave, Michael mumbled *Kaddish* to himself and sat down next to her eternal resting place.

He walked back into the house, reached into the cabinet above the refrigerator for his emergency pack of cigarettes, and returned to where he had just buried Aunt Clara and sat on the grass. He pulled a cigarette out of the pack, lit it and took a drag while he began to sob hysterically. He must have cried for over an hour. He sat beside Aunt Clara's grave until sunrise, when he slowly walked back into the house and sat at the kitchen table just as the phone rang.

"Who's calling me at 7:00 am?" he said rather than hello.

"Michael, it's Sharon. Oh, I forgot about the time change." Sharon Gorman worked as a writer on *Los Angeles Live* during the first two seasons. She and Michael hit it off immediately and had stayed in touch even after Sharon moved back to Washington, D.C., to write fiction. Her books had sold well, and she enjoyed her life in the nation's capital away from all the Hollywood bullshit.

"Hey, Sharon, how are you?" Michael said with no emotion.

"More importantly, how are you? I read about the show being cancelled," Sharon said.

Michael lit another cigarette, not caring about smoking inside. "Yeah, yesterday was a tough day, too. Dr. Sylvia Rose and Aunt Clara died."

"Oh my God! Michael, I'm so sorry. Were they in an accident?" she asked with alarm.

"Who?" he asked confused at her question.

"Sylvia and Aunt Clara?" She asked. "Were they in an accident?"

"No no. Sylvia died during her eighty-fifth birthday party. She blew out the candles, had a heart attack and fell face first into her cake," he told her.

Sharon started to laugh.

"It's not funny, Sharon," he said with annoyance.

"Michael, you of all people should see the humor in this," she said with a giggle.

Michael smiled and chuckled a bit as he thought about Sylvia's face covered in frosting for the *Chevra Kadisha* to clean up when preparing her body for burial.

"What happened to Aunt Clara?" Sharon asked.

"I came home and found her in her favorite chair, dead. I buried her in the back yard," he answered as tears streamed down his face again.

"How old was she?"

"She was sixteen. She led a good life. What a month. Show cancelled, good friend dead, dog dead."

"Well, they say things happen in threes," she said almost optimistically.

"Good, then that means you don't have bad news," he said, hoping for the best as he puffed on the cigarette.

"Actually, I do have some news."

"Sharon, please, I cannot take any more news," he pleaded.

"No. I have good news," Sharon assured him. "I just sold the movie rights to my latest book, and I had my lawyer put it in the contract that I get to pick my co-writer for the screenplay. Isn't that exciting?"

"Sharon, that is great news!" Michael said excited at her success and hearing something good for a change.

"But, here's the best part," she began. "I picked you!"

"What?" he asked, startled.

"That's right. I picked you. I think the producer already called your agent. That *alta cocker* is still your agent, right?" she asked.

"You mean Sid?" he asked. "Of course he is. But, Sharon, do you really want to move back to Hollywood?"

"Don't be silly," Sharon said sounding too giddy for a fifty-year-old. "You, my dear, are moving to D.C."

"I am? What makes you think I'm moving to D.C.?" he said in protest.

"Michael, what've you got holding you there? It will only be for a year. You can rent your house, and live here while we work together. The book takes place in D.C., so they will most probably do most of the filming here, also," she said, obviously with her mind made up.

"I see you have it all figured out," he said as he lit another cigarette.

"I do. My friend, Eric Sagman, has an apartment in the Mount Pleasant neighborhood near the zoo that he can sublet to you for up to a year while he goes on assignment in Brazil. It'll be fun. Didn't you spend your summers in D.C. with your grandmother?" she asked, with the excitement never leaving her voice.

"You don't forget anything, do you, Sharon? But D.C.? I don't know," he said, still doubting if he wanted to schlep cross-country to work on a screenplay.

"Michael, give it some thought. You don't have to be here until next week. It'll be fun!" she said.

"OK, Sharon, I'll think about," Michael said. "Next week?"

"And, Michael, I'm really sorry about Aunt Clara. I know how much she meant to you. Talk to you later, bye," and she hung up.

"Goodbye," Michael said, wondering if she heard him and hung up the phone.

Michael decided to take a shower as he was still wearing the clothes from last night. He stripped down, revealing a body sculpted from years of working out, even with the paunch he was carrying at the time due to his love of sweets, but with the television season just ending, it would allow him to finally resume a normal workout schedule. He stepped into the shower, and the hot water felt good, and he lingered for quite a while as he thought about moving to D.C. for a year. He stepped out of the shower, dried off and put on some shorts and nothing else.

As he sat down at his desk, he noticed Sam's headshot sitting there where he had left it when he found Aunt Clara just a few hours earlier. Michael thought Sam certainly took a great picture with his dark features, and he was certain Sam was Mediterranean. He turned the picture over to scan his resume. Sam Jacobs was thirty years old. *Sam Jacobs?* he thought. *He's Jewish – good looking and Jewish.* Fifty years ago, he would have had to change his name. Michael decided he would advise him to remove his age from his resume though. Sam had been the "man on the street" in this drama, "man in Pathmark" in that drama and various men in the crowd on other low-rated cable shows. He had graduated from the University of Alabama and grew up in Mobile. Michael thought Sam must have worked hard to get rid of his Southern accent as he had himself, although Michael had been told that when he chanted in Hebrew at synagogue he had a Southern accent. He wondered if Sam did. He thought about calling Sam's number, but he had been through too much in the previous twenty-four hours to be much fun. He called Sid instead, knowing he would be in his office this early on a Monday morning, working the phones and finding work for his cadre of writers and the few actors he still represented.

"This is Sid," he said, answering his own phone. He respected Sid because he wasn't pretentious and was very old school in his work ethic. He always answered his own phone and worked as hard as he did when he started as an agent half a century earlier even though he was now in his eighties.

"Sid, it's Michael."

"Michael, I was going to call you," he said excitedly.

"Did Sharon Gorman's producer call you?" Michael asked.

"Yesterday, but I was going to ask what all the commotion was at Sylvia's last night. I arrived late to the party, and they wouldn't let anyone up the driveway. What happened?"

Michael was surprised as Sid knew everything that was going on in town.

"You don't know?" Michael asked. "Sylvia blew out the candles on her cake, had a heart attack, fell face first into the frosting, and died."

"That was what I heard, but I thought it was a joke," he said. "Leave it to that old broad to go out with a bang, or shall I say a splat," he said laughing.

"It's true, Sid," Michael said annoyed at another odd reaction to Sylvia's death.

"I dated her in the fifties; did I ever tell you that?" Sid asked.

"No."

"Michael, between you and me, and never tell my wife this, but Sylvia was the best lay I ever had," Sid said, and Michael could picture him smiling on the other end.

"Thanks for sharing, Sid," he said while shaking his head.

"Michael, I'm sorry to hear about Aunt Clara. I know how attached you were to that dog," he said.

"Thanks, Sid," Michael said confused that Sid did not know about Sylvia but heard about Aunt Clara. "How the hell did you hear about my dog?"

"Helen Epstein told me," he said. Helen Epstein was Michael's next door neighbor. She was at least a hundred and nosy as the day she was born. She had been a silent film actress, acted in a few talkies and then became somewhat of a big wig at RKO before retiring.

"How the hell did Helen know?" Michael asked, knowing the answer.

"She saw you burying a box late last night and figured it must be your dog. She may be older than God, but she still has her wits," Sid said.

Helen actually called Michael's agent to tell him his dog died; how strange.

"Santa Monica really is a small town. Why did Helen call you?" Michael asked.

"Helen calls me every morning to find out the latest gossip in town," he replied.

"Sid, should I go to D.C. and help Sharon out with this screenplay? What's in it for me?" Michael asked.

"They made an offer I think you should take," Sid said, getting back to business.

"How much?" Michael asked.

"Well, it isn't as much as I would have wanted, but they are offering a piece of the profits," he said, not quite answering Michael's question.

Michael was good with money, having saved quite a bit over the years from his salary on *Los Angeles Live* and living modestly in a town filled with excess. He earned $400,000 for *Birthright* plus a good-sized portion of the profits, but this was Sharon's book, so he didn't expect the same kind of deal.

"How much, Sid?" Michael asked again.

"Keep in mind, Michael, that I can get you three percent of the film, so don't be disappointed," Sid said, still avoiding the answer.

Michael was getting frustrated. "Sid, answer my question. How much?"

"$150,000," he said with no emotion.

"Are you serious?" Michael asked with disappointment. "After taxes, I will be lucky to take home $70,000. For one year's work, that's crazy."

"Michael, take it. It'll keep your name in the spotlight and your head above water, while I get you some more work. If *Birthright* is as good as they say it will be, after it's released you won't need to look for work again as long as you live," Sid said trying to reassure him.

Michael couldn't believe it. He made over $75,000 an episode on *Los Angeles Live*. This was an insult. "Sid, forget it," he said.

"Michael, look. You're a television comedy writer with one screenplay under your belt. And, keep in mind, *Birthright* won't be released until next year. Once it's a success, then you can demand anything you want, but until you have proven yourself in film, you can't make big demands."

Big demands? Michael thought. Michael never made demands. His contracts stated his salary and a portion of the profits. He never asked for green M&Ms, special cheeses and only certain brands of bottled water. *What demands?* Michael just wanted to be paid what he was worth – for a change. "Get me $250,000 and four percent of the movie, and I'll think about it," he said as flatly as possible.

"Let me make a couple of calls, Michael, will you be home today?" he asked, as if expecting Michael would refuse the initial offer.

"Yes, or you can reach me on my cell. Bye, Sid." Michael said as he hung up. Move to Washington for $150,000, Michael was not that desperate.

Michael puttered around checking e-mails and doing laundry and realized he was at a loss for a routine without Aunt Clara around. At around ten, there was a knock on his front door. He looked through the window and saw it was Helen Epstein. He opened the door and invited her in, but she said she only had a minute. At close to a one-hundred, she was still in good shape. Her few strands of white hair were teased, and she wore pearls in her ears and a white sweater and slacks. Michael always marveled at her lipstick as it was drawn to mimic what must have been her lip-line fifty years ago into a bow-tie shape like many of the MGM actresses during the golden age of film. She didn't wear glasses and still drove her Lincoln all over town.

"Michael, I'm so sorry about Aunt Clara," Helen said as she took his hand. "If you need a companion, Hecuba just gave birth to a litter of kittens."

Michael thought it was so cliché, an old woman in a house full of cats. "Thank you so much, Helen, but I'm allergic to cats. I do appreciate it, though, but I'm not ready for another pet as it has not even been twenty-four hours," he told her.

She held his hand for a few seconds then said goodbye.

After he closed the door, the phone rang. It was Sid. "OK, Michael, this is what they are willing to do," he began.

"Go ahead," Michael said, knowing he worked his magic.

"$220,000 and three percent," Sid said. Michael didn't want to appear happy, so he took a quiet breath and paused for a minute. "Michael, I can't get any more," Sid said.

"OK, Sid, I guess that'll have to do. Tell them yes. But, Sid, I'm not happy about this," Michael said, trying to sound as diva-like as possible, but he knew that Sid knew him better than anyone.

"Whatever you say, Michael. I'll have them send the contracts to you this afternoon, and you can bring them by later," Sid said with relief in his voice. Michael had yet to turn down a deal Sid had secured and figured this was not the time to start.

"Sid, since I'm doing this, I need a favor from you," Michael said.

"Anything, kid, you're my best client," he assured him.

"There's this actor I met. He's good looking, and, Sid, I think you can find him some work. His name is

Sam Jacobs. I'll drop off his headshot and resume at your office this afternoon with the signed contracts. Do a favor for a member of the tribe," Michael said.

"First, we'll need to change his name," Sid said. "And second, did you fuck him and owe him a favor?"

"It's 2005, you don't need to change his name, and no, Sid, I didn't fuck him," Michael told him. "He parked my car last night. But if you find him some work, I'll fuck him and film it for you."

"Nothing would make me happier, Michael," Sid said as he hung up. He knew Sid needed a young actor to represent as Michael was the youngest client Sid had left.

Later that afternoon, after the courier dropped off the contracts, Michael ran some errands and delivered the signed documents with Sam's picture and resume. Sid liked the kid's looks and promised to give him a call. One thing Michael knew about Sid was that if he said he was going to do something, he did it. Michael also knew that if this kid had a brain, he would sign Sid on as his agent. Upon returning home, Michael's cell phone rang with a number he did not recognize.

"Hello."

"Mr. Bern?"

"Yes, this is Michael Bern."

"This is Sam. Remember, the valet from last night?"

"Oh yeah. Listen, you owe me a clutch," Michael said jokingly.

"No, I'm so sorry. What does it cost? I'll pay for it," Sam said as he started to panic.

"Calm down, kid, I was kidding."

"Oh," he replied.

"What's up?" Michael asked.

"Mr. Bern, I was wondering if maybe, oh … if you would … are you available to have dinner some time to discuss my career?" Sam stammered.

"I'll tell you what, Sam," Michael began, wondering if he should tell him he gave his information to Sid, "I'm leaving for Washington in a couple of weeks to work for a year. So, I'm going to be pretty busy the next few days, how about we get together, oh I don't know … tonight?" Michael thought that would confuse him.

"You're busy, but you want to get together tonight?" he asked.

"Yes, no time like the present. See if I don't see you tonight, I may never get to sit down with you to discuss your career. But, Sam, I have to ask you a question?" Michael asked.

"Sure, Mr. Bern," he said.

"Do you know what I do for a living?"

"Yeah, you're a writer. It said so on your card, and I read about you in the trades," Sam said almost proudly.

"OK, because I don't know much about getting a break for an actor. But let's see what we can come up with," Michael said.

"Where should we meet?" Sam asked.

"Meet me at Anna's Italian on Pico at eight. Do you know where that is?" Michael asked.

"I do, I almost got a job there," he said.

"Well, I worked there when I first moved here in 1985. I'll see you at eight," Michael said.

"Oh, Mr. Bern?" Sam asked.

"Yes, and will you please call mc Michael?" he said.

"Yes, Michael, did you get my headshot? I left it in your glove compartment."

"Sam, you shouldn't leave those in glove compartments. You don't know what kind of weirdo you'll meet in Hollywood. See you at eight," Michael said before hanging up.

Michael then took a six-hour nap when he realized he had not slept since the day before.

He arrived at Anna's Italian a few minutes before eight, wearing black slacks and a gray shirt, and he saw that Sam was already seated at a table waiting for him. He was more handsome than the night before, wearing a yellow shirt and jeans that hugged his slim but muscular frame quite well. Michael was impressed when Sam stood up to shake his hand, and he had a good grip.

Sonia, the two-hundred pound head waitress who moved faster than anyone on the floor, walked over to their table to take a drink order. Michael ordered a bottle of Chianti, knowing he would hardly finish a glass, just to see if Sam was a lush or a light weight, though Sam didn't argue about getting a bottle of wine for the two of them.

The wine arrived, and Sonia poured each a glass before taking their order. They both ordered the manicotti with a side order of garlic bread and decided to split a Caesar salad.

He likes the same foods as I. He's handsome, well-mannered and Jewish. He even has good table manners and chews with his mouth closed. If only he were ten years older, Michael thought to himself. "So, you wanted to talk about your career," Michael said.

Sam swallowed a bite full of salad before speaking. "Yes, I gave myself five years, and my time here is almost up before I go back to Mobile. I've only managed to get roles as an extra. I can't even find an agent."

"To get an agent, you need an acting job, and to get an acting job, you need an agent," Michael said, echoing the old saying about breaking into show business.

"I did get a call today from a Sid Goldman, but he sounds like an old guy, and I don't know how he got my name," Sam said.

"Really, Sid Goldman called you?" Michael asked trying to sound surprised.

"You know him?" Sam asked before taking another bite of his salad.

"Of course I know Sid," he said as he poked his fork at his plate. "He may be an old guy, but don't knock someone because of his age. He's the best in the business, and believe me, if that *alta cocker* wants you as a client, you'll be working in no time."

"So, I should go see him?" Sam asked.

"Sam, how long have you been here? Five years? You're parking cars and the man in the crowd here and the man in Pathmark there. How many agents have called you?" he asked as he put a bite of salad in his mouth.

"You read my resume?" Sam asked as he took a sip of Chianti.

"I had to before I handed it to Sid," Michael said, and Sam choked on the wine, bringing the napkin to his lips. "I'm sorry, did I say something to upset you?"

"You gave my resume to an agent?" Sam asked with surprise and a little excitement as he wiped his mouth and caught his breath.

"Isn't that why you left it in my glove compartment?" he asked as he took another bite of salad.

"Well, to tell the truth ..." Sam started to say.

"You wanted me to fuck you," Michael finished his sentence, taking another bite of his salad. He was enjoying the part of the suave older man making this kid nervous – a part he rarely, if ever, played. Maybe, he should have considered a career in acting.

Sam blushed at Michael's comment, and Michael smiled at him, putting his fork down and resting his hands on the table. "Listen, Sam. I'm really a nice guy, and you're a good looking guy and well-mannered from what I can see. I thought you were cute last night as I showed you how to drive my car, and I looked in the glove compartment right after I arrived home, knowing you would leave a headshot in there. Do you know how many headshots I've collected from valets over the last twenty years?"

"Probably hundreds," Sam said a little embarrassed.

Michael looked into his deep brown eyes and said, "Including yours, three."

Sam put down his fork and with surprise said, "Three?"

"Yeah, three," he answered. "People in this town know my name, but very few know what I look like. It's been to my advantage in that I get invited to some of the most exclusive parties, yet I can go shopping at Kroger's without anyone bothering me. That's why I like being a writer. Nobody notices me."

"But you're so hot! Don't they figure you are an actor or some Hollywood big shot?" Sam asked.

"Thank you, but I never considered myself hot. But, no, headshots are expensive, and most wannabes don't give them to someone unless they're sure it will get their foot in the door," Michael said as he resumed eating his salad.

Sam picked up his fork again and asked, "What happened with the other two who left them in your glove compartment?"

"I fucked them," Michael said without hesitation or looking up from his plate. This time Sam didn't choke. "But, if you're wondering if I gave them to my agent, I didn't."

Sam stopped eating and looked at Michael. "Why did you make the exception with me?"

"Because, Sam, there's something different about you. You see, making it in this business as an actor has little to do with talent. It's all about presence, appeal and charm. I think you have a natural charm about you, and if I'm right, Sid will see that, too." Sam blushed again as Michael continued, "And, you have a youthful quality, especially when you blush. I thought you were in your twenties until I read your resume. I couldn't believe you were thirty."

Sam finished his salad, put down his fork, and said, "I have to tell you something."

"What, Sam?"

"I'm not thirty," he said, setting off alarms in Michael's head, who wondered if he was sitting there with a seventeen-year-old.

"How old are you?" Michael asked with a frown.

"I'm thirty-five," Sam said. "I figured if I chopped off five years, it would increase my chances since I decided to try to be an actor late in life. I was a school teacher for seven years before I quit to move out here." Michael sighed with relief as Sam continued. "You're not upset that I lied about my age, are you?"

"Not at all," Michael said. "I was afraid you were going to tell me you were seventeen." He laughed, and so did Sam. "How old do you think I am?" Michael asked.

"Well, that's not fair because I know you have been here for twenty years. But, last night I thought you were in your early thirties."

"Good save," Michael said as Sonia removed their salad plates and brought the manicottis.

"Promise me you'll go see Sid," Michael said as they dug into their dishes. "I don't want to look like a fool."

"I will, I will," he said.

Michael really liked Sam, who like him, only drank a half a glass of wine. Michael told Sonia to take the rest of the bottle home with her, and after eating dinner with him, something told him Sam would make it big in this business if he got the right break. The rest of the evening was pleasant, and after dinner, Michael invited Sam back to his house.

They sat on the deck talking, and Sam asked, "Do you have a boyfriend?"

"No. I'm not boyfriend material. The guys I end up with are usually self-centered assholes who end up using me and discarding me when I've outlived my shelf life," he explained.

"Wow, I thought I was the only one who ended up in relationships like that."

Michael looked at him for a moment. They were very much alike, or at least he was like Michael ten years ago. He wanted to make a move, but he really liked Sam, so he didn't want him just to be a trick. As Michael pondered what path to take, Sam got up from his chair came over to Michael, leaned down and kissed him. His full lips felt great against his, and as they made out on the deck, Michael wondered what Helen Epstein thought of all this.

They parted lips, and Sam said, "I have an early day, and I better get going before I rip all your clothes off and have my way with you."

"What happened to that nervous, shy valet I met last night?" he asked.

Sam laughed as he gently tugged Michael's nipple through his shirt. Michael walked him to the door, and they made out some more before Michael opened it. Sam hesitated and patted Michael's chest, as if he were debating what to do next. He walked outside, turning before getting into his car and waved.

"Go see Sid," Michael yelled after him as he backed out of the driveway.

"I will, I will," he yelled back. "Call me before you leave for D.C."

"I will, I will," Michael said.

The next few weeks were hectic as Michael prepared to move to D.C. Sam and he never could quite get their schedules to mesh, and although they talked on the phone several times, they never managed to see each other again. Michael was not too disappointed, as he knew starting something before leaving would only make it more difficult. Here, he had met a really nice Jewish guy, and he was moving.

Timing is everything in Hollywood.

Chapter Four

Michael rented his house to one of his colleagues from *Los Angeles Live*, and he debated about whether to put his car in dry storage or take it with him. Since he didn't want to take a chance driving his Corvair cross-country, he went with his gut and stored it. Sharon told him he wouldn't need a car in Washington, and Michael figured if it turned out he did, he could rent one when necessary.

Michael arrived at Dulles International Airport around 2:00 pm on Friday, June 10, and took a cab to his temporary home in the Mount Pleasant neighborhood of Washington, D.C. The neighborhood looked like a nice area, and there were several people walking their dogs, which made him miss Aunt Clara even more. The apartment was actually the first floor of a townhouse located on Newton Street next to Bancroft Elementary School, and it was all brick with the ugliest blue doors and shutters Michael had ever seen. Eric Sagman said he would be home when Michael arrived to hand him the keys and all the necessary information. Eric had decided to sublet his apartment for a year, even though his assignment in Brazil could be as long as two years.

Michael exited the cab, pulled his bags from the trunk and knocked on the door to the apartment. When Eric answered the door, Michael's jaw dropped. He blinked several times, and so did Eric. They were the mirror images of each other. It has been said that everyone has a twin, but this was too weird, even for Michael.

Eric also stood six-foot-four with closely cropped hair, but where Michael's hair was still all black with a few gray strands, Eric's hair was all gray. Eric obviously worked out, but was carrying about twenty more pounds than Michael, some of it around the middle, which Michael also battled constantly, often yo-yoing up and down by twenty or so pounds a year, himself. Eric's eyes were also green, but they were obscured by Clark Kent style, black framed bifocals. Since Michael didn't wear glasses, he could be Superman to Eric's Clark Kent. Eric was wearing jeans and a green T-shirt, a matching green military style belt and Chuck Taylors in the same shade of green. He was just a little too color coordinated for Michael's taste.

After the initial shock, Eric opened the screen door and said, "You must be Michael. Come in, come in."

Eric's suitcases were neatly arranged by the door, and once inside, Michael was standing in the kitchen/dining room, and he put his suitcases down. The cabinets were white and built to the ceiling, and there was a green Formica table with matching green chairs. Everything in the kitchen – the pictures, the *chachkis*, the canisters and the like – had green accents. There were plants on a green baker's rack by the front window and taped to it were instructions on when and how to water them. Eric led Michael into the living room, and the first thing he noticed was that everything was arranged in threes. Michael glanced back to the kitchen and noticed all the pictures and other items were arranged in threes there as well. The living room had a futon, two matching chairs and a small bistro table by the back patio. Whereas everything in the kitchen was green, everything in the living room was either red or tan with *chachkis* and pictures to match. *It is true what Jews say, Art is what matches your couch, or in this case, your futon*, Michael thought.

Michael then completed the tour with the bedroom, again arranged in threes, but with everything accented in green and burgundy. The apartment was absolutely spotless, just as Michael's house was.

"How often does the maid come?" Michael asked.

"Oh, I don't use a maid. I don't like cleaning up after someone. It's amazing I'm subletting as I usually don't want anyone touching my stuff. I'm a little obsessive," Eric said.

Eric was very energetic, almost hyper, but extremely friendly. Oddly, neither mentioned the fact that they looked so much alike.

"Can I ask you another question?" Michael asked.

"Sure," Eric answered, "I have no secrets."

"Why is everything arranged in threes?" Michael asked gesturing around the apartment.

Eric looked around and laughed. "Well, if you must know, I have mild Asperger's syndrome or as some call it high functioning autism. I've learned to control it over the years, but some of my quirks come out screaming." Eric then laughed.

"I guess that makes life interesting," Michael said, having read up on Asperger's syndrome when a friend's child was diagnosed with it.

Eric was constantly on the move and handed Michael a list. "Yeah, I can't sit still. My grandmother used to say I was busier than a blue-assed fly, whatever the hell that means," Eric added.

Michael glanced at the piece of paper, which contained a list of emergency numbers, instructions on how everything worked in the apartment, including how if you baked a cake, set the thermostat twenty-five degrees higher than the recipe instructed and allow seven extra minutes of baking time. Every minute detail of living in this one-bedroom apartment was covered. Michael reached into his wallet and pulled out a check, which covered an entire year's rent, utilities and a security deposit. Eric looked at it, immediately endorsed it and pulled out a deposit slip filling it out as well. Michael was amazed at how organized Eric was.

"So, Brazil, I guess you're looking forward to that," Michael said.

"Actually, it's not as glamorous as you think. I'm going down there on a government contract to study and write about the impact of aid to poor villages in the country. I may never see Rio except when I land at the airport," Eric said. "And do you want to hear the weirdest part?"

"What?" Michael asked, intrigued by this twin of his with every move he made.

"I've been taking Portuguese lessons for six months now, and I still can't speak one word of it! Hilarious huh? Sending an Aspy – that is what they call us Asperger's people – to a foreign country with no working knowledge of the language," Eric answered and laughed again.

Michael looked over at his suitcases and noticed he had only three bags – of course, three. "Is that all the luggage you're taking for a year?" Michael asked.

"Look who's talking. You showed up with three bags yourself," Eric said pointing to Michael's bags.

"You're right, but I'm having the rest shipped," Michael answered, noticing that he had a "three-thing" going on, too.

"I shipped stuff also and guess how many boxes?" Eric said with a grin.

"Three," Michael answered.

"Wrong! Two!" Eric said. "Do you know for how long I was rocking and flapping my arms before I could allow myself only to send two boxes?" Eric then laughed again. That made Michael nervous – rocking and flapping his arms. Eric sensed his alarm. "Oh, come on. That's a little Aspy humor. I don't rock," he said then paused. "But I do flap my arms when I get excited." Then Eric winked. Just then, a blue van pulled up out front, and the driver blew his horn.

"Oh, there's my shuttle. My cell phone number is on the list if you need anything. I'll call once a month to see that everything's OK. Also, I didn't forward my phone, so if it rings, go ahead and answer it and give anyone my cell number. You can use the phone also, and the number is on the list," Eric said as he opened the door and walked to the shuttle with two of his suitcases.

Michael grabbed the third bag and followed him out.

"Do you think you forgot something?" Michael asked as Eric opened the door to the van.

Eric furrowed his brow and replied, "What?"

"The keys," Michael said holding out his hand.

Eric reached into his pocket and handed Michael a key chain with three keys. He pointed out the one for the door, the deadbolt and the one for the steel-reinforced screen door. "Make sure you lock all three. This may be Mount Pleasant, but it is neither a mount, nor pleasant ... discuss," Eric said as he closed the door to the van and they drove off.

Michael waved goodbye and passed a neighbor, who gave him a double-take as he walked back to the apartment.

"Eric, did you dye your hair?" the neighbor asked.

"No. Don't you think I would have dyed *all* the gray out?" Michael answered, not letting her know that he was not her neighbor.

He touched the *Mezuzah* on the front door frame and kissed his hand before entering the apartment.

Here he was, back in D.C. after almost twenty-five years. Michael had not been here since his maternal grandmother died, and he was actually looking forward to it. About an hour after Eric left, Michael's boxes arrived. What timing. Within two hours, he had everything unpacked and was settled in. *Now, who is obsessive?* He thought.

Michael called Sharon to tell her he arrived safely and would see her Monday when she returned from her mountain retreat in West Virginia. Then, he ordered some dinner from the Chinese take-out menu he found on the refrigerator and settled in for the night.

The next day was Saturday, and he spent most of the day walking around the neighborhood and running errands, grocery shopping and the like.

In the evening, Michael was restless, so he went online to see what the nightlife in Washington had to offer. It had been years since he had been out to a bar, but he lacked for anything else to do, so he printed out a list of bars and dressed in jeans, a black T-shirt and sneakers. He walked to 16th Street and hailed a cab and told the driver to take him to the D.C. Falcon on New York Avenue. Within twenty minutes, the cab pulled up to a nondescript building with a door that had written on it, "D.C. Falcon." He paid the fare and exited the cab.

The neighborhood looked a little dicey, and Michael was glad he was wearing sneakers in case he needed to make a fast getaway from a mugger. He walked quickly to the door and tried to open it, but it was locked. Michael pulled the list of bars from his wallet and checked the hours of operation. The D.C. Falcon was supposed to be open from 6:00 pm to 2:00 am, and Michael looked at his watch and saw it was a little after 10:00 pm. He looked around the door and saw a button that he figured was a bell, so he pushed it. Within a few seconds, the door opened, and a large bearded man, wearing a harness, leather chaps and a leather jock strap opened the door and eyed Michael up and down.

"Yes?" the bouncer asked.

"Are you open?" Michael asked as he looked inside and saw there was a sizable crowd in the darkened bar, most of whom were dressed in black or leather garb.

"Yes, there's a $10 cover to get in," the bouncer responded.

Michael reached for his wallet and stepped inside. He pulled a $10 bill from his wallet to hand to the bouncer, but the man shook his head no to Michael and said, "I can't let you in. We have a dress code."

Michael gave the bouncer a puzzled look and asked, "What's wrong with what I'm wearing?"

"You're wearing sneakers," the bouncer said pointing to Michael's shoes.

Michael looked at his shoes and didn't think they looked bad as they were gray with blue lettering and practically brand new.

"So?" Michael asked.

"The rules are black leather shoes or boots, preferably boots and absolutely no sneakers," the bouncer said as he opened the door, signaling for Michael to leave.

Michael turned around and walked out then he turned back to the bouncer and said, "I don't think you realize whom you just kicked out of your dump."

The bouncer responded, "From what I can see another pretty boy who wants to play with a daddy."

Michael shook his head and walked to the curb in the hope of hailing a cab before he was accosted by some hood. As he stood there, he heard the door to the bar open, but he didn't look back to see who it was. He heard footsteps behind him, and then someone tapped his shoulder. Michael jumped and yelled, then he turned and said, "I'm leaving, asshole, I'm just waiting for a cab ..." But, it wasn't the bouncer.

Standing in front of Michael was a man in his thirties, who was around five-foot-nine, with a crew cut, a goatee and, from what he could see in the dark, gray eyes. The man was wearing a black T-shirt that hugged a large muscular frame and jeans, similar to Michael's.

He smiled and said, "Do you call everyone asshole?"

Michael looked at his feet and saw the man was wearing black leather boots and pointing to them said,

"Why did they kick you out? You're wearing black leather boots."

The man looked at his boots, looked up at Michael and smiled, "Is that why you left? I was wondering why?"

"Yeah, and I'm going home to get my size seventeen, black leather stilettos, just to piss off the bouncer," Michael said as he turned toward the street again to look for a cab.

The man inched closer to Michael and looked up the street as well and said, "You won't get a cab just standing here. You'll need to call for one inside. They don't like coming to this neighborhood if they don't have to."

"Great," Michael said. "Where should I go then to catch one? I just moved here yesterday."

The man reached out his hand and introduced himself, "I'm Steve. Come with me into the bar."

"I'm Michael, but they won't let me in," Michael said shaking his hand and noticing the strong grip on this stranger who followed him out. "Weren't you leaving?"

"No," Steve said. "I saw you come in and then turn around and leave, so I decided to follow you out to see if I could meet you."

"It must be slim pickings inside tonight if you need to find a trick by watching the door for rejects," Michael said with a laugh.

Steve looked Michael up and down and said, "You're no reject. Come with me, I'll get you in."

"And, what makes you think you can get me in?" Michael asked without moving.

"I'm Mr. D.C. Falcon," Steve said as he walked back to the door and motioned for Michael to follow him.

Michael hesitated for a moment, then shrugged his shoulders and followed his new acquaintance to the door. Steve rang the bell, and the bouncer opened it, smiling at Steve but then throwing a frown at Michael.

"It's OK, Jim," Steve said as he grabbed Michael's arm to lead him in. "This is my date, Michael."

Michael walked past the bouncer and smirked as the bouncer huffed back at him, saying, "Yeah, well your date isn't dressed right."

Steve turned around and walked up to the bouncer, staring up at the big man who stood a good six inches taller. The bouncer bowed his head at Steve, who growled at him, "Boy. You know better than to sass me. Now, you apologize to my friend. He just moved here, and I wouldn't want him to think we're not respectful to our guests!"

The bouncer walked up to Michael who was watching this play out with much curiosity, got down on his knees, grabbed Michael's right hand and said, while looking at the floor, "Forgive me, sir. I did not mean any disrespect."

Michael, who was a little taken aback by the bouncer's behavior, looked at Steve for direction. "What do I say?" Michael mouthed.

"Put your left hand on the back of his head and tell him he's forgiven," Steve said as if anyone should know this.

Michael did as Steve instructed and said, "You're forgiven." Then he looked at Steve, who nodded approvingly, and took his hand off the bouncer's head and said as he then put it under his chin and tilted the big man's head up, "But, boy, I don't care if I come in wearing a party dress and Mary Jane's. You let me in next time."

The bouncer said, "Yes, sir." Then he stood up and walked back to the door.

Michael reached for his wallet and pulled out a $10 bill and walked over to bouncer and handed him the cover charge. He then walked back over to Steve and said, "I always pay my way."

Steve took a seat at the bar and motioned for Michael to sit next to him. Michael seated himself and asked, "What the hell was that all about with the sirs and the boys?"

Steve looked at Michael and said, "Role playing," as if anyone knew that.

Steve then ordered a bottled water, and Michael ordered a Diet Coke and paid for both and tipped the bartender. Michael noticed that people were staring at him as he sat there with Steve. "Why are people looking at me?" he asked.

Steve looked around and said, "Oh, I'm sort of a celebrity here, and my boyfriend and I are on a break, but they don't know, so they probably think I'm cheating on him. And, you *are* new meat."

"You have a boyfriend?" Michael asked, looking at Steve.

"We're on a break. It's OK," Steve said.

"I know it's OK; we're just sitting here talking," Michael said as he sipped his drink.

"So, where did you move here from?" Steve asked as he turned in his stool to face Michael, brushing his leg.

"Santa Monica," Michael answered. "I'm just here for a year working on a project."

"Really? What kind of project?" Steve asked as he put the bottled water to his mouth.

Michael studied him and wondered if he should answer his question or remain vague about it. He decided to go ahead and tell him. "I'm co-writing a screenplay with a friend of mine."

"Wow, that's cool," Steve said. "You ever done anything like that before?"

"Yeah," Michael said, offering nothing else. "What do you do when you aren't Mr. D.C. Falcon?"

Steve laughed at Michael's question and took another sip of his water. He didn't answer the question and ordered another bottled water, while Michael gave him a puzzled look.

"Is it something illegal?" Michael asked.

Steve paid the bartender, set the bottle down, opened it and took another sip. "I'm a security consultant for a government agency. Really boring, but it pays the bills," Steve said, finally answering the question. "So, what else have you written?"

Michael reached back for his wallet and handed Steve his card. Steve looked at it and raised his eyebrows. "You're the head writer of *Los Angeles Live*?" he asked, looking up at Michael.

"Was," Michael said, looking at the bottles on the bar. "The show was cancelled."

"Wow, for how long?" Steve asked obviously impressed.

"Eighteen seasons, I was there from the beginning to the bitter end," he answered as he sipped his soda.

"That's so cool," Steve said. "And now you write screenplays full-time?"

Michael looked at Steve. "For the moment. A movie I wrote will be released in January, and after I'm finished here, who knows."

Steve patted Michael on the back and said, "I'm sure you'll find something."

Michael leaned back and looked at him, saying, "Yeah, I should be able to scrape up some kind of living when I return in a year."

Steve smiled at him and said, "Is money tight now that the show was cancelled?"

Michael thought this was an awfully personal question and looked at him disapprovingly.

"Oh, was that inappropriate?" Steve asked.

"Kind of," Michael said.

"Well, it's just that you were trying to hail a cab, and I figured you can't afford a car right now, and you moved here to write a screenplay ..."

"You should never assume anything," Michael interrupted, tilting his head down to look at Steve. "I own a house in Santa Monica and a car. I just figured I wouldn't need one here, and in case you're worried about my eating noodles every night, I could retire today if I wanted to." Steve's eyes opened wide, and Michael took another sip of his drink. "Well, Steve, it was great meeting you and thanks for getting me in, but I think I better go home. Who can call me a cab, here?" Michael asked.

"I can drive you home," Steve offered.

"No, I don't want to put you to any trouble," he said as he got up from his seat.

"It would be no trouble," Steve said as he also got up. "Besides, I can see how a big Hollywood writer lives."

"You won't be impressed. I'm subletting an apartment from a friend of a friend," Michael said as he walked to the door. "So, can the bouncer get a cab?"

Steve grabbed Michael's arm, and said, "I'll take you home. Geez, what are you afraid of?"

Michael turned to look at him and said, "I'm not afraid of anything. I just don't want you to get the wrong impression."

"Hey, big guy, it's just a ride, lighten up," Steve said as he opened the door and led Michael out.

They walked to the parking lot around the side of the building, and Steve opened the driver's side door of a black Toyota pick-up, clicking the lock release for the passenger side door for Michael, who thought a real gentleman would have opened his door first.

"Mr. D.C. Falcon drives a Japanese truck?" Michael asked.

Steve started the truck with a laugh and said, "Where are we going?"

Michael gave him the address, and Steve drove him home. When Steve pulled up to the apartment, he asked, "Mind if I come in?"

"Actually, yes," Michael said. "I just moved here, and I'm a little tired. You have my number, give me a call. And, thanks for the ride. I appreciate it." He then stepped out of the truck, and Steve pulled off. Michael hoped he wouldn't call, figuring there was no reason to get involved with someone's boyfriend even if they were on a break.

As he closed the door behind him, his cell phone rang, and Michael didn't recognize the number.

"Hello," Michael said, wondering who would call after midnight.

"Hey, this is the guy who just gave you a ride home," Steve said.

"Oh, thanks again," Michael said. "By the way, what is your last name, Steve?"

He was silent then answered, "Smith, but my friends call me Smithy."

"Smitty?" Michael asked.

"No! Smithy," he corrected Michael.

"Nice to have met you. I'll call you Steve as Smithy sounds goofy," Michael told him.

"Nice to have met you, Michael; we'll talk later, bye," and he hung up. Michael figured he was not much of a talker on the phone, and he was certain he made that up. *Smith? Who is named Smith anymore? And, Smithy?* For his own mental well-being, Michael hoped Steve would never call him again and programmed his name into his phone, so he would know if he did.

Michael took a shower and climbed into bed, and his cell phone rang again. "Is this guy persistent or what?" Michael said out loud, but he noticed the caller ID indicated it was Sam. He answered, happy to hear his voice.

"Michael, how is Washington?" Sam asked, sounding as excited to hear Michael's voice as he was to hear Sam's.

"It's OK, although I've only been here a day. Why are you calling so late?"

"Oh damn," Sam said, "I forgot about the time change."

"It seems none of my friends can calculate time," Michael said with a chuckle. He had to smile as he wished Sam was there, so they could see each other again, having not been face-to-face since they had dinner at Anna's.

"Guess what?" Sam asked and answered quickly. "Sid got me an audition for a small part in a movie, and they liked me! It's only about three lines, but that's three more than I've had before!"

Michael was genuinely happy for him. It was a start, albeit a small one, but at least he would get to speak. "That's great, Sam," Michael said. "It could lead to more work. Who's the director?"

"Peggy Martin," Sam replied. "Can you believe it? I'm going to be directed for forty-five seconds by Peggy Martin! I can't thank you enough for telling Sid about me!"

"Wow, Sam, a Peggy Martin film. This is big time. I know her very well. She was member of the ensemble on *Los Angeles Live* the first five seasons," Michael told him, making a mental note to give her a call. "What's the part?"

"I play a bumbling valet at a Hollywood party. How is that for typecasting?" Sam said, and Michael could actually hear him smiling.

"Well, I know you'll nail that part! My car is still whining from you turn at the wheel," Michael said half-jokingly. "Well, Sam, it's after midnight here, so I'm going to bed. Keep in touch and tell me how it goes. When do you film your scene?"

"Monday!" he yelled. "Oy, I have such diarrhea I am so nervous."

"Nervous is good," Michael said. "It's when you get too over confident that you screw up. You'll be great, and Peggy's a sweetheart. Break a leg! Good night."

"Good night, sexy man," Sam said. "I'll call you later this week to tell you how it went."

"All right, kid, take care."

Michael was genuinely happy for him. Sam was a really nice guy, and Michael also hoped that if he became successful, it wouldn't go to his head. Michael had seen so many people become such egomaniacs once they had a small taste of success. He wasn't that sleepy, so he called Peggy Martin, knowing it was only after nine on a Saturday night, and she was known to stay home more than go out partying.

"Hello?" she answered with her well-known nasal, whiny voice.

"Peggy, it's Michael Bern," he said to his old friend, who was now one of the most respected directors in the business.

"Michael, how are you? Did I hear you moved to Washington? What the hell are you doing there?" she asked.

"I'm co-writing a screenplay with Sharon Gorman. Remember Sharon?" Michael replied.

"Oh yeah. I always liked her. Who's directing it?" Peggy asked.

"I'm not sure as we haven't even started writing yet. I just arrived yesterday, Peggy."

"Let me know who as soon as you know," Peggy said. "So, why are you calling me? I thought Stanley King directed all your pictures?" she asked sarcastically.

"If by all, you mean one, yes, for the moment," Michael said.

"I was an idiot not to go for that one. Word around town is that it's going to be a huge hit," she said, making Michael nervous because whenever a film was declared a hit six months before its release, it was surely going to be a flop.

"Well, I'm making no predictions. But that's not why I called," Michael said. "You have an actor, who I think is playing a bumbling valet on your picture."

"Oh yeah. Good-looking kid and loaded with personality. I was impressed by him seconds after he read for me," Peggy said, putting his mind at ease. "He's never had a speaking part. I wonder how that *alta cocker* Sid found him?"

"Peggy, are you sure you aren't Jewish? What Italian says *alta cocker?*" Michael asked. "Anyway, I just wanted to put in a good word for Sam. He really is a nice kid and deserves a break."

"What, are you worried I'll make his life a living hell? Why are you so concerned? Wait a minute, did you fuck him?" she asked.

"No," Michael insisted. "I discovered him." There was silence. "Peggy?"

"I was banging my head to see if there was wax in my ears," she said half-jokingly. "Since when do you discover people?"

"I don't, but this kid parked my car at Sylvia's party a few weeks ago, and something told me he had a chance, given the right circumstance," Michael assured her.

"OK, Michael, for you, anything, but only if you promise to insist I direct your next picture," Peggy said demandingly.

"You have a deal," he said.

"Good night, Michael, and I'll be kind to the kid," Peggy said.

"Thanks, Peggy," Michael said. "I won't forget this, good night."

Peggy, Sid and Michael were proof that there were actually nice people in Hollywood. They always looked out for up and coming talent. Unfortunately, in most cases, these brats would turn into divas the minute they earned six figures. Michael helped a young actress get a small part on *Los Angeles Live* a few years ago after she pleaded with him at a party in the Valley. She did pretty well, but she never thanked him. A year later, after she was cast in a few prime TV roles, Michael ran into her again at a party, and she acted as if she never met him. Michael wished he could say that was the only time that happened, but it wasn't. Michael walked up to her toward the end of the party and said to her, "Be nice to everyone on the way up because you'll meet them all again on the way down!" She gave him a look as if he were covered in shit and feathers and walked away. She is now in rehab after playing bit parts in *Lifetime* movies, and from what Michael has seen in recent pictures, she looks like hell.

Michael liked helping people, and although he was bitten in the ass on many occasions due to his generosity, he hadn't hesitated to help Sam. If he also turned diva on him, then so be it. Michael was used to it, and what goes around comes around.

The next day, Michael read Sharon's novel, *Romancing the Capitol.* He had to admit to Sharon that he had not read it yet. She gave Michael a hard time about it but forgave him after chiding him for an hour. He liked the book, which was about two senators from opposite sides of the aisle who fall in love – a Republican woman from the South and a Democratic man from the Northeast. Sharon's narratives were well-written, but there was not a great deal of dialogue in the book, so

Michael knew their work was cut out for them. By mid-afternoon, he had finished reading it and called Sharon to tell her he liked it and to send him the treatment and any scenes she had already drafted.

Michael then went out for a walk in search of a gym to join. Steve had told him on the ride home about Results the Gym on U Street, so he walked down 16th Street to U Street and spotted the large yellow banners in front of the gym. After getting a tour and learning they opened at 5:00 am, Michael decided to join without going to any other gym in town. The next morning, which was a Monday, he woke up at four-thirty and began a routine of working out at five and getting home by six-thirty. The gym was only a twenty-five-minute walk from Mount Pleasant, so it was convenient enough, and the mornings weren't crowded with the after-work, spandex wearing, happy-hour club boys he so despised.

Michael was feeling more at home in D.C.

* * * * *

Michael spent two weeks every summer in Washington visiting his Nana Mary, his maternal grandmother. She was a tall woman like his mother, and she did everything left-handed but write. The story was that when she was in grammar school, they tied her left hand behind her chair to force her to use her right hand. They tried to do the same with Michael's mother, who was also left-handed, but Nana Mary complained, and they let Hannah use her left hand.

Nana Mary always wore blonde wigs over her thinning but extremely long gray hair. She also wore thick glasses over her blue eyes and orange tint lipstick. (She was also the blonde, blue-eyed Jewess, who had to read the *Jewish Daily Forward* backward to the neighbors in Baltimore before she could marry his grandfather.) Nana Mary was also one of the best-dressed women Michael knew. "I never buy cheap drek," she declared, always shopping in the finest stores. Yet, she was tight with a buck when it came to anything frivolous and lived comfortably all her life. She never smiled, and he rarely heard her laugh as she was the most serious and humorless person he ever knew.

There were pictures of Nana Mary and Grandpa Michael Summers all over the apartment, and in all of them, she was actually smiling. She mourned his death for the entire twenty-five years she was a widow. Arlene, who was a friend and neighbor of Nana Mary's when she lived in Newport News (where Nana Mary's family had settled in 1905, and where she returned in the 1950s after living in Washington most of her life,) once told Michael his grandparents were the most devoted couple she ever met, and that his grandfather's death hit her very hard, which is why she moved back to Washington after his death.

Nana Mary had few friends, or at least that was the impression Michael had. When he visited her, no one ever dropped by. When he would visit Grandma Rose Bern, her friends were always dropping by for coffee or just to chat, but Nana Mary did not have a life like that.

However, she was an amazing woman in that she worked until she was eighty-two as the head secretary for Leggum and Gerber, a large real estate company located in Cleveland Park, even after her eyesight started to fail. In 1968, she had cataract operations on both eyes, when it was still considered a dangerous and major operation. Michael remembered her crying before the surgery because she thought they were going to take out her eyes. She also insisted they leave her wig on during the surgery, and she emerged from the operating room with it cock-eyed. They had compromised; she could wear it as long as she took out the pins. The recovery was six weeks, and she could not look down for the entire recovery period. Whenever she chose new frames for her glasses, she had to put them over her old frames, so she could get an idea what they looked like.

Nana Mary chained-smoked Kent cigarettes, as many as four packs a day, and often would fall asleep, burning a cushion on her Louis XIV furniture right under her *tuchus*. She often had cigarette burns on her dresses as she could not see the ashtray. Michael asked her if she realized when she burned a hole in a dress, and she said very seriously, "Only after I feel it burning my skin."

When she moved back to D.C. after Michael's grandfather died in 1960, she lived at the Kennedy Warren. When they built the Van Ness East in the mid-1960s, she moved there, and in 1970 she moved to Van Ness North with a view of Connecticut Avenue. When Michael visited, their days were pretty routine. They would have breakfast. Then she would send Michael to People's Drug Store to pick up whatever sale item she found in the flyer that day. Then, he would go to the pool until noon, while she sat in the shade keeping from burning her fair skin. After that, they would go to the Chevy Chase Neiman Marcus to see if the latest styles of Eva Gabor wigs had arrived. They would get home by four, so they wouldn't miss the *Merv Griffin Show*. They never missed Merv. Then they would go to the Hot Shoppe and eat dinner, come back home, watch more television, have ice cream sodas, and go to bed. Although it was boring being there with only *alta cockers* around as no one Michael's age lived in her apartment building, it was a pleasure to be away from his mother and her husband, Bart, whom Nana Mary hated as well.

The only down side was that Nana Mary would take every opportunity to complain about everyone and even Michael's father, Adam, saying his grandfather never liked Adam. She would then say, "I cannot believe Florence got a divorce. How can anyone get a divorce? No one in my day got a divorce." And, every night, Michael would hear this same speech.

One night, she sat Michael down and told him a story that to this day, he has not forgotten:

"Michael, when I was a little girl," she began, "we lived in downtown Newport News. One day, this girl I knew from *shule* invited me to her house. When I got there, I noticed potato peels in the corner of their kitchen along with other scraps from preparing numerous meals. I went home and told my mother about it, and she said I could not be friends with that girl because they lived like pigs. I know your mother is not the greatest housekeeper, but she should be ashamed of herself. I never kept a house like that, so I have no idea where she got it from. Michael, you need to be sure your house is clean, or you will never have any friends."

From that day forward, Michael did all the laundry and cleaned the house, so he would always have friends; ironically, his mother did not allow him to have friends over to the house.

At the end of the two weeks with Nana Mary, Hannah would drive up to bring Michael home. During the entire three-hour drive home, Hannah would quiz Michael about what he told Nana Mary, "What did you talk about?" "What did you say?" "What did she tell you?" He often wanted to say, "Mother, if you're worried about what we talked about, why don't you stay up there with us?" But, Michael never had the nerve to say anything, and he never told Nana Mary anything either.

Nana Mary retired in 1985, and within a few months, she was dead. Nana Mary should never have retired as work, buying wigs, watching Merv, and complaining about how Bart never worked, was all she had to keep her alive. Michael often thought he inherited his work ethic and some other quirks from Nana Mary.

She left half her estate to Michael, but while on her death bed, Hannah had her sign numerous papers giving her power of attorney and access to all her accounts. When all was said and done, Michael received a check for $2,170 from her estate three years after she died, and he later learned that his mother blew through the remaining $180,000 in less than a year as Bart never had any money, and what he did have he drank or gambled away. Nana Mary worked hard all her life and saved money on a secretary's salary, only to have her daughter squander it all and rip off her only grandchild.

Chapter Five

Sharon and Michael spent the majority of the next few months e-mailing the script back and forth, refining, re-writing, deleting, and adding, until they had a first draft around mid-September to submit to the studio. Michael pondered going back to California early, since he wasn't needed in Washington anymore, but Sharon said they would probably send it back for re-writes over the next few weeks. However, Michael was not looking forward to spending a Washington winter re-writing a script.

His life was pretty routine at this point. He would get up at four-thirty, go to the gym, come home, have breakfast, work on the script or other writing assignments Sid had secured for him, re-writing scenes for movies, and writing monologues or other bits and pieces for various TV shows. He ghost wrote so much stuff that summer and fall that he wondered if anyone realized how busy he really was, rather than lamenting the end of a great career. By six, he would turn off the computer, have some dinner, watch some television, and go to bed, but Michael was beginning to miss the Hot Shoppe, shopping at People's Drug Store, and watching *The Merv Griffin Show*.

By mid-October, the director asked for a re-write of the ending of *Romancing the Capitol*, so he was stuck for a while. One morning, he had just arrived home from the gym and was bored. He turned on the computer to check his e-mail, and he saw one from someone named MrDCFalcon2005. At first Michael thought it was an advertisement, but the name rang a bell, and he realized it was Steve Smith. He had not heard a word from him since the night they met in June, and here it was four months later, and he received an e-mail.

Michael opened it, found it was short and to the point, and the time and date stamp indicated it had just been sent. "Hey big guy, how ya been? What are you up to? Woof to you."

Michael thought a few minutes before replying and eventually sent back, "I'm home from the gym and getting ready to do some work. What made you e-mail me out of the blue?"

Michael figured Steve wouldn't reply right away and checked his other e-mails when a reply from Steve arrived almost immediately.

"Want to meet up?"

Michael frowned at the screen. He hadn't heard from the guy for four months and now he wanted to meet. Michael also noticed that Steve didn't say why he e-mailed out of nowhere, so he wrote back, "Now?"

"Yeah," Steve wrote back. "Can I come over?"

Michael thought for a moment. He got up from the computer and walked into the kitchen to pour himself a cup of coffee when he heard his cell phone ring. He saw it was Steve who was calling, and he waited a few seconds before answering it.

"Hello, Steve," Michael said in a monotone manner.

"Hey big guy. So, you want to get together?" Steve asked again.

"One, it is six-thirty in the morning, and two, what about your boyfriend?" Michael asked.

"I'm always up this early, and he and I broke up," Steve answered. "So, should I come over?"

Michael thought for a moment. It had been a while since he had sex, but he also knew that this was not what he wanted, especially this early in the morning.

"Michael, you still there?"

"Yeah, I'm still here," Michael answered.

"So, what do you say?" Steve asked.

"To be honest, Steve, I don't feel like fooling around right now ..."

"Who said I wanted to fool around? I just want to come by and say hi," Steve assured him.

Michael wasn't sure if Steve was being entirely honest, but he invited him over anyway.

He decided not to change from his jeans and sweatshirt he had put on after showering at the gym, and it was a good thing he didn't because there was a knock on the door within five minutes. He looked through the peep hole, and it was Steve. Michael opened the door, and Steve walked in wearing black sweat pants with a white stripe down each leg and a black sweat shirt.

"How did you do that? Weren't you sitting in front of your computer?" Michael asked.

"Oh, I got in my car after I asked if I could come over, hoping you would say yes," Steve answered as he walked into the living room.

"Pretty sure of yourself, aren't you?" Michael asked. "Want some coffee?"

"Oh, I don't do caffeine. Nice place, really clean," Steve said as he looked around.

Michael took his coffee and sat down on the futon, placing his cup on the table next to it. Then Steve took off his sweat shirt and stood right in front of Michael.

"I thought you just wanted to say hi," Michael said as he admired Steve's hairy, muscular body. "By the way, nice body."

Steve ran his hand over his stomach and said, "I'm fat. I think I need liposuction."

Michael looked at Steve's belly, which wasn't quite a washboard, but wasn't fat either. It was as if he had been temporarily transported back to Hollywood, where someone who was one pound overweight was considered obese. Steve then sat sideways on Michael's lap, and

Michael didn't protest as Steve put his hand behind Michael's head and leaned in to kiss him.

As they parted lips, Michael looked into Steve's eyes and wondered what he was doing with this thirty-year-old, and he knew that keeping it casual, if they proceeded to the bedroom, would be for the best.

"You work fast," Michael said.

"Yeah, I know what I like," he responded.

"It took you four months to see what you like, then five minutes to go after it," Michael said as he stroked Steve's thigh.

Steve got up from Michael's lap and walked toward the bedroom, slipping off his sneakers and sweat pants, and standing in only a black jock strap, which hugged the roundest, hairiest butt Michael had ever seen and said, "Tom and I were in couple's therapy most of the summer."

Michael did not move from the futon as he asked, "What would your therapist think of this?"

"Doesn't matter. We're on another break, and we decided to open up the relationship," Steve said as he turned and removed his jock strap and settled on the bed, yelling to Michael, "So, are you going to join me or what?"

Michael stood up and removed his sweatshirt slowly revealing a body that he had worked to perfect for more than two decades, then bent down and removed his shoes and socks before walking into the bedroom where Steve was lying on his back and sporting a nice, thick, long erection.

"Damn!" Steve said upon seeing Michael shirtless. "For a guy in his forties, you are smokin' hot."

"For a guy in his forties?" Michael asked with a smile as he unbuckled his jeans and dropped them along with his white briefs.

"I guess it's true what they say about Jewish boys," Steve said as he sat up and ran a hand down Michael's torso and grabbed his stiffening organ, which was thicker and longer than Steve's. "You ever measure this thing?"

"Please, yours is pretty huge," Michael said as he leaned down and grabbed Steve, milking a bit of precum from the tip.

Steve then slipped his mouth over Michael's erection and proceeded to give him the slowest and most sensual blowjob he had experienced in a while. Michael also knew that if Steve kept up what he was doing, he would blow any second, for it had been a while since he got laid. He put his hands on Steve's cheeks, easing him off his dick, then bent down and kissed him passionately. Michael sucked on Steve's tongue, then ran it over his lips before shoving into Steve's mouth, doing things with his full Semitic lips that Steve had never expected. When they parted lips, Steve was speechless and looked up at him with wonder. Michael then got down on his knees and grabbed Steve's hard dick, gave it a couple of strokes, then put his warm mouth on it.

"Oh my God!" Steve practically yelled, but Michael was not surprised because he was known for two things he did better than just about anyone, kissing and sucking dick. "You are fucking amazing ... holy shit ... I don't know what you're doing ... but God damn ..."

Michael would have preferred to edge Steve, but he did have work to do, so he brought him to the brink pretty quickly and released his cock only a second before Steve came in shudders. Michael then stood up and stroked his own cock, coating Steve's torso only seconds later, having enjoyed giving pleasure to such a hot man with such a nice cock.

It took Steve a few minutes to recover, and afterward, they showered together before Steve left. The whole thing lasted no more than fifteen minutes.

The next morning, Michael went to the gym as usual. As he walked in the door, he heard his cell phone ringing. He never took it to the gym, figuring no one would call that early, proving that after all those years in Hollywood, he had not become so entrenched in show biz habits that he was tethered to his phone twenty-four-seven.

"Hello, Steve," he answered after looking at the ID.

"Hey, Michael."

"Steve, what are you doing calling me again this early?" he asked a little annoyed.

"Open your front door," Steve said.

"What?" Michael asked turning around to face the door.

"Open your front door," he said again, insistently.

Michael walked over to the front door and looked into the peep hole and saw Steve stepping out of his truck still talking on the cell phone, so he opened the door.

"Surprised to see me?" Steve asked into the cell phone.

"Yes," Michael said as he hung up the phone.

Michael let him in, and Steve was dressed in a suit with an ID tag around his neck. Michael chided himself for not looking at it before Steve put it in his pocket to see if Steve Smith was his real name.

"What are you doing?" Michael asked as Steve walked toward the living room.

"I was on my way to work, and I thought I would drop by and say hi," Steve said as he turned around and smiled.

"Where exactly do you work?" Michael asked as he followed him into the living room, wondering why Steve would stop by a day after having sex with him. Tricks never did that. There was the seventy-two-hour rule, and one never stopped by unannounced. Had the rules changed, and no one told Michael? Was this an East Coast thing?

"So, what are you doing?" Steve asked, ignoring Michael's question, as he sat down on one of the chairs and removed his shoes, not waiting for an invitation to make himself comfortable.

"I just got home from the gym, and I'm going to have some breakfast and get to work," Michael answered as he stood there watching him.

Steve then stood up and walked over to Michael, his head coming to Michael's chest as there was at least seven inches difference in their heights. Steve started running his hands up and down Michael's torso, but Michael pushed him away. "Listen, Steve, I like you, but I'm not comfortable with you coming over unannounced, when you either have or don't have a boyfriend."

Steve ignored Michael and proceeded to undress and said, "Hey, like I said, we're on a break and probably breaking up anyway. Besides, I can't seem to separate sex from friendship."

A red flag went up in Michael's head. *He can't separate sex from friendship?*

Within a minute, Steve was naked, and Michael reluctantly joined him.

They started making out while standing next to the bed, then Steve lifted Michael up and tossed him on his back on the bed. He lay on top of Michael, and they made out for quite a while. When they finally parted lips, Steve whispered into Michael's ear, "I want you to fuck me."

Michael's eyes popped open. "What?"

"I want to sit on that big, fat Jewish dick and ride it. I want to feel it up my asshole," Steve growled into Michael's ear.

"Listen, I'm not really into anal sex," Michael said as he tried to squirm out from under Steve, but Steve was a bit stronger, or he didn't try hard enough.

"Come on, don't you want to fuck my big hairy ass?"

Michael stared at Steve for a second, then said, "The condoms and lube are in the nightstand," remembering where Eric said they were on his amazingly complete list. As Steve leaned over to grab the necessities, Michael wanted to slap himself. He didn't know what kind of hold this guy had on him to make him do something he didn't particularly enjoy.

Steve ripped open the condom pack with his teeth, then slipped it onto Michael's stiff cock. He then squirted a bit of lube on his hand and a liberal amount on Michael's sheathed tool. And, without a bit of hesitation and in one swift movement, Steve sat on Michael's cock and took it all the way in, smiling the entire time.

"Oh man, your big dick feels so good inside me," Steve moaned as he proceeded to ride up and down, while Michael did his best to try and enjoy the situation, but this was one thing that did little to turn Michael on.

He just could never get into the appeal of anal sex. He tried being a bottom a couple of times, but he didn't enjoy it in the least, and as a top, he found it boring, especially since condoms caused his dick to go numb, so there was very little pleasure in the situation.

Steve's eyes were closed, so he couldn't see the bored look on Michael's face, and they remained closed while he stroked then came only minutes after impaling himself. He slipped off Michael and lay beside him and said, "That was amazing, now you."

"Now, me, what?"

"Come," Steve said as he slipped the condom off Michael and stroked him. It took Michael a while, but he did finally come.

Again, they showered together, and Steve was gone. This time it took twenty minutes for all to transpire.

Afterward, Michael was a mess. This kid was only thirty. The worst part was the fact that Steve dropped by just to surprise Michael made him start to have feelings for Steve.

Two days later, Steve showed up at Michael's front door again. This time, he walked in, undressed and proceeded to seduce Michael without any invitation. The following week, however, Steve had spent the night at his boyfriend's house and come over to Michael's straight from there. Upon hearing this, Michael asked him, "You just had sex with your boyfriend, and you show up at my door?"

"Oh, we didn't do anything. That's one of the problems. He always wants it, and I have a low sex drive," Steve said as he removed his clothes, talking as if he were reporting on the weather.

Low sex drive? Michael thought. Steve didn't have one around him. Talk about confusion.

They made out for quite a while then Michael sucked on Steve's dick before Steve once again asked Michael to fuck him. Michael obliged, this time doing it doggy-style. The way Steve moaned, you would have thought Michael was a pro at topping guys, and he never told Steve how much he really didn't enjoy anal intercourse because it was all about Steve's pleasure.

After they were done, Steve said he was leaving on a work-related trip to Texas in a couple of days, and he would call Michael when he got back. Michael was glad Steve was leaving as he seemed to be losing control over this situation, and the further away Steve was, the better Michael would be. The following week, Steve called from Texas just to say hello. Michael thought that simple act was one of the sweetest things he ever experienced, but little did Michael know that it would be the last time Steve would ever call while out of town.

Is this guy for real? Is he falling for me? Michael thought. *What is happening here?* Michael knew he was falling for him, or he wouldn't have allowed him to drop by unannounced. He also knew that if they became lovers, it would only be a matter of time before Steve left Michael's apartment to have a tryst with someone else on the way to work. This was Steve's obvious MO.

They e-mailed each other quite a bit, sometimes talking dirty and sometimes just saying hi. Michael did notice somewhat of a pattern around this time. If he asked Steve a question, it was never answered. Steve wouldn't even dance around it; he would just ignore it. Michael asked him what he was doing for Thanksgiving, as he was worried Steve would be alone, and wanted to invite him to go with him to Sharon's house. Michael didn't tell him about the invitation as he did not want to sound too clingy.

Michael just asked, "What are you doing for Thanksgiving?"

He asked him about four times, until Steve finally answered, "Tom and I are going out for Chinese with a bunch of friends."

Michael thought he and Tom were on the outs, but then Steve told him they were working things out, and Michael's heart sank as he realized he was in way too deep, and that he was definitely falling for someone else's boyfriend.

They did not see each other for the first few weeks in November, and on November 22, Steve called Michael to wish him a happy birthday, and Michael was surprised Steve remembered his birthday as he only mentioned it in passing. Michael told him to have a Happy Thanksgiving, and Steve even called him on Thanksgiving morning to say hello. Then, Michael noticed another pattern beginning to take shape. Steve never answered the phone when Michael called. Steve actually preferred e-mail to actual conversation. On the rare occasion they did talk on the phone, it was Steve who called.

Michael was available to Steve, but Steve was not available to him. He started to realize he had relinquished all control over his feelings and time to someone who was someone else's boyfriend. But, for some reason, Michael could not extricate himself from this situation entirely.

The Friday after Thanksgiving, Steve called Michael from work and asked if he could stop by on his way to the gym. Michael, who at this point was starting to crave any moment with Steve, while becoming leery of continuing this situation, said yes anyway. When Steve arrived, Michael sat on the futon, and Steve sat on his lap sideways as usual, but still dressed in his work clothes.

Michael looked into his eyes and asked, "What the hell is going on here?"

Steve looked into Michael's and answered, "Oh we're just friends having some fun." He then leaned in for a kiss, and they made out as they practically ripped each other's clothes off.

Once in the bedroom, they continued to make out, but when Steve uttered the usual, "I can't wait for you to fuck me," Michael stopped.

"I'm not in the mood to fuck today," he said, proud of himself for expressing his feelings.

"That's cool," Steve said, surprising Michael by letting it go, then scooting up Michael's chest until his cock was resting on Michael's chin, "Then suck me, boy."

Michael obliged giving Steve a great deal of pleasure, while he became quite oral himself, saying things like, "Yeah, you like that daddy dick, don't you boy? ... come on, milk my bone ... take it all down your throat."

Michael got so into the dirty talk that he did something he hadn't done in years. He swallowed Steve's load, which just about made him scream, "Holy fuck! Oh shit! God damn!" And, Michael came without even touching himself.

Steve caught his breath and hopped off Michael's face and looked down at the pool of cum on Michael's belly, "You really liked that didn't you, boy?"

But, Michael said nothing. He suddenly felt dirty and ashamed at what he did.

This time, he let Steve shower alone and was pretty quiet, barely saying goodbye as Steve left.

Afterward, Michael made up his mind that would be the last time he would see Steve. This was not healthy for him, and he knew he was falling for a guy who was unavailable and crossing a dangerous line with him. The following Friday, Steve e-mailed Michael asking if he wanted to go shopping with him on Saturday. Michael hesitated before answering and foolishly e-mailed, "Sure, call me. I should be home all day."

The next day, Michael did something he hadn't done in a decade. He actually stayed home all day, waiting for a man to call him. He never once dialed Steve's number, and by around four, he realized Steve had no intention of contacting him.

Steve finally contacted Michael around five-thirty, and by e-mail, telling Michael he just got back from shopping and asking how Michael's day was.

Michael e-mailed back, "Weren't you going to call me to go with you?" and he wondered why he was giving Steve so much control over everything?

He e-mailed back, "Don't be like that; I just needed time alone."

Without hesitation this time, Michael e-mailed, "Steve, I don't think I can see or have contact with you anymore. I waited here all day for someone else's boyfriend to call me. This is not healthy for me, as I am not comfortable with this whole situation. You and your boyfriend have issues to work out, and I need to get on with my life. I really like you, but I am too old to be doing this. Please understand, Michael."

Michael was proud of himself for cutting it off. However, he then sat at the computer waiting for Steve's response rather than go out for the evening. Michael realized he was now becoming more obsessive while he was also becoming more miserable.

Why are my relationships never happy ones? He thought. *What the hell is this situation with Steve?*

Steve responded two hours later with "OK." That was it, just OK. No goodbye, no protest, just OK. Michael was not even upset. It was over. It was time to move on.

Throughout all of this, Michael had told no one that he had met Steve Smith or that they were fooling around. He did not even share it with Dr. Mikowsky.

The secrecy had begun.

Chapter Six

Most of December was dull for Michael as he continued to work in the apartment and occasionally meet with Sharon, but he did not go out very much. He considered buying a car or renting one for the time he was there, but kept putting it off, finding one excuse or another not to do it. Michael would talk to a few guys at Results the Gym, but working out in the morning did not lend itself to establishing friendships as he pretty much kept to himself, and everyone there in the wee hours of the morning was concentrating on working out and getting to their jobs on time.

This was surprising as Michael was such a social person when he was home in California, but he had changed – Washington had changed him. He was so used to the show biz environment that he didn't know how to function in a city full of lawyers and federal workers. He just didn't fit in. He missed being in a writer's room at a studio. Although that was work, it was always fun, even when they worked past midnight. Michael would bring Aunt Clara to work with him, and she would sleep most of the day in his office or in one of the chairs in the writer's room. He missed having a dog, but Michael knew he should wait until he returned home before considering adopting another pet. There were days he would not leave the apartment except to go to the gym or pick up dinner from the Chinese take-out on Mount Pleasant Street.

He wanted to go home.

As he was getting ready to go to Sharon's for a New Year's Eve Party, he decided to check his e-mail, yet there was nothing of any significance, except an e-mail from *GayDC Weekly Magazine* asking him to vote for the "Hottie of the Year." Michael opened the e-mail and clicked on the link and looked at the profiles of the five finalists, and not surprisingly, Steve Smith was one of them. Michael looked at all five guy's profiles and interviews, and Steve's was the most confusing. He said he was "desperately lonely" and hoping to find a love interest and balance that with his need to be alone. Michael wondered what the hell that meant. *Did he and the boyfriend break up? How does one become desperately lonely yet want to be alone?*

"Oy, am I glad I ended that situation, whatever the hell it was," Michael said out loud.

Steve's pictures were perfect, and Michael had to admit Steve was the most photogenic person he knew outside of Tinsel Town, and one of the sexiest men he had ever met. But, Michael also wondered how someone posing in a jock strap or leather chaps and nothing else could work for a government agency, albeit as a contractor or a consultant, and still have a security clearance. *Didn't they know everything about everyone?* Maybe Michael was right, and that was not his real name. But still, Michael was aware that the government even knew when one took his last crap!

Michael decided to vote for Steve. Then he did something he knew he would regret. He e-mailed Steve to tell him he voted for him and wished him a Happy New Year. Michael then shut down the computer, determined not to sit there waiting for a response.

"No more of that behavior for me," Michael said to himself.

Michael called for a cab, which arrived in fifteen minutes and took him to Sharon's party. He was never much for New Year's Eve, as he was never much of a drinker, usually stopping after one. He was quiet to the point of being almost anti-social for most of the evening, and he was not in the greatest of moods. He attributed it to being a little homesick and nervous about going back to California for the premiere of *Birthright* in a few days. Michael did engage in small talk with a few people, but he really wasn't himself, so he would use the excuse of helping Sharon and duck into her kitchen to help with the food, leading most of the guests to think he was a snob, which couldn't be farther from the truth.

After midnight, just about everyone left, and Michael stayed to help Sharon clean up. She was picking up cups and putting them in a trash bag, while Michael put all the leftover food into containers and into the refrigerator. Her boyfriend, Wes, who also didn't drink, acted as designated driver and drove a few of the guests home, so Michael and Sharon were the only ones in the condo once the party was over.

Sharon walked into the kitchen and leaned against the counter looking at Michael. "OK, Michael, what's wrong?" she asked with her arms crossed over her ample bosom.

"Why would anything be wrong?" Michael asked as he continued the task of putting away the leftovers.

"You haven't said a word all night. You pretty much nodded at people and then would retreat into the kitchen and make like you were helping me," she said. "You're usually the life of the party. Everyone gravitates around you while you tell jokes and stories about your mother and her friends or some weird situation you've managed to fall into."

Michael glanced at her for a second, then placed the last container in the refrigerator, poured himself a diet soda, and sat at the kitchen table. "Do you have any cigarettes?" he asked, ignoring her question.

"Michael, I thought you didn't smoke," Sharon said as she tied up the trash bag she had brought into the kitchen.

"Only when I'm a little stressed," he answered.

"You and your secrets. I have some, but we have to smoke on the patio," she said as she walked toward the refrigerator. She then tried to reach into the cabinet above the refrigerator but was having no luck. Michael walked over to the refrigerator and opened the cabinet and found her pack of Marlboro Lights and handed them to her.

"Now, who has secrets?" he asked with a slight smile.

They walked out onto the patio, and it was unusually warm for a December night in Washington. The view from her Adams Morgan condo was magnificent. One could see the Washington Monument and the Capitol Dome, and they could still hear a few partygoers whooping it up around town. Michael lit her cigarette and then his own, and they smoked in silence for a while.

"OK, Michael, what's up?" she asked with her brow furrowed and looking directly at him.

"I don't know, Sharon. I guess my coming out here was a mistake," Michael said, avoiding her gaze.

"Why do you say that?" she asked.

He took another puff and answered, "Well, I never really took the time to digest all that happened, what with the show being cancelled and Aunt Clara and Sylvia dying. I just hopped on a plane and came out here. I'm really lonely here. I don't know that many people."

"You know me, you idiot," she said indignantly.

"That's not what I meant," he said. "I don't go out to the bars. I'm not meeting anyone. I sit in that apartment all day writing. The only time I get out is when I go to the gym in the morning."

She looked at him and put out her cigarette in a plastic ash tray she had sitting on a table just for these occasions. "When you say you're not meeting people, do you mean men?"

Michael put his cigarette out and immediately grabbed another one. She gave him a look and proceeded to do the same. Did he mean men? Did he mean friends? Why was he so lonely? In Hollywood, Michael went to one party after another. He met people all the time, and he rarely stayed home on a Saturday night. But here in Washington, he had become a hermit. *What has happened to me?* Michael thought.

"I guess that's part of it. I just have no social life either," Michael said.

"Michael, when was the last time you had a real boyfriend?" she asked.

"It's been a long time," he answered.

"Why?" Sharon asked, interrupting his thoughts.

"I only attract selfish jerks, who can't love me as I love them. I gave up on dating as I was tired of falling into the same patterns all the time," he answered. Intellectually, he could see where he was going wrong, but emotionally, he had no control.

"Did you ever think that rather than attracting them, you are attracted to men who can't love you back?" Sharon asked.

"No. I figured I was a magnet ... and now, you sound like my therapist," Michael said, as if her question were ridiculous.

"You're not a magnet, Michael. You're a walking billboard," Sharon said. "I've listened over the years to your stories about Roy and Doug and Philip, and it's always the same thing. These guys only stay with you because you make yourself available to them. You change in an effort to make them fall in love with you. But, they'll never love you. They use you. They only love themselves. They know whatever they do you'll stick around and allow yourself to be treated like shit."

Michael was starting to get upset. Sharon was harsh, but she had also touched a nerve. Michael lit a third cigarette and wondered if in fact she was right?

"I allow myself to be treated like this?" he asked looking right at her.

"Yes, Michael," she said. "You allow yourself to be treated like shit. Only you can walk away from these situations. You have to learn to stand up for yourself and not allow people to walk all over you."

He continued to look at her but remained silent.

"Look, Michael, I love you as if you were my own brother, but sometimes I wanted to scream when I heard about how this one treated you and that one treated you. I don't get it ... At the risk of being rude," Sharon continued as she lit another cigarette, "Would you like to see *my* therapist?"

"You have a therapist?" Michael asked with a smile – the first time he smiled all night.

"You're not the only one with secrets, Michael," she said with a smile back to him as she took a puff.

"That's OK, Sharon, I know I can call my therapist any time, and he'll talk to me."

"So, why don't you call him?"

Chapter Seven

On New Year's Day, Steve replied to Michael's e-mail about *GayDC Weekly Magazine's* "Hottie of the Year." Steve thanked Michael and then said he was glad to hear from him as he was thinking about him and missed him. Steve also said he was imagining Michael having sex with him on a weight bench. Michael told him he was just sorting things out and hoped he was well. There was no response to Michael's reply, and he was actually happy about that as he still knew deep down that he had fallen for Steve and the further he stayed away, the better it would be for both of them.

Michael flew back to LA the second week of January for the premiere of *Birthright*. It was good to be home, even if just for three days, although it was weird for Michael to be staying at a hotel. He did check on his tenant, and the house was being kept relatively neat but not up to Michael's standards. He suggested a cleaning lady, and the tenant agreed. Michael also reminded him to call the landscapers as the yard was beginning to resemble a jungle. He informed his tenant that he expected to be back on schedule, June 1.

Once back at the hotel, Michael called Sam to see if he wanted to go with him to the premiere, and he said enthusiastically, "Yes, of course!"

He knew it would be good to see Sam again, and he could catch up on his career as Sid had managed to get him a small recurring role on a sitcom as a sexy delivery driver, who showed up at an office every few episodes, sending all the employees into apoplexy because of his good looks and the tight uniform they made him wear. It was not a memorable role, and ten years into his career, people would probably say, "He looks familiar." Then, during a retrospective of his career forty years from now, they would show a clip of him as the nameless delivery driver, and everyone would say, "That was Sam Jacobs?" Michael imagined it happening just like that, and it was not much of a stretch by Hollywood standards.

Sam showed up at Michael's hotel room, wearing a black suit, gray shirt and a black and silver tie. He looked like a Jewish James Bond. His hair was shorter, but he was as handsome as ever with his dark features and full lips. Sam stepped in and hugged Michael tightly as if he missed him like no one else.

"Oh, Michael, I cannot thank you enough for everything you've done for me," he said with tears in his eyes. "Meeting you was the best thing that ever happened to me."

"Come on, Sam," Michael said as they let go of each other, and he placed his hands on Sam's shoulders, "You did this all yourself; you just needed a break. I'm so proud of you. I saw you on the show, and you looked so great, and you were funny, too. I think you have a fantastic career in comedy ahead of you."

Sam hugged him again, and at six-feet even, he was probably not used to looking up at someone as tall as Michael. Sam placed his hand behind Michael's head and pulled him in for a kiss. Their lips were perfectly meshed. They kissed for quite a while before Michael realized they would be running late.

"Sam, you got the job; you don't need to throw yourself at me," he joked.

"I like you, Michael," he said. "Even if you did nothing for my career, I would still want to be close to you."

He really was a sweet guy, and if Michael weren't so jaded from two decades in Hollywood and bad relationships, he would have allowed himself truly to believe him. Michael tried, but the cynic in him managed to come through. The one thing he did know about

Jewish guys was that they fell hard and fast. Michael was also like that. They really do make the best husbands as they are truly devoted and filled with guilt, too. If Sam's parents were dead (the best match *is* a Jewish guy with dead parents), Michael was intent on proposing marriage. And, Sam would be perfect for Michael. So, why could he not stop thinking about Steve?

"Listen, are you worried about being my date tonight? Everyone knows I'm gay, and your career is just getting started," Michael said to him, wondering if he would back out.

"Are you kidding? It's 2006, and I don't care," Sam said. "If I don't find work because of who I am, then fuck it. I don't want to work," he said with a smile as he put his arm through Michael's, who locked the hotel room door behind them.

"I admire your attitude," Michael said. "You don't have to play the 'is he or isn't he' game."

As they walked up the red carpet at the Kodak Theatre, no one seemed to know who Michael – or Sam – was. Michael liked being anonymous but worried that Sam might be disappointed.

"I'm sorry I'm not adding any scandal to your career," Michael whispered into his ear as they made their way into the theatre. "That's what you get for being a writer's date. No one cares."

"Hey, fellah," Sam said, "I am here for you, not to further my career; this is your night."

Wow, selfless and supportive, Michael thought as he looked into Sam's dark eyes, *so why am I still thinking about Steve?*

Photographers were snapping shots at Onah Wilson and Johnny Lawrence, the stars of the picture, saying look here and look there, so they could get "candid" pictures. Onah and Johnny would pose this way and that way, looking ever so natural. Michael couldn't stand the phoniness of it all. One photographer asked

Michael to step out of the way as he was blocking his view, and Stanley King, who happened to be standing next to Michael, shouted and pointed at Michael, "Do you know who the fuck you're talking to? That is Michael Bern, he wrote this goddamn movie, you moron!"

Immediately, cameras starting flashing in Michael's direction, and he tried to smile naturally, but it was of no use. He was no supermodel or screen idol. But Michael did manage to scream at them, "And, this handsome hunk is my date, Sam Jacobs. Remember that name. Sam Jacobs!" Sam looked at Michael with a smile, and Michael told him through clenched teeth as he looked this way and that, "Smile pretty for the camera, Sam; this'll be your world some day."

While smiling for the paparazzi, Sam said, "And, I hope you're in my world when it happens."

After they finished snapping, Michael walked up to Stanley and tapped him on the shoulder. "Thanks, Stanley, I just hope they airbrush the shots of me," he said as they rushed into the theatre.

Michael had not seen the final cut, only the rushes when they were filming in North Carolina in 2004-2005. He had bugged Stanley about the picture, constantly being assured by the director that all was OK, and the writer need not worry about anything. Michael was generally pleased with the film. There were parts he would have changed, but the cinematography was beautiful, and Onah and Johnny were perfect in the starring roles. The reviews the next day were glowing, and there was talk of an Oscar nomination or two, including best screenplay.

After the premiere, Michael and Sam went to a party at Stanley's house, but Michael had a hard time enjoying himself as he could not stop thinking about Steve although he was with a perfectly wonderful man, who never left his side all evening and was the perfect gentleman at the party. Whenever anyone came up to talk to him, he tried to make small talk, but he was not his usual social self. Thank God for Sam, who could carry on a conversation with anyone as he was intelligent, funny, and well-spoken, too. What a catch. Michael observed Sam with a smile, impressed by his ability to be comfortable in any situation.

What the hell is wrong with me? Michael thought as Sam talked to a couple of actors. *This is supposed to be the highlight of my career, and I'm feeling so down and antisocial even though Sam is here to support me.*

They went back to the hotel after the party, and Sam came up to Michael's room for a while to talk. They chatted about the evening, and since they both had to get up early, Sam for rehearsal, and Michael for an early flight to the East Coast for another premiere, they again parted ways without ending up in bed. Michael just didn't want him to be a trick. He really liked Sam and thought if they ended up in bed together, it would ruin what was developing into a great friendship. Sam didn't seem to mind, and Michael believed Sam sensed he was a little depressed.

Michael was living the old Jewish saying: "I'm just not as happy as I thought I would be."

As he opened the door for Sam, he said as he reached up to stroke Michael's cheek, "Michael, you seem down, not like the big flirt I met last year."

"I'm sorry, Sam," Michael said as he looked into his dark brown eyes. "I guess I'm not looking forward to going to Richmond for another premiere, and I wish I could stay here and sleep in my own house and not a hotel. I really don't travel well," he said, avoiding the real reason for his mood.

"I understand," Sam said. "When you come back in the summer, you'll feel more at home and be back to your normal self."

Sam was so understanding, and Michael knew that if he were in his shoes, he would run from this depressed mess of a man who could not enjoy the highlight of his career. After Sam left, Michael prepared himself for his early flight to Virginia's capital, which was chosen as the venue for the "second" premiere because *Birthright* took place there. Michael called Sam early in the morning before he left and invited him to visit him in Washington, so he could show him around. They talked for a while as Michael made his way to check out of the hotel, and he realized talking to Sam put a smile on his face and made him feel better. But, he could not get Steve out of his thoughts.

Michael flew into Richmond and rented a car. The premiere was that night, and he planned to stay only one night before flying back to Washington. This premiere was very low key, and without Stanley King there to tell them who he was, only two photographers took his picture. Again, the audience loved the movie, and the critics were raving about the performances and the script. At this high point in his life, Michael should have been thrilled and excited, but his depression had taken him over. Michael managed to smile politely when introduced, but those who had never heard of him assumed he was a man of few "spoken" words. If only they could have had the opportunity to know his real personality, the one he had before arriving in Washington.

The next morning as Michael prepared to go back to the airport, return the car, and fly to DC, he decided to take a side trip. He called the airline and changed his ticket for the following day and extended his car rental as well. He planned to drive to Hampton and Newport News for the day. The trip would only take an hour, and he thought the drive would do him some good.

As he merged onto I-64 early that morning, memories of driving along that route flooded his mind. Michael was reminded of how customers in the Williamsburg restaurant where he worked in the early 1980s would comment on all the trees on the Lower Peninsula that was home to Williamsburg, Jamestown,

Hampton, and Newport News. He thought about the last time he was in his hometown in April 2004 for Aunt Florence's funeral and how her death brought about a major shift in his life. Upon returning to LA after her death, he began therapy and completed *The Girls*, his "opus" that was rejected by every major studio, and learned more about himself than he wanted to know at the time. But, even with the breakthroughs in therapy, there was so much more he had not confronted, and he vowed upon his return to LA next summer to resume therapy and find out why he went through these dark periods whenever he became involved with a man.

Weren't relationships supposed to be happy? Wasn't finding "the one" supposed to bring one eternal bliss? Would he ever meet his soul mate? Michael doubted it, and he had resolved himself to the fact that he would be single for the rest of his life.

He drove past all the Newport News exits and once in the Hampton city limits, took the exit for Kecoughtan Road toward Rosenberg Cemetery, a century-old Jewish burial ground established by Russian immigrants who pursued the American dream via Hampton Rhodes Harbor in the mid- to late-1800s. The gates to the cemetery were open, although it was deserted. Michael pulled in and parked next to the first row after the oldest section of the cemetery. He took a deep breath before exiting the car and walked down the row until he spotted the dark tan granite stone. He had been unable to make the unveiling in April 2005, so this was the first time he had visited since being a pallbearer at the funeral almost two years earlier. Michael picked up a stone and stood before the large head stone, which read "Friedman." There were three footstones, and buried on the left and written on the footstone was, "Florence 'Flossie' Friedman Greenberg Mirmelstein Einstein Kennof, Devoted and Beloved Mother, Grandmother, and Godmother, June 20, 1927–April 24, 2004." Michael chuckled at the fact that they included all her married names. But upon reading "Godmother" on her marker, he was so touched that tears streamed down his face as he placed a stone on her grave. Michael was Aunt Flossie's only godchild, and this simple act of putting that title on her grave warmed his heart and made him miss her even more. On the lower right side of the marker were two dancing figures and the inscription, "She danced her way to Heaven," a reminder for all eternity that she collapsed and died while ballroom dancing, her favorite pastime.

"Oh, Aunt Flossie, I miss you so much. I wish you were here right now to cheer me up. I think about you every day," Michael said out loud for only the resting souls to hear.

He stood there for a few minutes, thinking about his favorite person in the world. He then walked a few rows back and placed a stone on Arlene Feld's grave, which was to the left of her mother-in-law, Minna Feld, who was buried between Arlene and William Feld, Arlene's ex-husband. Michael's eyes filled with tears again while thinking about Arlene, his mother's oldest friend, and someone he cared for very deeply. As he wiped his eyes, he decided not to seek out any other graves at this cemetery that day.

Michael returned to the car, exited the cemetery and decided to visit one more burial ground before heading back to Richmond. He drove onto Jefferson Avenue and turned left on Denbigh Boulevard, heading for Route 60, and within a few minutes, he spotted Peninsula Memorial Park on his right and turned in to the main drive. The Reformed Jewish section was on the left, and as he drove around, he parked the car. The cemetery was empty, which he found unusual for such a large burial ground that had sections for just about every religion and their respective denominations.

"Must be a slow death week," Michael said to himself, as he stepped out of the car and walked across the drive to gather some gravel he spotted on the other side. He picked up a few stones and walked back over to the Reform Jewish section, which was distinguished from the rest of the cemetery not only by its location near the road, but also by the use of in-ground grave markers as opposed to headstones. Michael had only been to this cemetery once before, in 1981, when his cousin Lenny died from a mysterious illness that they would later learn was AIDS as it would not even make national headlines until June of that same year. Amazingly, he located his marker without any trouble – "Lenny Bern, 1960-1981." Michael placed a stone on the marker and noticed a few other stones had also been placed there. He wondered if he knew who had visited him.

As Michael walked to the right of Lenny's marker, he noticed a grave he had never visited. He paused to look at the marker and pondered if he should put a stone on it.

It was his mother's grave – "Hannah S. Stein, Loving Mother and Wife, July 28, 1927-June 2, 2001." Michael shook his head. "Loving Mother and Wife?" he said out loud. Michael had read about people who screamed at their parents' graves letting go of anger they had bottled up for decades, but although he could be quite a drama queen when the situation called for it, he did not have the urge at that moment to lay on the histrionics – besides, there were no other people around to enjoy what could have been an entertaining display. He always believed that if one were to put on a scene, one should at least have an audience.

For the last sixteen years of Hannah's life, he did not speak to her, and Michael thought he had let go of the hurt and the pain, but looking to the right of her grave, the pain returned. There was Karl Stein's burial place. Next to his mother was the man who had broken his nose and knocked out his front teeth, causing him to leave Newport News and not return for almost two decades. His heart beat so loudly, he could hear it. He then struggled to keep from yelling and instead stepped on Karl's marker while he placed a stone on his mother's. As he stood back up, tears welled up in his eyes.

He then looked around, turned his back to the road, unzipped his pants, pulled out his penis, and took a piss on Karl's grave. While the urine streamed over Karl's resting place, he said out loud, "Why, Mother, why? Why did you hate me so much? What did I do to cause you so much pain?"

He stood there shaking the last drops and crying for quite a while before he put his penis back into his pants, and zipped up.

He wanted to know what made her the way she was. Was her childhood as horrible as his? Why did she marry violent, narcissistic men, who mirrored her own selfish personality? If she didn't want children, which obviously she did not, why did she? She certainly waited long enough to have Michael, giving birth at thirty-five, when all her friends already had teenagers to contend with. He wiped his eyes and thought his coming down here was a bad idea – although his bladder was now relieved.

* * * * *

In April 1962, Hannah Bern discovered that at thirty-five years old, she was two-months pregnant for the first time. After six years of marriage, she had resolved herself to the fact that she would probably never have children and never really gave it much thought. She knew she needed to break the news to Adam, but wasn't sure of the best way to do so.

As she relayed the story to Michael after dinner one night when he was sixteen years old, Adam, Michael's father, came home drunk late one night. Hannah was sitting at the kitchen table, smoking a cigarette and playing solitaire, when Adam entered the room, staggering. He was around five-foot-nine, with reddish brown hair and a slight build, and his eyes were cold and empty.

"Where have you been?" Hannah asked without looking up.

"Playing poker, why?" Adam asked as he opened the refrigerator and pulled out a bottle of beer.

Hannah looked at her husband, whom she had grown to hate, and blurted out, "I'm pregnant."

Adam looked at her with rage in his cold, dead eyes, and yelled, "You're just telling me that because I'm drunk." He then hurled the bottle at Hannah's head. Fortunately, she ducked just in time as the bottle crashed against the kitchen wall.

"And, that is when I realized I was stuck with your father," Hannah told Michael as she finished the story and lit another cigarette.

She never added another word to that story.

* * * * *

Michael walked over to a few more graves of people he barely remembered, but laid stones on their markers as well, as a sign of respect. Then, he found Morton Sapperstein's grave. Michael smiled when he thought back to Rona's husband. He always had a *ferbissina punim* or sour look on his face, but he was really a nice man, who was so devoted to Rona. If only he had made love to her as often as she wanted. Michael laughed as he thought back to Rona in the Emergency Room, when Morton had a heart attack, and her removing her robe and standing in front of everyone, including a bunch of college kids, in a red lace bra and panties, wearing gold high-heeled slippers, showing everyone the reason Morton went into cardiac arrest. Even though she was fifty-eight at the time, she looked great. With this memory, Michael actually laughed for the first time in a long time.

He walked back to his car, and before starting the engine, he turned on his cell phone to check for any messages. There was one from Sam, telling him to have a safe trip and that he looked forward to seeing him again. Michael smiled when he thought about Sam. He then scrolled through the numbers and located one he thought he should call while in town. He hit the send button and waited while it rang, choosing not to start the car yet.

"Hello," a woman's voice said on the other end.

"Mrs. Wonderful?" Michael said.

"Mr. Perfect, where are you? How are you?" Doreen Weiner Eidleman asked.

"Aunt Doreen, I am in Newport News for the day, do you want some company?" he asked.

"Of course, I'd love to see you. Let me give you directions," she said excitedly.

He wrote down the directions to her home in King's Mill. After years of living in Hilton, Doreen finally bit the bullet and moved to the neighborhood, where all the snobs lived, and if he were not mistaken, Rona Sapperstein had done the same after Morton died.

Michael started the car and drove up Route 60, forgoing the Interstate as this would only be about a twenty-five-minute drive. He realized along the way why he never liked Newport News – once voted the ugliest city in the United States – as he passed one strip mall after another and the occasional mobile home park. Oddly, there were upscale neighborhoods dotting the landscape between the strip malls and trailers. Before long, he was at the entrance to King's Mill, and he rolled down the car window and introduced himself to the guard at the gate as he was handed a temporary visitor's pass.

He followed Doreen's directions and pulled up in front of her house, which was situated off the main road and abutted the golf course. There was a small courtyard in front and two houses situated on either side of hers at ninety-degree angles, all with red brick and white trim. Michael walked past a champagne-colored Cadillac, knowing it was Doreen's as she always drove the largest Cadillac available and bought a new one every two years. He rang the bell and heard another familiar and loud voice, which made Michael smile in anticipation.

"I'm coming, I'm coming," the woman yelled from the other side of the door, before she swung it open.

"Aunt Rona!" Michael exclaimed. "What are you doing here?" Rona smiled with her large mouth and rows of large teeth, still framed with the brightest pink lipstick in town. She was still tall with a slim figure, dressed in a brown sweater and winter white slacks with her signature amber jewelry in her ears and around her neck. She still wore multi-colored plastic framed glasses with pink-tinted lenses, but she had allowed her once curly red hair to go gray, almost white. She wore it short now, and it actually made her more attractive. She swung open the screen door and gave Michael a huge hug, kissing him on the cheek, and he knew that lipstick would take forever to wash off.

"Oh my God! What a hell of a surprise! Doreen, get out of the can, he's here!" Rona yelled after letting Michael go and dragging him into the living room.

Doreen's house was open and airy, just like a photo spread in *Architectural Digest*. It was decorated in whites and beiges with a hint of green and yellow accents. The living room had a large patio door on one side overlooking the golf course and a cathedral ceiling. Ironically, that golf course was where his mother's second husband, Bart, was killed after being struck by lightning on the eighteenth green. There were two large white leather sofas, and Rona motioned for Michael to sit down.

"Doreen, wipe your ass and get down here!" she yelled, always crass and with a big mouth to go with it.

"Shut up, Rona, I'm coming," Doreen yelled from upstairs.

Michael looked up and wearing her blonde hair as she had since Vidal Sassoon styled it in the late 1960s, Doreen appeared at the top of the stairs, wearing a sweater and slacks in her signature peach. She had two small gold hoops in her ears and a matching necklace, and on her hand was a diamond that was even larger than the one she wore twenty years earlier. She descended the stairs slowly, as Michael got up to greet her. He knew she had back surgery and a quadruple bypass in the past few years, but she still looked fantastic, although even shorter than her original five feet. Michael hugged her before she reached the bottom step, so she could reach him for a kiss on the cheek.

"Mr. Perfect," she said. "You look fantastic. How old are you, now?"

"Mrs. Wonderful, you know how old I am. I'm forty-three."

"Oy vay! Lie, I tell you, lie," Rona said from where she was sitting on the couch. "You make us feel so old."

"Please, you two don't look a day over sixty," Michael said as they sat down on the couch.

"That's because we're both over seventy-five," Doreen said, laughing. "Can I get you anything? I made lunch. You're staying for lunch aren't you?"

"Of course, he's staying for lunch. He wouldn't just drop by and leave," Rona chimed in.

"Yes, I can stay for lunch," he answered as he smiled at them. "Rona, where is your house?"

"Next door," she said. "They're renovating it, so I'm staying with Doreen for a couple of months."

Michael looked at both of them and wondered how they could stand to live together for that long. They both had very strong personalities, and where Rona was loud, Doreen was always on, even with a heart condition and back problems, she was still quite animated and the center of attention. As with all his mother's friends, he loved these two women. He could not remember a time when they weren't in his life. And, here they were, two elderly women, yet they were as energetic and lively as he remembered them twenty years before.

"He needs to eat; he looks skinny," Doreen said.

"Are you kidding, I am at least twenty pounds overweight," Michael answered, sounding a bit like his mother, which he would never admit and having not stepped on a scale in quite a while, even though his clothes were starting to fit loosely.

"No, Doreen is right, you're too thin," Rona said as she got up to go to the kitchen. "I'll get you a snack to tide you over before we have lunch." Michael heard a bag opening and its contents being poured into a bowl after Rona went into the kitchen.

Doreen leaned toward Michael and whispered, "That bitch is driving me crazy. One more day in my house, and someone is going to end up dead. Do you know she snores as loud as she laughs? I can hear her two bedrooms over."

Rona returned with pretzels in one bowl and mustard in another as Doreen leaned away from Michael, who almost cringed as this was his mother's favorite snack. He had a vision of her dipping the hard pretzels in the mustard and eating them slowly, and it about made him wince at the thought of doing the same.

"Rona, how can you serve him that dry *drek* without something to drink?" Doreen asked as she got up slowly to go the kitchen.

Rona picked up her purse and pulled out a cigarette. She then went over to the patio door and opened it, standing in the doorway as she lit up. She took a puff and whispered in Michael's direction, "I should have stayed with Neil and his wife. Do you know what it is like living with that tramp? The woman has had two heart attacks, bypass surgery and walks with a limp, and she still has the *alta cockers* coming over all hours of the night for a screw!" She then exhaled and raised her eyebrows as if to confirm what she said.

"What are you whispering about, Rona?" Doreen asked as she returned with two sodas. She handed one to Michael and kept the other for herself.

"You couldn't bring me one?" Rona asked as she put out her cigarette after a few puffs, blew the remaining smoke in the direction of the patio, closed the door and stepped back inside.

"You especially know where the kitchen is, Rona. Every time I walk by the refrigerator, all I see is your asshole and pockets," Doreen said with a smirk to her friend.

"I'm surprised you left your bedroom long enough to notice, Doreen," Rona said as she went back to the kitchen for a soda.

Although they were bickering, Michael knew they were still the best of friends and would do anything for each other. Sixty years of friendship is hard to ignore or let go.

"That woman can eat and eat, and she never gains any weight. I'm telling you it's unnatural," Doreen, who struggled to maintain her full figure, whispered to him. "It's a good thing I have money, or I would be out on the street with all she eats."

"Doreen, remind me to call Neil and tell him to send over some more food from the deli," Rona said as she returned with her soda in hand, indicating Doreen had not really paid for any of the food. Rona then sat on Michael's other side.

"Does Neil still run Sapperstein's Deli?" Michael asked, deciding not to eat any of the pretzels.

"Going on ten years," she answered as she raised her glass to take a sip.

The two remaining women from his mother's forty-year Tuesday night Mah Jongg game were sitting on either side of Michael, and he was happy to be there.

When he was a kid, he never would have imagined his sitting on a couch as an adult between Rona and Doreen as they bickered about living together. It was almost surreal. A friendship like theirs was very rare. It was sad, too, as three of their best friends were gone, Arlene, his mother, and Florence, as well as all their husbands. They were the only ones left. *What will happen when either of them dies?* Michael thought.

Doreen started to cry and pulled a tissue out of her sleeve. Then Rona also cried and pulled a tissue out of her own sleeve. He remembered the "sleeve tissue dispensers" and how he wondered as a little boy if all these women had holes in their forearms.

"Why are you two crying?" he asked with alarm.

"Oh we are just a couple of sentimental old farts, Michael," Rona said between sobs.

"Your being here just brings back so many memories, and we are just so happy you turned out so well," Doreen said as she patted Michael's knee and dabbed her eyes. Not wanting to be outdone, Rona also patted his knee. And, he noticed them looking at each other to see who could pat the most affectionately. He never felt so loved. But what did they mean by happy he turned out so well? Were they worried about him? Did he really want to know?

"OK, you two *yentas*, stop crying, or I'll start," Michael said, wanting this tear-fest to end since he had already been crying earlier that day.

"You're right," Doreen said. "Rona, stop crying, this is a happy occasion. Michael didn't drop by to see us blubber."

"You started it," Rona said indignantly.

"Do you two argue a lot?" Michael asked.

"All the time," Doreen said as if surprised by his question.

"We wouldn't have it any other way," Rona said as if there were any other way to conduct a friendship.

"And your friendship survives all that bickering?" he asked with wonder, as he did everything possible to avoid arguments or fighting and especially yelling. Michael couldn't imagine having a friendship based on bickering.

"Of course," Doreen said. "We're like sisters. That is how we show our love. She can say anything to me, and I to her." Then Doreen leaned toward Michael, shook her finger and said, "But, God help anyone else who says anything about Rona."

"And, you, Rona?" Michael asked.

"Please, half the gossip around town about her, I started, myself," she said and laughed that loud laugh Michael missed so much. Doreen also joined in the laughter, and he was infected by the humor as well, as he laughed and truly was glad to have made this special side trip.

Doreen stopped laughing long enough to yell at Rona, "Careful, Rona, or those teeth'll come flying out."

"How many times do I have to tell you these *are* my teeth," Rona yelled at Doreen, then looked at Michael and said, "After all, I paid for them." They started laughing again.

"Can you believe it? They actually made her a set that matched those horse teeth she had," Doreen said as she got up and looked at her friend.

"Somewhere, there is an Osmond with a toothless grin," Rona answered back.

"Or Mr. Ed," Michael said.

"Good one, Michael," Doreen said as she went into the kitchen slowly.

Rona slapped Michael's leg and got up herself. He followed them into the kitchen and sat at the dinette, happily watching as they prepared lunch, constantly tripping over each other and bickering about what plates to use and what containers to open. Rona put a plate of egg salad and a tray of sliced challah on the table, while

Doreen placed a bowl of large, kosher pickles, followed by bowls of potato salad and coleslaw. Rona then placed a bowl of potato chips and a plate of pimento stuffed olives on the table.

"I hope there's enough food," Michael said, missing these large Jewish meals.

"Rona, did you pull the kugle out of the oven?" Doreen asked.

Rona then opened the oven and pulled out a kugle and placed it on the table. There was no room for plates at this point.

"Kugle? I haven't had good kugle in years," he said with delight.

They both stopped to look at the table, then in unison, they said, "The whitefish."

Rona then retrieved the whitefish from the refrigerator, and Michael was certain they had no room to eat. Rona, sensing his concern, immediately rearranged everything, as per her years of restaurant management experience, and amazingly they had room for the plates, cutlery, and napkins. When the iced tea was poured, Michael was confident he was back in the South. A few states north, and they would have been enjoying cream soda.

They both sat down, and Michael said, "When do the other guests arrive?"

They looked at each other and then at Michael and laughed again, while he prepared himself for Rona's teeth to come flying in his direction or land in the egg salad.

"Go ahead, Michael, don't be shy, eat," Rona said. "We wanted to be sure we had all your favorites."

"You have this food in your house all the time?" he asked as he took a slice of kugle, followed by some whitefish and egg salad. Michael had not eaten like this since he could remember.

"It pays to have a roommate with a deli in the family," Doreen said ironically as she filled her plate with whitefish and egg salad and took a piece of challah.

Rona made a sandwich with the challah and egg salad and took two slices of kugle. She then piled on the white fish, potato salad, and coleslaw and topped off her plate with a pickle. Doreen gave her a look then looked at Michael, rolling her eyes in Rona's direction.

"Rona, do you have enough food on your plate?" Doreen asked, sarcastically.

Rona looked at her plate then reached for the potato chips, and after grabbing a handful, declared unapologetically, "Now I do."

Michael smiled at the two of them as they began eating in silence. Between bites of the kugle, which was among the best he ever tasted, he asked, "When you said you were glad I turned out all right, what did you mean?"

Rona swallowed her mouthful of food and Doreen put down her fork as they looked at each other. It was as if each knew what the other was thinking.

"What?" Michael asked as he put down his fork.

Rona put her sandwich down and looked at Michael, and Doreen also stared in his direction.

"What?" he asked again, looking at each of them.

Rona spoke first, "Michael, we can only imagine what it must have been like growing up in your home. Hannah was our dear friend, but we worried about you all the time."

"When your mother told us she was pregnant," Doreen began then paused, "we girls, Arlene, Florence, Rona, and I, made a pact to look after her child."

"Why would you do that?" Michael asked.

They both hesitated and sat back.

"You can tell me," he said. "It's no secret I never spoke to my mother again after I left home in 1985, and you know what happened to make me leave. I won't get upset."

They looked at each other before Rona said to Doreen, "I think we can tell him. Enough time has passed."

Doreen inhaled deeply, exhaled slowly then began, "Michael, your mother loved you the only way she knew how. Unfortunately, that wasn't enough."

"Doreen, you're dancing around the issue," Rona said. "He's an adult; he's over forty; he can handle this."

"Handle what?" Michael asked, wanting to know what secret they were hiding.

"Michael, your mother never wanted to have children. As a matter of fact, your father didn't either," Rona began. "When your mother became pregnant after so many years of marriage, she wanted an abortion, but Arlene, Doreen, Florence, and I talked her out of it. That was when we agreed to look after you. That is why you were always invited over to our homes to play with our kids and stay over night and go on vacations with our families."

"But, it wasn't enough," Doreen said, interrupting Rona. "Florence told us about the bruises and how you would get quiet and go and sit for periods of time without talking to or playing with any of the other kids. You were closer to her than any of us, and she tried in vain to get you to open up, but she also knew your mother would harm you if you revealed anything."

"I actually asked your mother if I could have you for my own, before you were born," Rona said.

"So did I," Doreen said, trying to outdo Rona. "And, Florence even spoke to a lawyer about having you removed from your mother's house and getting custody of you when you were ten or eleven."

Michael was stunned. All this time, he thought they didn't know. Michael never questioned why he was always being invited to stay at their homes, go on their

113

vacations, and attend their family gatherings. All this time, he sometimes resented them for not rescuing him, when in fact, they *were* rescuing him.

"What did the lawyer say?" Michael asked, wanting to know more.

"He told Florence that it would be impossible, and your mother would probably move away with you if she did something like that," Rona said.

"Why did you stay friends with her?" Michael asked, continuing to look at both of them.

"As the years passed, all of us started to dislike her, but we had an agreement that we would put up with her as long as you were living at home," Doreen said, looking at Rona.

"Once you moved out, we drifted apart from your mother, and for the last several years of her life, none of us really talked to her," Rona said. "You stayed in touch with Florence, so we knew you were OK."

Michael started to cry, and he picked up a napkin to wipe his eyes. He had been through so much emotionally this day.

"Michael, don't cry," Rona said, "We didn't mean to upset you."

Between sobs, he told them, "You haven't upset me. I just wish I knew. I'm actually thankful you did what you did. I just wish I could have thanked Arlene before she died. She must have thought I was a brat for not thanking her. Seriously, thank you, both of you."

Rona and Doreen started crying again as well and dabbed their eyes with more tissues from their sleeves.

"Michael, Arlene knew you appreciated her," Rona said as she cried. "She knew more than anyone. She had two grown children already out of the house, yet you still would ride your bike to her house to visit. Arlene loved you like one of her own. Why do you think she always wanted to perform with you in the 'Cabaret'? She loved you and knew you loved her."

"More than one of her own," Doreen said sarcastically. "You turned out better than her own children." Rona laughed at Doreen's comment, and Michael smiled a bit, too, while continuing to cry.

"Talk about a couple of *shmeggegies*," Rona said as she laughed.

"Do you know that when I was little, I used to scream every time Arlene came over to the house?" he said, remembering a story from his childhood.

"That's because you thought Lucille Ball had come for a visit right out of the television, and it scared you," Doreen said. "I think that is why Arlene changed her hair color. You really scared her, too, the way you would scream and run."

They laughed at one of the few funny moments from when Michael was a child.

"I cannot thank you enough," he said. "All these years, I always thought nobody really knew what I was going through, and now I find out you girls were looking out for me all along."

"Eat, eat, enough of this sad talk, Michael, you have a great life now," Doreen said as she resumed eating her lunch.

They finished lunch, and he was stuffed as he had not been stuffed in years, but Michael made room for the prune Danish they served for dessert. He loved prune Danish. Although Michael protested, they made him take a couple of containers of food home with him, packing them in a cooler with dry ice. Only Rona, who was always prepared for any occasion, would have a cooler and dry ice on hand. As Michael kissed them goodbye, hugging them both and walking to his rental car, they cried once again. He asked them to visit him in Washington, and they said they would try. They both stood there waving at Michael, and as he started the car and looked back, he could see they were bickering about something, and then Doreen walked back into the house and attempted to slam the door in Rona's face. These girls were friends for life.

Michael drove back to Richmond and caught a flight the next day for Washington. It seemed ridiculous to fly as he was only in the air for about twenty minutes. He took a cab back to Eric's apartment and decided not to turn on the computer and check his e-mails. He had been through enough, and he didn't want to deal with his feelings for Steve at the moment.

The next morning, Eric's landline rang. It hardly ever rang, and Michael would usually pick it up when it did to give whoever called Eric's cell phone number, unless it was a telemarketer.

"Hello, Eric Sagman's residence," Michael answered.

"Eric, is that you?" an older woman's voice asked on the other end.

"No, Eric is in Brazil. I am subletting the apartment," he answered.

"Oh, I knew that," she said. "It is just that your voice sounds just like his. Is this Michael Bern?"

Michael's voice sounded like his also? And, if this woman knew he was in Brazil, why was she calling Eric's landline and not his cell phone?

"Yes, this is Michael. Can I give Eric a message?" he asked.

"Actually, this is Eric's mother, Harryette Sagman," she said.

"Oh, is something wrong?" he asked.

"No, no, nothing's wrong," Mrs. Sagman said. "Michael, what was your mother's name?"

What was my mother's name? Why the hell would she ask me a question like that? Michael pondered. "Why do you want to know?" he asked.

She hesitated for a moment then answered, "I think I knew your mother."

116

She knew my mother. This is odd. "Her name was Hannah Stein," Michael said.

"Oh," Mrs. Sagman said, "Was that her maiden name?"

"Well, no," he answered. "But, you see, my mother was married three times. Her maiden name was Summers, then she married my father, Adam Bern, then Bart Shimmer, and her third husband was Karl Stein."

"So your mother *was* Hannah Bern?" she asked as if a light bulb lit up in her head.

"Yes," Michael answered as he sat down, wondering how this woman knew his mother.

There was an awkward silence before she spoke again. "Michael, is your mother still living in Newport News, Virginia?"

"Well, she's buried there. She died in 2001."

"Oh, I'm so sorry," Mrs. Sagman said.

"Thank you," Michael said, never knowing how to react to that sentiment.

"Did you know Florence Greenberg?" she asked.

Michael took a deep breath and answered her question, "Florence died in 2004. She was my godmother, however, we called her Flossie," knowing she sensed the sorrow in his voice.

"I'm sorry, you must miss her very much," she said.

"Thank you, I do," Michael said.

"Michael, would you mind if my husband and I came over this afternoon to meet you?" she asked.

He was curious as to why she would want to meet him, so he answered yes, and she said they would drop by around two.

Michael tried to get some work done and e-mailed Sharon a couple of scenes. She asked what he was doing the rest of the afternoon, and he told her just some errands. Michael didn't want to go into Eric Sagman's parents' stopping by although she probably knew them, since she and Eric were friends. Then, he thought of something that had not occurred to him before. Sharon knew that Eric and Michael looked so much alike, so how come she never mentioned it? Michael did have a suspicious mind sometimes, dizzy, but suspicious nonetheless.

He showered, shaved and changed into a pair of kakis and an orange turtleneck wondering if he would clash with the décor. Right at 2:00 pm on the dot, there was a knock on the front door. Michael was surprised they could find parking so easily. He opened the door, and a woman he presumed was Eric's mother was standing there. She was about five-foot-six with dark red hair, and he guessed her age to be around seventy or seventy-five. Standing behind her and using a walker was apparently Eric's father. He looked to be in his eighties or even close to ninety. Although stooped over to support himself on the walker, he was a tall man, not as tall as Eric or Michael, but taller than usual, but may have been as tall when he was younger. He had thick white, wavy hair and wore large glasses with coke-bottle lenses that barely revealed green eyes with long gray lashes. Eric, who wore bifocals, must have inherited his father's eyesight as his mother did not wear glasses.

Eric's mother walked in first and introduced herself, and his father slowly entered behind her. Michael closed the door and asked if they wanted to sit in the kitchen, thinking it would be more comfortable for his father. They decided to go into the living room instead, and his father sat on one of the chairs, and Mrs. Sagman and Michael settled on the futon.

"I forgot my manners; can I get you anything to drink?" Michael asked standing up.

They both said no, so he sat back down.

"Sharon was right, Seymour, look at him," Mrs. Sagman said.

"Yep, he does look just like Eric," Mr. Sagman responded with a raspy voice.

"Sharon told us you did, but we didn't believe her," Mrs. Sagman said.

"Sharon talked to you about me?" Michael asked.

"When were you born, Michael?" Mrs. Sagman asked, ignoring Michael's question, very curious about Michael and not hesitating to ask him questions.

"November 22, 1962," Michael answered.

"Yep, Seymour, that would be about right," she said, looking at her husband as he shook his head yes.

"Mrs. Sagman, why are you so curious about me?" Michael asked still not sure why he was sitting here with these people.

Again, she was silent. Then she took his hand. "Eric was born on December 4, 1962," she said.

Michael really wanted these people out of the apartment as they were starting to creep him out.

"Michael, I have to tell you something you may find upsetting or unbelievable, but coming here today has confirmed it for us," she said.

"Go on," he said, wondering if he really wanted to know the reason for her visit.

"My husband knew your mother," she began, and again she paused. "We were married in June 1962, after I found out I was pregnant with Eric. Yes, even in those days, girls got into trouble."

He suddenly felt as if he were on one of those horrible tabloid talk shows, but he sat there quietly waiting for the bomb or Jerry Springer to pop out of the closet.

"At the time I got pregnant with Eric, my husband was having an affair with your mother," she continued.

Michael's heart stopped. His stomach knotted up, and he thought he was going to throw up. He also had a feeling what was coming next. She sensed his uneasiness and probably saw the color drain from his face.

Mrs. Sagman put her hand on Michael's, squeezed it and said, "You and Eric are brothers ... actually half brothers. I am convinced Seymour, my husband, is your father."

Michael's jaw dropped to his lap. When he arrived in Washington, he was Michael Bern, an only child. When he woke up this morning, he was still Michael Bern, an only child, whose father was killed by a runaway golf cart three months before he was born. Now, he was the result of an affair that happened forty-three years ago? His mother had three husbands, and now none of them were his father?

"Michael, are you OK?" Mrs. Sagman said to him.

"How long have you known?" he asked, after clearing his throat and trying to talk. Neither of them said a word. "Please, I need to know. How long have you known?" he asked again, with more strength in his voice.

"Michael, didn't you think it was unusual that your mother and father were married almost six years before they had their first child?" she asked.

Again with the goddamn questions, he thought. "No," he said, as he never wondered about that until his recent visit with Rona and Doreen.

"Your father may have been sterile ... it was only after the affair with Seymour that Hannah became pregnant. Had I not become pregnant at the same time, she may have left your father and married him," she continued, still with little emotion in her voice.

Michael started to shake and stood up. He paced back and forth trying to process what he was being told – his mother, his father, affairs, dead husbands, sterile husbands, half-brother, and a single pregnant mother. It was too much to take in, and he started to get angry.

And, now with an audience, he knew he was about to make a scene.

He started yelling at them, "You are my father? Eric is my brother? What the hell is this? You waltz in here and tell me my father, whose grave sits next to an empty plot in Hampton, Virginia, waiting for me, is not my father! Then you tell me your husband could have been my father had you not been knocked up! Now, I am supposed to just swallow all this? My father is dead and buried. Everyone said I looked like my father, although I never saw the resemblance ... I ..."

And then, Michael stopped.

He just stared at them as they looked at him with alarm. Then he thought about something ...

* * * * *

It was a Tuesday night in March 1979, and all the girls were over at Hannah's house playing Mah Jongg. Michael came downstairs for a drink and walked into the den to say hello. Arlene was sitting out and standing at the side-bar fixing herself a plate of food, while his mother, Rona, Doreen and Florence were getting their *mo-jo* on the tiles.

"Hi, girls," Michael said as he perused what his mother was serving – egg salad, tuna salad, chips, soda, pickles and the like.

Arlene, who had recently dyed her hair blonde and started wearing it in a teased flip, gave Michael a kiss and said while pinching his cheek, "He gets more handsome every day, Hannah. Who in your family does he look like?"

"Don't be silly, Arlene, he looks like his father," Michael's mother said with a cigarette dangling from her lips and mixing up the tiles.

Florence looked up at him, took off her large purple-framed glasses and said, "I don't know, Hannah. He doesn't even have the same hair color as Adam, and his eyes are green. No one in Adam's family had green

121

eyes." She then resumed mixing the tiles with the other three girls.

"Then there's the height. Adam was shorter than you, Hannah, especially when you wore heels," Rona said as she put out her cigarette and turned to look at Michael.

"Hannah, he must look like someone on your side," Doreen said as she also looked up at Michael. The four girls were examining Michael while his mother kept her focus on building her wall.

Hannah asked without looking up, "Doreen, do all of your kids look like Sammy?"

The women grew silent, as his mother made one of her usual snide comments. It was no secret that Doreen was always having affairs, and although her sons looked like Sammy, her daughter looked like Dr. Lawrence Eidleman, a man she had a long-term affair with and would eventually marry after Sammy died in 1992.

They remained silent and resumed building their walls, until Arlene started again as she was the only one looking at Michael now, "I still say, Hannah, he reminds me of someone."

Rona, Florence and Doreen looked at Michael again, but his mother continued to concentrate on building her wall.

Rona then spoke, "He looks like that Seymour fellow who used to work with Adam."

Hannah was clearly annoyed at this point and stopped building her wall. She looked up at the girls and said, "Don't be ridiculous, he looks like my mother's father, see the picture over there?" She pointed at an old photograph on the bookshelf, having already contradicted herself by saying he looked like his father and now her grandfather. It was a wedding picture from 1895, taken in Russia. Nana Mary's father was tall with dark hair and a mustache. Michael did not think he looked like him, and something told Michael, neither did the other girls.

"Can we change the goddamn subject and play some Mah Jongg. This conversation is annoying me," Hannah said.

Rona, Doreen and Florence resumed building their walls. Hannah had to maintain control, and for some reason, everyone did as she ordered when she got into one of these moods.

* * * * *

Michael stood there in the living room, staring at them and asked Mr. Sagman calmly, "Did you work with my father?"

He spoke up, "Yes, I did, until we moved up here in the summer of 1962."

"And, you knew all along you were my father?" Michael asked, not really wanting to know the answer.

Mr. Sagman looked down at the floor and nodded yes.

Michael grew angrier and yelled at him, "And, you knew what a controlling abusive bitch my mother was, and you did not even come to see me to check on me? You allowed me to grow up in that hellhole, not knowing what became of me? And, I am supposed to accept this as if everything is springtime and roses? I should kick you two out of here, but it is your son's apartment. I wish to fuck I never came to Washington. I don't fucking believe this! Do you know how horrible my childhood was? Do you have any fucking idea? Do you know how screwed up I am to this day because of that living hell? Do you? Do You?"

Neither said anything as their eyes opened in horror, as they were not expecting such an outburst. Michael imagined Eric never lost his temper, since he seemed in the few minutes he met him to be a happy-go-lucky guy. Michael was shaking uncontrollably at this point, so he walked into the kitchen, reached into the cabinet above the refrigerator for his emergency pack of cigarettes and walked out the front door.

He stood there smoking for a while before Mrs. Sagman came out to check on him.

"You really shouldn't smoke, it'll kill you," she said as if she were his mother.

He looked at her and said, "You are not my mother. I had a mother, and God knows I don't want another one."

"Look, Michael, I know this is difficult. Believe me. I wanted for years to contact you, but Seymour wouldn't let me. He was afraid of your mother. From what you just said in there, you probably were, also. I didn't know her well, but I knew she was secretive and controlling with a horrible temper. She probably preferred to keep your father's identity a secret also."

He blew the smoke in her face. "My mother was only concerned with herself. She never answered questions. Never! She would lie right in front of me and everyone for that matter. And, no one knew what it was like in that house because we had to put up a front. She controlled everything, including what she believed to be the truth," Michael said as he put out the cigarette and immediately lit another one.

"I know," she said.

"She also hated me," he said.

Michael bent down and grabbed her hand. She appeared nervous as he did this, but Michael placed it on the back of his head anyway.

"Do you feel that bump?" he asked.

"Yes," she said, her voice shaking.

"That's from when my mother's second husband shoved my head through a wall while she watched." He then took the same hand and put it on his wrist. "Feel this bump on my wrist?" She nodded her head yes again. "That is where he twisted my hand until the wrist broke in three places." Then he told her to look at his nose. She did, and he saw tears welling up in her eyes. "That is where her third husband punched me in the face repeatedly." Michael then pulled out the bridge work that held in his front teeth. She looked at him and started to cry. He then put his teeth back in place. "I wish you could look inside my ears," he continued. "When I was three, they had to reattach my ear drums, and I have always suspected that was due to a head injury I sustained at my mother's hands."

She was clearly upset at this point and pulled a tissue out of her sleeve. That little act made Michael sympathize with her.

"Mrs. Sagman, I'm sorry, I didn't mean to upset you. I'm just in shock," Michael said, now worried he had acted like a lunatic.

"You don't need to apologize," she said. But for some reason, Michael always did apologize even when he was not wrong.

"Look, I'm not upset that I found out he was my father. I really don't care to tell you the truth. I never really had a father, and at this age, I don't want one. I'm just upset that I could have had a different life."

But Michael *was* upset to find out Seymour Sagman was his father. Why did he always hide his true feelings?

"Michael, I think we should go. You need time to digest this, and Seymour is an old man, and I am not sure if he's up to any more excitement today," she said as if Seymour were more upset than Michael was.

"Can I ask you a question?" Michael asked.

"Yes," she said as she opened the screen door.

"Does Eric know?"

"We plan to call him as soon as we get home," she said. She went inside to get her husband, while Michael lit yet another cigarette. As they walked outside, Seymour grabbed Michael's hand and said he was sorry before they walked to their car, but Michael just nodded.

Michael was numb, he was upset, he was in shock, and he needed to call Dr. Mikowsky. He went back into the apartment and called Sharon first.

"Hi, Michael," she answered cheerily.

"Sharon, did you know?" Michael asked as if she knew about the Sagman's visit.

"Know what?" she asked.

"That Eric and I are brothers, and his father is my father?" he asked.

"I didn't know that, but I had my suspicions that you were somehow related," she began speaking quickly, knowing Michael would get upset. "Hear me out. I thought it was creepy when I first met Eric sixteen years ago, but everyone it seems has a twin. He did not look that much like you then because he wore glasses and his hair was really long. You had a goatee, and he didn't. But, when I saw you last, and you had shaved your goatee, and he had cut his hair, I knew there was something odd there. So, I called his mother and told her I had a friend who looked almost exactly like Eric. I told her your name, and she wanted to know your mother's maiden name, but I couldn't remember it. When I sold the movie rights to my book and asked you to help me write the screenplay, I thought this would be the perfect opportunity for you two to meet. I figured if you were related you would figure it out, but you just found it curious. So, I called his mother and told her if she wanted to see for herself, she should give you a call," she finished without taking a breath.

"That's it?" Michael said expecting more.

"Yeah, I didn't know much about your family history and you are pretty closed-lipped about your childhood, only telling funny, happy stories about it, so I figured I would just let things happen," she said, hoping Michael would not get mad at her.

"So, I didn't have to move here to help you with the screenplay?" Michael asked, getting angry again.

"Oh, no, I do need you here, as it takes place in D.C., and I think it helps you get a feel for the book," she said trying to assure Michael that he made the right decision to come to Washington.

"Sharon, I appreciate everything you've done for me over the years, and you have been a good friend, but this is just a little too *Parent Trap* for my taste," he said, wondering if he should just pack up and go home immediately.

"I know, I know, but I couldn't think of a better way to get you two to see each other. If your plane had been late, you never would have met," she said, knowing Michael was thinking of leaving.

"I guess it's all about timing," he said. "But maybe I should go back to California." Had Michael not moved here for a year, he would never have found out about his real father, and he never would have met Steve. What else could possibly happen?

"Michael," she pleaded. "Don't be rash. Stay a little longer. I like having you here. Please."

"OK, I just need some time to think this over," he told her, said goodbye and hung up the phone.

He then dialed Dr. Mikowsky, and he hoped he had two hours to talk to him. He had an hour.

"Michael, why are you upset that you got angry? You had every right to be angry," he said as Michael imagined him writing on one of his legal pads.

"I just don't like losing control of my emotions like that. I never yell. I never get like that. They must think I'm nuts," Michael told him again worrying about upsetting them and putting his feelings aside.

"It is not important what they think. They kept a secret from you for over forty years. They come in and give you life-altering news, and you can allow yourself to feel," Dr. Mikowsky said. Michael always liked him because he never said, "What do you think?" He expressed his opinion.

Allow myself to feel? Michael thought about this. Did he not allow himself to feel? He liked being in control. People thought he was easy-going, calm, rational, and that is how he wanted to be perceived.

"Michael, is there anything else I need to know that has happened since you moved east?" he asked as their time wound up.

"No, that is the only shocking news I have," Michael told him. He didn't want to mention Steve or even his visit to Rona and Doreen. He then realized he also never told him about Sam.

Around 6:00 pm, Michael's cell phone rang, and the caller ID said it was Eric. He hesitated before picking it up.

"Hello," he said as if he didn't know who was on the other end.

"Michael, it's Eric. How are you?" he asked cheerily in what Michael presumed was his normal mood. He really was a happy person. Michael thought Eric couldn't possibly be related to him.

"I'm fine. Did your mother tell you about our little visit today?" Michael asked, knowing the answer.

"Yeah, what a bombshell, huh?" Eric replied, using the same adjective Michael used to describe the news to Dr. Mikowsky. "I have a brother. This is too cool."

"Cool?" Michael questioned while he walked toward the kitchen to get his cigarettes. "What makes it cool?"

"I always wanted a brother, but when my parents realized I was, how shall we say, 'special,' they decided I was enough of a handful. Didn't you always want a brother?" he asked as if Michael dreamed of the day a sibling would arrive.

Michael thought about the question. He knew that if his mother had another child, he or she would be a Shimmer, Bart's baby, and things would have been worse for Michael if that were possible. They would favor that baby and forget Michael existed, or worse, there would be two children in the house to be mentally and physically abused. However, at the time, Michael thought all children were treated as he was. He figured once the doors were closed, all kids were beaten until they submitted and all families kept their secrets.

"Michael, did you hear me?" Eric asked.

Michael purposely ignored the question. "Eric, tell me. What was it like growing up in your house?" he asked, fearing the answer. Maybe his childhood was as horrible as Michael's, and it would not make a difference.

"I had a pretty good childhood. My parents did their best to provide me with a happy life," Eric answered.

Michael's heart sank as Eric confirmed his belief that his childhood could have been different had Eric's mother not been pregnant.

"My mother told me about what you said about your growing up," Eric continued, trying his best to be sympathetic. "I'm sorry, Michael. I don't know what to say."

By now, he was standing outside smoking cigarette after cigarette. "You don't have to be sorry. It had nothing to do with you," Michael answered. He wanted to blame Eric's father, but what good would that do, now? "Did they ever spank or hit you?"

"My parents? Never," he answered as if it were a ridiculous question. "They didn't believe in spanking and hitting children. I was grounded a lot for doing stupid things, but I was never hit."

"And you turned out all right?" Michael asked.

"Well, if you say so. I *am* pretty weird," Eric said with a laugh.

Weird was good. Living in fear of breaking the rules was not. Apologizing and begging for forgiveness to avoid a beating was not. Carrying the scars and memories for a lifetime was not.

"Michael, you turned out all right from what Sharon has told me," Eric continued. "You've won awards and have a great career."

"You don't know the half of it," Michael replied. "I have managed to create a persona of a normal, well-adjusted guy, but I'm pretty fucked up when you peel away the layers. But hey, you don't need to hear about that."

"Michael, you can talk to me anytime. I like knowing you're my brother," he said, still pleased with the knowledge that Michael existed.

But, something told Michael that talking to Eric would only make things worse as he would constantly compare Eric's upbringing to his.

* * * * *

It was the summer of 1973, and Michael was staying over at Florence's for the weekend. Her son, Scott, and he were getting ready to go to the pool, and she was joining them. She had since moved from her home in Hampton to an apartment at Towne Square in Newport News. Her three older children were out of the house, so she was raising Scott alone. She was engaged to Dr. Martin Mirmelstein at this point, too.

When they arrived at the pool, Michael took off his shirt, and she stopped him, took off her large, purple sunglasses, and looked at his back, placing her hand on it as well.

"Michael, what are these marks on your back?" she asked as she examined them. Scott walked around behind him to look also.

Not wanting to get in trouble, he said, "I fell down." Even then, he was a terrible liar, but Michael knew that if he told her the truth, she would call his mother, and he would get another beating for revealing a secret. Michael's mother always said, "We are private people." *Private? The woman thinks she is Jackie Kennedy or something.*

"Michael, you didn't get these from a fall," she said as she touched the marks.

"Really, Aunt Flossie," Michael said. "I fell. Can I go into the pool now?"

"No," she said. "Sit over here with me. I want to talk to you."

Michael always did as he was told, so he sat down on a chaise lounge. She was wearing a purple one-piece bathing suit, and he found himself staring at her enormous breasts in an attempt not to look her in the eyes. Scott, who didn't want to miss anything, sat down next to him. Even at almost eleven years old, Michael was already taller than both of them.

"Mickey," she said, using her nickname for him, "Who did that to your back?" She then reached for his hand, and when she did, she noticed the bruises under his arms. "What is this? Are you getting into fights?"

"No, no, Aunt Flossie, I've never been in a fight, never," Michael protested, having never been in a fight and vowing never to get in one as long as he lived.

She took her sunglasses off again and put her hand under his chin to make Michael look her in the eyes. "Mickey, tell me the truth. Who did this to you?"

"I am telling the truth. I fell," he said, and he began to cry. "Why don't you believe me?"

She pulled a tissue from her bag and handed it to him. Michael wiped his eyes as he continued to cry. He was determined not to tell her the truth.

"OK, Mickey, if that is what you say, I believe you. Go swimming," she said with a frown

Michael knew she did not believe him, but he also knew that she would never say anything to his mother, as she knew that if she did, he would be punished. She told them she would be back in a moment as she walked back to her apartment to make a phone call. Michael also knew that Aunt Flossie knew a lot more about being beaten than he was supposed to know, but that was a secret he had kept to himself for almost four years at that point.

* * * * *

Two mornings later, Eric called again.

"Hi, Eric, what's up?" Michael asked upon answering the phone.

"Michael," Eric began, sounding upset. "I have some bad news."

Was he coming home early and Michael would have to vacate the apartment? That was hardly bad news, as Michael was ready to return to California at any moment. "What is it?" he asked.

"My father died in his sleep last night," Eric said. Michael noticed he said "my father" not "our father."

"I'm so sorry, Eric," Michael said, not feeling any sense of loss for a man whose only contribution to his life was a single sperm.

"Thank you, Michael. He was ninety-six years old and not in good health. My mother would like for you to come to the funeral, which will be tomorrow. They're waiting for me to come home. I'm flying back today," he said. "Would you come to the funeral?"

Michael didn't want to give him an answer. He needed to think about it, and he was doing the math in his head. Seymour Sagman was ninety-six. That meant he was fifty-three years old when Eric and Michael were born, making him eighteen years older than Hannah.

"Are you going to stay here? I can go to Sharon's while you're in town," Michael asked avoiding the invitation and marveling at the age of his father, wondering how many other illegitimate children there were out there.

"No, I'll stay with my mother," Eric said. "Please consider coming to the funeral. I'll call you when I get in."

"Bye, Eric, and let me know if you need anything," Michael said before hanging up. Why did he offer his help? Michael guessed he was just being polite as no one ever told you if they actually needed anything.

Michael spent most of the day wondering if he should go or not, and he eventually decided to go as he was curious about what they would say about Seymour Sagman at his funeral. Michael was also curious to see if any other siblings showed up.

They sent a limousine to pick Michael up, and when the chauffeur opened the rear door to let him in, he was surprised to find Eric and his mother already in the car. Michael was not comfortable with this and almost backed out, but she grabbed his hand and thanked him for coming. He sat down to her right as Eric was seated on her left. Michael and Eric wore almost identical navy suits and blue shirts, with eerily similar yellow print ties. Michael didn't know how much more of this situation he could take. Eric smiled, but they said little on the way to the funeral, which was held at Jewish Memorial Gardens in Maryland. As they pulled up behind the hearse, Michael noticed what must have been two-hundred people waiting by the grave for the family to arrive and for the rabbi to lead the casket to the grave, stopping seven times to show the reluctance to say goodbye to the old man who knocked up two women in the same year.

As Michael stepped out of the limousine, he was aware of the startled looks on some of the attendees' faces, and he chuckled at their reactions when Eric stepped out the other side and walked around to stand next to his mother. While they stood there, Michael looked around to see if he had any more twins at the cemetery, but most if not all the other people there were over seventy, and many were over eighty. He didn't see any familiar faces. Eric and his mother asked Michael to sit with them, but he was not comfortable sitting in one of the chairs for the mourners, so he stood off to the side. Thankfully, they did not argue. The last time Michael sat with the mourners was at Bart Shimmer's funeral in 1985, and he only did that because he was glad Bart was dead.

They lowered the casket, and the rabbi began the short service. Michael loved Jewish funerals because the actual service was rather abbreviated, but unfortunately, the eulogies would sometimes go on forever. Eric was asked to give the eulogy for his father, and he was clearly upset and choking back tears as he spoke.

"My father, Seymour Sagman, was a good man, a loving father, a devoted husband, and a pillar in the community," Eric began. "One of my earliest memories of my father was his teaching me to ride a bike. As many of you may not know, I have coordination issues, and riding a bike was very difficult for me, but he was so patient, never losing his cool, and working with me for not one but five days until I mastered riding my bike. He then bought a bike, and we would go riding together ..."

Michael didn't want to hear anymore, so he worked his way to the back of the crowd, while many of the people stared and whispered to the people standing next to them as they looked in his direction. Michael knew they were all trying to figure out who he was. He managed to slip away quietly and wandered around the cemetery. Michael could still hear Eric speaking, but he was far enough away not to be able to discern what he was saying. As Michael walked to another section of the cemetery, he sensed someone was following him. He turned around, and there was a slight woman, who looked to be the same age his mother would be if she were still alive, even though it was obvious this woman had undergone numerous face lifts. She had short brown hair and wore a simple but expensive black dress with matching gloves, coat and hat.

"Are you Michael Bern?" she asked as she removed her dark glasses. Michael didn't recognize her, but she may have seen his picture in *People* magazine after they took a photo on the red carpet at the premiere of *Birthright*, so he didn't act surprised.

"Yes, do I know you?" Michael asked.

"I have not seen you since you were a baby. I'm Eleanor Summers," she said holding out her hand. Michael shook her hand and thought she might be related to his mother, who was also a Summers. "I'm your mother's first cousin," she confirmed.

"Small world," he said, realizing how much he hated that expression. "Did you know Seymour Sagman?" Michael asked.

"Sort of," she said. "I also know he was your father."

Here was another person who knew the secret. How many were there?

"How did you know that?" Michael asked, still wondering if everyone in attendance knew.

"Your mother would send me pictures of you over the years, and the Sagmans belonged to my synagogue. You and Eric were too similar-looking for it not to be true. I also knew your mother had an affair with Seymour before he moved here," she told Michael, not in the least worried about shocking him with her news. "I kept my distance from them over the years, but when I saw that his funeral was today, I wanted to come with the hope of running into you."

This time, Michael was not angry or upset. He had reached a point where he did not care. He had a father for two days who was now dead. Michael also had a father who died before he was born, and he really had no emotional connection to either of them.

"Will you be staying with your family?" she asked, as if he were part of the Sagman family.

Michael was beginning not to like this woman although they were related. "No, *my* family is all dead. I'll be going back home after the funeral as I have work to do," he said to her, and she gave him a shocked look.

"Michael, your family is not dead. I'm your family, and Eric and Harryette are your family. You shouldn't say that," she said as if scolding a child.

"Miss Summers, I know you mean well, but this is not my family, and frankly, I don't know you. No one from any of the many sides of what seems lately to be an expanding family of mine ever came to see me when I was a child, therefore, my family is dead to me. Now, if you will excuse me, I would like to go up to the cemetery office and call a cab," Michael said as he walked away. He pulled the pack of cigarettes out of his jacket pocket and lit one as he walked toward the office, but this newfound cousin of his kept following him, so he turned around, and she stopped. "I would appreciate your leaving me alone. I have been through quite a bit in the last week, and I don't want to meet or talk to any more so-called relatives. And, if you don't mind," Michael continued, pointing to the others at the grave side, "tell any other relatives I have over there that I do not wish to meet them either. OK?"

Michael then turned around and walked to the office and asked them to call him a cab. As he stood outside the cemetery office waiting for the taxi, he noticed Eric walking his way. Michael really could not deal with anymore "family" today, but Eric walked up to Michael and stood there silently.

"You want a cigarette?" Michael asked him, just being polite.

"Sure, but don't tell my mother," he said. Michael handed him the pack, and he lit a cigarette. Michael could swear Eric turned a little green after taking his first puff.

"Eric, I called a cab. I'd prefer to go home now. I hope you don't mind," Michael said as he looked over to the grave side and saw a few old men shoveling dirt into the grave as the other guests got into their cars and slowly made their way out of the cemetery. To exit, they had to pass where Eric and Michael were standing, and all of them looked and pointed at the two of them as if they wouldn't notice. Michael rolled his eyes at their curiosity.

"That woman, Eleanor, told me what you said, Michael," Eric said, breaking his silence.

"I didn't mean to hurt your feelings, Eric, but having all these relatives come out of the woodwork is not sitting well with me," he told him.

"You didn't hurt my feelings," Eric said, but something told Michael he had. "I'm just disappointed because I thought we could get to know each other, but I kinda get the feeling you'd rather not." Eric looked at Michael as he took another puff.

"Eric, I would like to get to know *you* better. You're the only one who didn't know the big secret," Michael said. "I just don't want to get to know people who knew I existed and never acknowledged me. I seem to be nothing but a curiosity to these people, and to meet my mother's cousin, who said she knew the secret all along was too much."

"From what I could tell, Eleanor is a dumb ass. I mean the woman appears to be one shank bone short of a seder plate," Eric said. And, they both started laughing.

"She thought going over and talking to you would make you feel better. She has no clue what you're going through."

"And, you do?" Michael asked, lighting another cigarette, realizing he would probably be looking at grass from the other side not too far from where he was standing if he didn't quit chain smoking soon.

"I think I do," Eric said. "I think I'm going through the same thing. After the initial excitement of finding out I had a brother, I began to wonder how many other siblings I have out there. My father must have been pretty potent to knock up two broads in a matter of months, and he was fifty-three when he did that!"

"Was he married before he met your mother?" Michael asked him, figuring a fifty-three-year-old heterosexual bachelor was rare.

Eric looked at Michael with wonder. He stomped the cigarette on the ground and looked away for a second. He then turned to face Michael again and asked, "They didn't tell you?"

"Tell me what?" Michael asked, dreading what other secrets would be revealed to him that day.

"I don't know, Michael, if I should tell you, but what the hell, nothing else could shock you at this point," Eric began. "My father married your mother in 1945 when she was eighteen and he was thirty-six. They were only married six months and had it annulled."

Michael's mouth dropped open. He was not ready for this. His mother was married to Seymour Sagman for six months in 1945? He was dumbfounded. She really did hide things from him. No wonder Eleanor knew of the Sagmans.

"Is there more?" Michael asked.

"They were married in D.C. After the annulment, your mother moved to Newport News. My father moved there a couple of years later, hoping to reconcile with your mother, but then she married again. Apparently, they started having an affair around the same time he met my mother," Eric told him.

"How long have you known this?" Michael asked.

"My mother told me in the limousine on the way to pick you up this morning," Eric said.

"No wonder you know what I'm going through," Michael told him as his cab pulled up.

"Michael, come back to the house with us. Please, do it for me," he pleaded.

Michael opened the taxi cab door, and as he stepped inside, he changed his mind. He handed the cab driver a twenty and apologized for taking up his time as he decided to go back to the house with Eric. After all, Eric was his half brother, and he also wanted to see pictures of what he looked like growing up.

As Michael got back into the limousine with Eric and his mother, he turned to both of them and said, "I'm only going to your house because Eric asked me. You must promise me one thing, Mrs. Sagman."

"What is that?" Mrs. Sagman asked as she checked her make-up in her compact.

"Don't introduce me as Seymour's son," Michael said.

"OK, Michael, if you promise me one thing," she said.

"What?" he asked, not sure he would agree to whatever she wanted.

"You will call me Harryette," she said as she closed the compact and smiled at him.

"OK, Harryette," Michael said, smiling back at her.

"Can I introduce you as my brother?" Eric asked.

Michael leaned over and looked at Eric and said, "Let me think about that one."

They chuckled a bit as they rode back to the Sagman's house on Helsel Drive in Silver Spring. They lived in a modest three bedroom ranch style home with a deck and a large back yard. There were dozens of people already in the house when they arrived, and there was food everywhere. Michael excused himself to the bathroom, and he lingered in there as there were pictures of Eric at various stages in his life. There was a headshot with his name etched on the bottom, Eric Buddy Sagman. Michael guessed him to about twenty in the picture as he looked like him at that age. There was a shirtless picture of him on the beach. He had a nice body in his youth, a little thin, though. Michael had a similar picture in his home, and he was also a bit thin at the time. Eric had really packed on the pounds since then, but so had Michael. Neither was fat, just a little fuller – though Eric was fuller than Michael. But, the picture that struck Michael the most was his baby picture. It was as if he were looking at his own. Michael stared at it for quite some time, marveling at how much they looked alike. Michael never looked like anyone in his family, but here he was staring at what could have been his identical twin. Michael did notice one significant difference between pictures of Eric growing up and pictures from the same period in his life. In Eric's, he looked happy, always with a big smile and a sparkle in his eyes, but in Michael's, the smile was strained and his eyes appeared empty. Michael didn't begrudge him his happiness, nor was he jealous.

Michael stepped out of the bathroom, and there was an elderly woman standing there. She told him how sorry she was about his father before going into the bathroom, and he didn't feel like correcting her. Eric and his mother were seated in the living room, so Michael decided to look at the pictures they had hanging on the wall opposite where they were seated. There was a picture of Eric at around ten or eleven sitting on the ground with a pug.

"You had a pug?" Michael asked Eric as he turned around to look at him.

Eric stood up from the couch and walked over to where Michael was standing, looking at the picture. "Yeah, that's Kelly. She was my fourth birthday present. She lived sixteen years. Imagine that. I was twenty when she died." He then touched the picture, remembering his dog.

"I also had a pug," Michael said. "Her name was Aunt Clara. She died right before I moved here, and she also lived sixteen years. Weird, huh?"

Eric looked at Michael and furrowed his brow. "What is your favorite color?"

"Green," Michael said.

"Mine, too," Eric said with excitement. "What is your lucky number?"

"Twenty-four," Michael said, "But I know that's not yours. Yours is three."

"No, Michael," Eric said with a smile, "My favorite number is twenty-four. It's divisible by three. Everybody I know has a favorite number like five or seven, but never a two-digit number. I felt so weird in first grade when I picked twenty-four. No one else could count that high, but being an Aspy, I was special." Eric smiled as he said this feigning superiority for comic effect.

Michael looked at him and tried to come up with something else they might have in common. "What is your all time favorite TV show?"

"*Bewitched*," Eric said, waiting for his reaction.

"Oh my God," Michael said slowly. "That is why I named my dog Aunt Clara. OK, you can introduce me as your half brother, now." Michael smiled at Eric, happy to be related to him at last.

"Great!" Eric exclaimed as his eyes lit up.

Just then, an elderly woman with horribly teased hair and too much make-up came up to them. "Which one of you is Eric?"

"I am, Aunt Rose," Eric said. "This is my half brother, Michael Bern."

Michael reached out his hand to shake hers and she looked at him as if she just saw a ghost. "You two look exactly alike."

"Well, to tell you the truth, Aunt Rose, my hair is gray, and I wear glasses," Eric said. "And, Michael is gay."

Michael looked at him confused as he was convinced Eric was gay, too. Aunt Rose walked away, and Michael said to Eric, "You're straight?"

"Get a grip, Michael," Eric said, "I'm so gay the mailman knows. I was just teasing Aunt Rose. She's a little senile."

Michael liked his sense of humor. It was more sarcastic and dryer than his, and he thought Eric should have been a comedy writer. But most comedy writers come from a dark past, so he might not have had much of a career after all.

Michael stayed for a few more hours talking to some of the guests, who didn't know if he was Eric or not. Not once did anyone ask what he did for a living, as they were more curious about his looking like Eric. Not having to deal with the thing he dreaded – having to explain who he was and what he did for a living – turned out to be a relief as Michael didn't have to hear about this one's daughter who should be in movies and did he know this director and could he get that one an audition. Whenever that happened, he would see the look of disappointment on their faces when he would tell them he was a just a lowly television comedy writer with no real connections – at least none he would admit to.

Eric drove Michael home in his mother's Cadillac, and one thing they did not have in common was the way they drove. Michael always obeyed the speed limit and all the rules, but Eric took it to the extreme, driving with his head near the dash and in the right lane with old women passing him as if he were standing still. Eric was obviously terrified to be driving his mother's car in the city.

"You don't drive much, do you?" Michael asked.

Not taking his eyes off the road, Eric said, "I hate to drive. I only got a license because my father said I would need one some day. I don't even own a car. I never have. I haven't driven a car in almost seven years."

"Well, that's one thing we don't have in common. I love to drive," Michael said, and upon hearing that, Eric pulled over immediately, got out, walked around to Michael's side, opened the door and practically ordered him to drive.

Michael settled behind the wheel, trying to remember the last time he drove a Cadillac, also realizing this was the first time he would drive a car into Washington as they continued down Connecticut Avenue in Silver Spring. Michael also wondered if the experience would rival the Hollywood Freeway in a Corvair.

* * * * *

When Michael was eighteen, he still had not learned to drive because his mother didn't have time to teach him, and Michael never would have thought to ask Bart. Michael did think about asking Aunt Flossie to teach him to drive, but she had such a reputation as a bad driver that he decided that would be worse. As luck would have it, Hannah and Bart went away for a week and left him home alone, and they knew Michael would never throw a party for fear of the repercussions. One of the nights they were away, Aunt Doreen invited him over for dinner. Her daughter, Marci, was her only child still living at home at the time, and she thought they would make such a nice couple, but Michael knew by then he was gay. Marci was fifteen at the time, and she adored him because he worked at Baskin Robbins, and she loved ice cream.

After dinner, Doreen suggested they go see a movie. Michael asked if she could drive them, and she looked at him as if he were crazy.

"Michael, you don't need a chaperone. This is Marci. I changed your diapers; I trust you," she said.

"Aunt Doreen, I don't know how to drive," he said almost embarrassed to admit it.

"What? Aren't you eighteen? Hannah has not taught you how to drive?" she said to him almost frustrated at the thought of his not learning to drive. "That does it, come over tomorrow at ten. I am going to teach you how to drive. Then, we are going to get you a license."

"Aunt Doreen, I don't think my mother would like that, and who would pay for my insurance?" he asked.

"I'll handle your mother, and if need be, I'll pay for your insurance, too," Doreen said as she got up from the dining room table and asked the housekeeper to bring coffee and dessert into the den.

The next morning, Michael biked over to Doreen's, and after eating a bagel and lox to make her happy, although he already ate breakfast (realizing then that as long as he was around the girls he would always have a weight problem), they began Michael's lesson.

"Aunt Doreen, thank you for doing this. I was going to ask Aunt Flossie ..." he began.

"Are you *meshugina*? Florence needs someone to teach *her* how to drive. I'm the best driver of the girls, so you are in good hands with me. Besides, do you want to learn how to drive in a Chevy or a Cadillac?" she asked.

"A Cadillac of course," he said as he sat down behind the wheel. Michael had to move the seat all the way back, and Doreen laughed when he finally found a comfortable position.

"All right, Mr. Perfect, here is what you do," she began as she showed him how everything worked in her car with all its buttons and knobs. She was a great teacher. Doreen had him drive all over town, on the interstate and in parking lots, she taught him how to parallel park until he got it right on the first try, which was no small feat in a Yellow Cadillac Fleetwood with a white vinyl top, and within a week of daily driving, she declared him perfectly roadworthy and took Michael to the DMV to get his license, and he passed on the first try.

When his mother and Bart returned, Michael showed her his license. For once, she was not upset that Doreen took it upon herself to teach him how to drive. Michael guessed she was glad she didn't have to do it, herself.

Doreen and her husband Sammy gave Michael her 1979 Cadillac when they were ready to buy a new one at the end of the summer, and they even paid for his insurance. Hannah never protested, and Michael only let her drive his car once, when he was in the hospital and could not stop her. He drove that car all through college, and after he arrived in LA in 1985, he gave it to a stage hand, who had just learned how to drive herself. It was Michael's way of giving back.

* * * * *

Michael cruised down Connecticut Avenue and enjoyed being behind the wheel of such a large luxury cruiser again. He even considered buying another Cadillac when he moved back to California. Eric also seemed a lot more relaxed with Michael behind the wheel. Once in Mount Pleasant, Michael looked for a parking spot. He spotted one near the apartment that would accommodate Eric's mother's car with little room to spare, and proceeded to parallel park it perfectly on the first try. Michael had such a proud look on his face, especially since the last time he parallel parked a Cadillac was 1985.

"That was amazing, Michael," Eric said as Michael put the car in park and handed him the keys.

"I was taught how to drive in a Cadillac by the best driver among the girls," Michael said as he stepped out of the car.

"What girls?" Eric asked as he exited the car.

"My mother's friends. My Aunt Doreen taught me how to drive. Thanks for letting me drive. It actually brought back a nice memory and made this day worth it."

Eric came in for a minute to chat. Then, he called his mother and told her to send his cousins Mel and Tony to pick him up and drive her car back. He was in no shape to drive, with his nerves still rattled from the ten minutes he drove already that day. Michael felt it was nice to know Eric wasn't completely perfect.

After he left, Michael decided to give someone a call. The phone rang four times before it was picked up.

"Hello?"

"Aunt Rona, it's Michael."

Then she screamed, "Doreen, Michael's on the phone, pick it up!" Michael had the cell phone hands-free earpiece in and thought he would have to have eardrum surgery again after she yelled.

Doreen picked up and yelled, "Rona, how may times do I have to tell you not to pick up my phone!"

"It was ringing, what the hell do you want me to do?" Rona said.

"Wait. Let it ring, dammit. You don't give me a chance to pick it up," Doreen yelled to Rona.

"What if it is an emergency, or one of my kids?" Rona yelled to Doreen, while Michael listened.

"What if it is one of my kids? This is my goddamn phone! I'll answer it," Doreen yelled back.

"Vaysmir, Doreen, pick up your fucking phone from now on, I'll just sit here while it rings and rings. And, don't get pissed when one of your boyfriends hangs up waiting for you to get up off your fat ass to answer it!" Rona yelled.

"I'm surprised you could hear it with your head in the refrigerator all the time," Doreen yelled.

"Girls, girls, quit yelling at each other," Michael yelled into the phone.

"Who's yelling?" they asked in unison.

"This is yelling, Rona? He thinks we're yelling. Were we yelling?" Doreen asked.

"I wasn't yelling. Why would he think we were yelling?" Rona asked.

"Girls, I'm still here," Michael said.

"Talk, what's new, Michael?" Doreen asked.

"Yes, Michael, how are you?" Rona asked.

Pausing to be sure they were done, he finally said, "Guess where I was today?"

"Where?" they both said.

"Seymour Sagman's funeral," he said with no inflection in his voice.

"Seymour who?" Rona asked.

"Sagman, Sagman," Doreen mumbled then exclaimed, "Oh my God!"

"What?" Rona asked. "What, Doreen?"

By now, Michael had stepped outside to have a cigarette as they continued talking around him.

"Rona, Seymour Sagman used to work with Adam Bern, Michael's father," Doreen said. "Remember the tall guy who had a thing for Hannah?"

"Wait a minute, Doreen; he could not possibly be alive; he would have to be at least ..." Rona began.

"He was ninety-six," Michael said. "He died two days ago,"

"So, why were you at his funeral?" Doreen asked.

"My brother asked me to go," Michael said, again with no inflection.

"What?" they both asked simultaneously.

"My brother. Did you two know I have a half brother named Eric Sagman?" Michael asked.

"Michael, what the hell are you talking about?" Doreen asked.

"Oh my God," Rona said. "Doreen, do you remember what Seymour Sagman looked like? He was tall with black hair and green eyes."

"Oh ... my ... God and with a big booming voice ... like Michael's," Doreen said slowly.

"Oh you think that is a coincidence?" Michael said. "My half brother was born two weeks after I was. His mother is Harryette Sagman. Apparently, Seymour knocked up my mother and his mother at the same time. But wait, that is not the best part. You should see Eric. He looks exactly like me." There was silence. "Aunt Rona, Aunt Doreen, are you two still there? Did I shock you?"

"No, no, Michael," Rona said as if pondering what he just told them. "You confirmed something. We always suspected your mother was fooling around with Seymour Sagman ..."

"And, you never looked like your father," Doreen interrupted. "This explains so much. Oh, your mother was good at keeping her secrets."

"So, Harryette, Harryette?" Rona asked as if she were talking to herself.

"Rona, she was Harryette Erlach. Remember, kinda plain looking with red hair. She was a saleswoman at Feld's Department Store," Doreen said.

"She worked for Aunt Arlene and Uncle William?" Michael asked.

"Oh, yes," Rona said. "I remember her. She was such a nice girl, a little quiet, but very nice."

"Apparently not so nice," Michael said. "She got knocked up and had to get married."

"Michael, do you know how many girls gave birth six months after their weddings back then?" Doreen asked.

"Your generation didn't invent sex," Rona said.

"Well, I guess that wasn't fair of me to say," Michael said apologetically.

"Don't worry about it, Michael," Doreen said. "I was just surprised that such a quiet little mouse like Harryette would get in trouble."

"So, what is she like now?" Rona asked.

"Very nice," Michael said. "She is a very nice person, and Eric is a great guy, too. But, I haven't told you the best part."

"There's more?" Doreen asked.

"Tell us, tell us," Rona the yenta demanded.

Michael took a deep breath, and then he told them, "My mother was married to Seymour Sagman in 1945 for six months. They had the marriage annulled, and he moved to Newport News with the hope of remarrying my mother. They apparently were having an affair for some time."

"Oh my God," they both said in unison.

"How is that for a bombshell?" Michael asked.

"Michael, you should write a novel about all this," Doreen said.

"Or at least a movie," Rona chimed in.

"Nah, no one would believe it," Michael told them.

Chapter Eight

Michael reluctantly decided to stay in D.C. until he and Sharon completed the final draft of *Romancing the Capitol*. He hated the title, but it was Sharon's baby, so he kept his mouth shut. As he was sitting at his desk working on a re-write one late January morning, his cell phone rang. He looked at the caller ID, and it was Steve. *Should I answer it? Should I let it go to voice mail?* Against his better judgment, Michael answered it.

"Michael, how are you?"

"Well look who's using the telephone," Michael said sarcastically.

"You know I hate answering the telephone," Steve said, not bothered in the least by Michael's remark.

"How have you been, Steve?" he asked.

"I'm getting ready to have liposuction. I'm so excited."

Michael leaned back in the chair as he couldn't believe what he was hearing. "What the hell is wrong with you? You don't need liposuction. You have a perfect body. If I looked like you, I would do everything naked – sleep naked, work naked, drive naked. Are you nuts?" he said to Steve.

"Michael, this is something I have wanted and needed for a long time; support me on this," he responded as if pleading for his approval.

"Where are you having it done?" Michael asked.

"In Virginia Beach with the same doctor Tom used. He's taking me," he answered, confirming that he and Tom were still together.

"So, you two are still together?" Michael asked anyway, convinced he knew the answer.

"Well, no we are just friends now. We decided that was best," Steve said in attempt to assuage Michael's fears.

Do I really want to get involved in this again? Should I just say good luck and hang up? "Steve, I hope this doctor is good," Michael said, truly concerned as he knew what a major procedure liposuction was.

"Oh, he's the best. He said I'm a perfect candidate," Steve answered with excitement in his voice.

"Steve, I work in Hollywood, and I can tell you that every plastic surgeon says that. You could ask for a sex change, and you'd hear that," he told him.

"Don't be silly," he said, a little annoyed.

"Well, I hope you thought this through. That's a dangerous operation."

"Hey, you want to come with us. I know you have family down there," Steve said, the excitement returning to his voice.

Michael could not believe Steve remembered he was from that area? "Actually, I *had* family in Newport News, but there's no one left there now, and I was just there a few weeks ago to visit some old friends. To tell you the truth, driving down with you and your ex doesn't sound appealing to me. Where would I fit in the picture?"

"I understand. Hey will you come over and jack off for me when I'm recuperating?" he asked, as if Michael would consider that.

"Oh sure. Call me, I will be right over, wearing a gold lame thong and a sports bra," Michael said in dead pan. "Listen Steve, I'm on a deadline, and I have to go. Good luck with your surgery although I think you're wasting your money,"

"Don't be like that," Steve said as if Michael were being snotty.

"No, I think you don't need it, but if this is something you want, I can't stop you. Seriously, I hope you checked this doctor out. I have to go, goodbye." Michael said as he hung up before Steve could say goodbye.

Talking to him was all right, but Michael knew he couldn't see him because if he did, he would lose control and fall back into a pattern he wanted to avoid. Michael got up from the desk and walked into the kitchen, first reaching for the pack of cigarettes on top of the refrigerator, but changing his mind, he poured himself a glass of water and leaned against the counter.

"Why would a grown man with a perfect body go through that kind of procedure?" he said to himself. "Is appearance that important to him? Does he have issues with his self-esteem that need to be addressed professionally?"

Steve did go through with the liposuction and e-mailed Michael from the hotel where he and Tom stayed overnight in Virginia Beach. It turned out Steve was getting on Tom's nerves, so Tom would go out to get away from him. He sent before and after pictures, and although still swollen, there was a difference, yet Michael still thought a strict diet would have achieved the same result.

They stayed in regular e-mail contact for the next few weeks, and at the end of February, Steve called Michael one Saturday afternoon out of the blue.

"Hey, buddy," Steve said.

"Wow, you're using the telephone, again," Michael said, wishing he had let it go to voice mail.

"What are you doing?" Steve asked, ignoring Michael's comment.

"I'm working," he said as if he did anything else these days.

"Do you want to go shopping?"

Here we go again, Michael thought, so he asked, "When?"

"Now!" Steve answered.

Should I drop everything and go shopping because Steve wants to go? Against his better judgment, Michael said yes, jumped in the shower, put on his best jeans and a green turtleneck and made up his mind that they would not end up naked after their excursion. Steve arrived in about twenty minutes. He was wearing a sweat shirt and sweat pants, obviously straight from the gym, and Michael tried to keep his distance, but Steve managed to hug him anyway.

"How have you been, buddy?" Steve asked as he let Michael go.

"I've been good," Michael answered. "You know, I must really like you, if I am willing to drop everything to go shopping on the spot."

"Hey, I'm the same way," Steve said. And, Michael wondered if the tables were turned, would Steve have gone with him.

Steve lifted up his shirt to show him his flat stomach, and Michael acted impressed. As much as he wanted to touch it, he resisted. He also remembered what Steve said about how he couldn't separate sex from friendship.

"Where are we going?" Michael asked, changing the subject from his body to shopping.

"To Virginia," Steve said as if they were going cross country.

They got into Steve's truck and chatted about nothing of importance. At one point, Steve put his hand on Michael's thigh, and he flinched. He really did not want Steve touching him, and Michael wished he were not in his truck at that moment. He knew he was headed for trouble.

"You don't want me touching you?" Steve asked as he took his hand off Michael's knee.

"No, that's OK," Michael said, not wanting to hurt Steve's feelings and ignoring his own.

Michael really didn't know what he wanted. What he wanted to know was why he hungered for even a few minutes' time with this man. Why did he have such intense feelings for him when it was obvious a relationship with him would never work?

As they walked through the stores, Michael would pick up a shirt and look at it, and Steve would tell him he didn't need it. Or, Michael would look at some other item, and Steve would say the same thing. Michael ended up buying Oil of Olay from Target and protein powder from the Vitamin Shoppe. *For this, I had to go to Virginia? Why didn't I buy the shirt? It was just a black T-shirt, and no gay man can have enough black T-shirts. I am an award winning television and screenwriter, who makes a lot of money. I can shop anywhere. Can't I make my own decisions? I could have bought anything in the store I wanted. I've shopped on Rodeo Drive for God's sake!* Michael thought to himself as they walked back to the truck.

It was true Michael was like his Nana Mary in that he never bought anything frivolous, and he was excellent at saving money and not paying retail (even on Rodeo Drive), but he never bought *drek* either. The one time he wanted to by a $10 T-shirt, he let a man talk him out of it.

Michael asked as they drove up 14th Street on the way home, "So, is this where you live?"

Steve smiled and said nothing. For some reason he didn't want Michael to know where he lived. When Steve turned onto Newton Street, he pulled up to the apartment and parked his truck in the first available space.

"What are you doing?" Michael asked, thinking he would just drop him off. "Why are you parking here?"

"I'm coming in for a while," Steve said as if there was no argument and Michael had no choice.

Michael let him come in. He put away the exciting items he had purchased and offered Steve something to drink. Steve just wanted water, and he drank it in one gulp and handed Michael the glass to refill it, which he did. He walked into the living room and sat on the futon, and Steve went to sit on his lap sideways as he always did. Michael tried to stop him, but Steve insisted, and frankly, he didn't resist that much. Michael knew he was losing control, but he did nothing about it.

"I missed you, big guy," Steve said as he looked into Michael's eyes, and Michael looked back into Steve's sexy gray eyes.

"Listen, Steve, I really don't want to fool around with somebody's boyfriend anymore," Michael said, trying to stop what he knew was going to happen.

"Oh, Tom and I are done. We're through. I'm a single man now," he said, trying to assure Michael.

Then Michael thought that is not enough because if he were to get involved, he would be the rebound guy and probably get dumped in six months. Steve then kissed him passionately, and Michael was totally under his control. The next thing Michael knew, they were getting undressed, and as they were climbing onto the bed, Steve told him to be careful as his midsection was still tender. Michael assured him he would be gentle, and he was as they mostly made out, sucked and jerked each other off.

Afterward, they showered together, and Michael asked him if he wanted to go out to dinner as his treat, but Steve said he had plans. He dressed quickly, kissed Michael goodbye and left.

Michael was confused and angry with himself, and he was also miserable. *Why was it when I fall for someone, I'm never happy?*

Within fifteen minutes, Steve sent Michael an e-mail that said, "That was hot." So, Michael figured he must not live that far from him.

Michael replied, "Yes, it was." And, the downward spiral began as a pit formed in his stomach – a pit that would keep growing and growing.

They e-mailed back and forth for the next week, and he told Michael about this guy he chatted with online and that guy he chatted with online, and each time, Michael's heart sank a little more. Steve continued not to answer his questions, and he also never answered his phone, so Michael resigned himself to knowing this would be an electronic friendship, relationship, or whatever the hell it was. If he were a fuck-buddy, they would have fooled around, and Steve would be gone and not heard from until the next tryst, which could take place six months later or even a year, according to the rules. But they had actually gone out and done something, albeit only shopping, but that was something in Michael's mind.

The first Saturday in March, Steve called Michael around 2:00 pm and again asked what he was doing. Michael said he was writing, and Steve asked if he could come over. By now, Michael realized he had spent just about every weekend alone. Sharon would go to her cabin in West Virginia every weekend to be with her boyfriend, Wes, and Michael was always working.

By this time, Sid had secured Michael a deal with HTO to develop a one-camera sitcom, so Michael had begun drafting different ideas for a treatment then a pilot. Work or no work, he told Steve he could come over, and they were naked within minutes of Steve's arrival.

Steve lay on his stomach as Michael ran his tongue from the bottoms of Steve's feet up his calves to his round, hairy, muscular butt. He then did something he rarely if ever did as he parted those round cheeks and proceeded to rim Steve as he reached around and stroked his hard, thick cock. Steve was moaning more than Michael had ever heard him moan before, and he was begging Michael not to stop. Michael continued this until Steve came, foregoing his own orgasm.

As usual, they showered together, and Steve left.

The following Monday, Steve called him in the afternoon on his way to the gym after work. Michael answered, wondering why he was calling on a weekday.

"Hey, Michael, guess what I just did?" Steve asked.

"I can't imagine," Michael said as he turned away from the computer and leaned back in the chair.

"Well, I was picking up some stuff for a business trip from our office in Southwest, and I ran into this really hot guy I know there, and we went to the bathroom, and the next thing I knew we were making out. He's so hot and Jewish like you. Isn't that hot?" he told Michael as if he were supposed to be as excited as Steve was.

"Are you sure there weren't cameras in the bathroom?" Michael asked, hiding his jealousy as his heart sank even further and the pit in his stomach grew larger at the thought of Steve making out with some guy in the bathroom.

"No, they don't have cameras," he said confidently. "I hope to see him again and maybe go out on a date with him."

Michael was despondent as he wanted to know why Steve didn't want to date him and who exactly he *was* in Steve's life. Was Michael just some trick he used for his own pleasure? *Why don't I end this right here and now?* Michael thought. *What do I see in him?*

"That's nice," Michael said, not revealing how he really felt.

"Hey, listen to this," he said. "I have wanted to buy another home as an investment, and I was thinking you could go in on it with me. I trust you more than I've ever trusted anyone in my entire life. I would so much like to do this with you. What do you think?"

He won't go out on a date me, but he will buy a house with me? Michael thought. *He trusts me like no one else? What in the hell have I gotten myself into?*

"Steve, I already own a house in Santa Monica, why would I want a house here?" Michael asked.

"As an investment," he said. "I have a goal of owning more real estate by the time I'm thirty-five, and with your help, I could do this."

With my help, he could do this, Michael thought as he saw but ignored another red flag. *How could I possibly invest in property with someone who does not answer my calls? What if something went wrong with the house after I returned to California? Why am I even thinking about the possibility of it? Do I want to be tied into something like this with someone who has never told me where he lives?*

"Let me think about it, Steve," he said. "This is a big decision, and I don't make decisions like this without thinking about them."

"OK, big guy," Steve said. "I'm in front of the gym, so I have to go."

The following Saturday, Michael took a chance and invited Steve to see a play. Instead, Steve said he was going out "to be bad," so Michael didn't push it or ask if he could come along. Michael realized then that Steve never wanted to be seen with him in public. He always had plans, usually related to a leather event. Michael didn't see him that Saturday, but on the following Sunday, Steve called, and Michael got the usual, "What are you doing?" and he of course said, "Writing," and Steve came over.

By now, Michael knew he had fallen so in love with Steve it scared him. Steve came over, and they got naked, but didn't start with the sex right away. As they lay there, Steve told Michael how he went out the night before, and he could not get anyone to even look at him let alone make out with him.

"I cannot give it away," Steve said as if Michael were supposed to sympathize with him.

"You should have called me."

"Oh, I don't think of you that way," Steve said as he looked into Michael's eyes.

"But it's OK to call me in the middle of the afternoon for a fuck? What were we doing here, Steve?"

"I've been wondering the same thing ... Michael, I trust you like nobody else. I feel a connection with you I've never felt with anyone. You mean so much to me."

There was that word again – trust. Michael turned over to his side, facing away from him, and Steve spooned him and asked, "What's wrong?" while he stroked Michael's chest and stomach.

"This will never work," Michael said.

"I know," Steve replied without hesitation.

That was not the response Michael wanted to hear. He was hoping Steve would say, "Oh, Michael, it could work. We could spend the rest of our lives together, buy a house, adopt six children and live happily ever after." As a writer, Michael should have known that only happens in movies. He wrote lines just like that, himself. But, Steve's reply was just, "I know."

"Then, why are we doing this?" Michael asked as he turned his head to look at Steve.

"Can't we just have fun? Why does everything have to mean anything?" Steve asked as if they were of the same mindset.

Why does everything have to mean anything? Because that's how it works, Michael thought. *There are rules to how things work, and everything must fit perfectly in the confines of those rules.* That is what Michael believed, but he didn't say it out loud.

* * * * *

In October 1971, Michael was still enrolled at South Morrison Elementary School, which was only a quarter mile up the street from his house on Dresden Drive. Bussing had just begun that year, and one day at school, one of the black students who lived downtown, said, "You white kids have it easy. You get to ride a bus up the street. I had to walk thirteen blocks to our school downtown."

She was right. The white students who lived within blocks of South Morrison were picked up by school busses for what would have been a short walk, while before bussing, the black students who lived downtown had to walk almost three times that distance to get to their school. Things were still separate but not equal. After she told Michael that, he decided he would walk to school in protest.

"You absolutely will not walk to school," his mother screamed. "You will wait for the bus. If I hear you walked to school, you'll be very sorry."

Michael tried reasoning with her that it was unfair to the black kids, but she would not hear of it. Whenever Michael tried to argue with his mother, she never heard a word he said. Hannah made up her mind, and that was that. The next morning, Michael walked to school in protest. It only took him twenty minutes, and he felt good about himself. But, that evening, Michael learned again what it meant to break the rules.

At dinner, Hannah's husband, Bart, said, "I didn't see you waiting for the bus this morning like your mother told you. Where were you? Did you go to school?"

"I walked to school," Michael said rather proud of himself.

Bart got up from the table, grabbed Michael and took him to his room. Bart told him to stand in the middle of the room and drop his pants and underwear and take off his shirt. He then got behind Michael and removed his belt. Michael put his hands back to cover his buttocks, but Bart yelled, "Move your goddamn hands! Put them on your head."

Michael did as he said, and Bart proceeded to beat him with the belt on his buttocks, back and thighs over and over again, yelling, "That will teach you to break the rules in this house!" Michael refused to cry, which made Bart beat him even more. When Michael finally did scream in pain, Bart stopped. When Bart was done, the beating was so bad that Michael was bleeding.

Later that night, Michael apologized to Bart for breaking a rule and even told Bart he was thankful that he taught him a lesson by spanking him.

* * * * *

Michael didn't answer Steve. He just kissed him, and they had the most passionate sex they had ever experienced with each other. They made out for a long time before Michael slowly eased Steve onto his back, and Michael licked and kissed every inch of Steve's torso from his neck to his armpits down his stomach, and down his thighs to his feet. Steve returned the favor covering every inch of Michael with his mouth.

They kissed while he mounted Steve and locked eyes as Michael slowly fucked him. They came together, and Michael fell onto Steve's sweaty body, satiated and content.

Michael heard people say they made love, but he never understood the real difference between sex and making love until that afternoon. When he and Steve showered and Steve left, Michael had no idea that it would be the last time he would ever have sex with Steve, nor did he realize he would not see him again for over two months.

The next day, Steve e-mailed him that he was leaving on four different work-related trips, and each weekend, he was tied up with leather events – "forgive the pun." Michael looked at his calendar and realized the first opportunity he would have to see him would be May 20 – a little more than a week before he would be returning to California. Michael's heart sank further, and the pit in his stomach left no room for anything else. At that very moment, Michael stopped eating. Little did he know what lay ahead, and little did he know how both of them would change.

They e-mailed regularly, usually dirty stuff about what they wanted to do to each other. With each e-mail Michael would hunger for a response. If it were not for Sharon's screenplay and the pilot he was writing for HTO, Michael would have sat at that computer staring at the screen, waiting for the chime to tell him an e-mail had arrived every moment of the day.

Michael felt he was beginning to go insane, and he knew he was not in his right mind. He would pace in the apartment, walking in circles, forgetting what he was doing. He did laundry without putting clothes in the washer, put food in the microwave and not turn it on, made coffee without putting water in the machine; he was off his regular routine, and he was not sleeping. He was starved for some kind of contact with Steve. He was deeply in love and sadder than ever. Michael was despondent, miserable, and more depressed than he had ever been in his life. He kept wondering how he could stop feeling the way he did. He thought love was supposed to make people happy, so why did love always make Michael depressed – and lonely?

Then, one Monday in the beginning of April, Steve was home between trips. He e-mailed Michael that he got into an argument at the gym with his ex, Tom, and he felt bad and would text message him.

"Text message him?" Michael responded in an e-mail. "Call him if you feel bad." He wanted to meet Tom and find out how Steve treated him. Michael then e-mailed Steve, "Maybe I should come over there and fuck your brains out!"

Steve responded, "Maybe that is what I need."

So, he e-mailed back, "Address please."

Steve e-mailed in response, "LOL."

Michael then lost it and e-mailed: "Why won't you tell me your address? Why do we only see each other when you want to see me? Why are you always the one in control?"

Where the hell did that come from? Michael thought. He rarely lashed out like that at anyone.

Steve then responded, "What is the matter, big guy?"

Michael then e-mailed him, "If I call, will you answer your phone?" He was getting snippy, but this was the most backbone Michael had had in a long time, especially when it came to Steve.

Michael called, and Steve answered, "Michael, what's up?"

"Steve, I'm going to tell you something that will probably scare the hell out of you," he said as he choked back tears.

"What? You can tell me anything," Steve said.

Michael thought he was going to start crying, but he held it together. "The one thing I didn't want to happen did ... Steve, I've fallen in love with you."

"Oh, Michael, I love you, too, but I'm not *in love* with you," Steve said without hesitation.

"I know," Michael said, "and that is why I cannot have any more contact with you for awhile. I need to work through this. I cannot make you fall in love with me, and it is making me depressed."

"Why are you saying that?" Steve asked. "I'm not going anywhere. We can work through this. I want you in my life." He was clearly upset that Michael wanted to retreat.

"Then, why won't you tell me where you live?" Michael asked.

"Oh, I don't know," Steve said. "I just don't like having people in my space. Tom didn't know where I lived until we were together six months."

Michael let it go. He knew he shouldn't have, but he did. Steve then started talking dirty to him and said they should stay in contact because he wanted Michael in his life and that he was good for Michael. He did manage to put him in a good mood for the next few days, so maybe he was good for him, Michael thought.

They e-mailed back and forth for the next couple of days, but after hearing Steve tell Michael how he met two guys and played with them on his trip to Arizona, he knew he needed to extricate himself from the situation. He was jealous and wondered if Steve had any regard for his feelings or was he trying to get Michael to fall out of love with him by telling him about his trysts? Steve clearly had no regard for anyone but himself. He kept stringing Michael along, and he let him.

That Thursday, when Steve returned from Arizona, Michael sent him the first of a series of emotional e-mails.

The first one read:

"Dear Steve,

"Although you said we could work through this together, I don't think this will work. I need to go into personal retreat and work through my feelings.

"The good news is that although I fall in love very hard, I can fall out rather quickly as long as I sever all contact.

"Please understand this is not about you. I don't know if you have ever been in love with someone who is not in love with you, but it is difficult for me now. Very difficult.

"Please understand.

"I will contact you in a few months to see how you're doing.

"Love,

"Michael."

Michael knew it was total bullshit. He had never been in love like this before in his life. He was not going to get over Steve in a few months. This would take a long time, and Michael was not sure he would ever fall out of love with him. The only truth was that he needed to have no contact with him.

The next morning, Michael came home from the gym, turned on the computer and saw that Steve had sent an e-mail overnight in response that said, "Michael, you are being so dramatic. Only you can snap out of this. Don't shut me out."

"Dramatic? I'm not dramatic. Look who's being dramatic. OK, I am dramatic, but that's not the response I want," Michael said out loud. "I want 'Michael, don't do this, I need you, I want you, I love you.' Now, that's being dramatic? Believe me, I know drama!"

Within a minute of reading it, his cell phone rang. "Oh no," Michael said. He looked at the caller ID, and sure enough, it was "on-my-way-to-work-morning-boy."

"Hey, I was just in the twenty-four-hour grocery store, and I saw Matzah on sale and thought of my Jewish friend Michael. How are you?" Steve said, cheerily.

"Are you outside my door?" Michael asked, praying Steve was not, but looking through the peep hole to be sure.

"Would you like me to be?" he asked with a chuckle.

The emotional part of Michael did, but for once, the intellectual part took over. "No, that's the last thing I need. Please, Steve, let me be alone for awhile."

"Are you mad at me?" Steve asked.

"No, I could never be mad at you," Michael said, knowing full well that he had and could and probably would be mad at Steve again, unless he left him alone.

"OK, mister, you take care of yourself, I'll talk to you later," Steve said and hung up.

"Did he not hear a word I said?" Michael said out loud as he put the phone down. "I said leave me alone. I need my space. Why can't I have my space? Why does this guy have such a hold on me? Why does he insist on staying in touch?" Michael then realized he was talking to himself quite a bit lately when he should be talking to a professional.

He decided to send Steve another emotional e-mail. As a writer, one would think Michael knew better than to keep writing long e-mails. He should have just stopped and not responded to him. But no, Michael had to fix things.

"Dear Steve,

"I am not being dramatic. As I see it, I have three choices:

"1. I go on personal retreat and try to get over you, so we can be friends.

"2. I stalk you until you get a restraining order.

"3. I stay in contact in the vain hope you fall madly in love with me. I never eat or sleep and waste away to nothing.

"I am going for option one, although option three promises a new lean and mean physique! Please, let me do this. I do love you, and I want you in my life for the long run, but if I don't take some time away, I will start doing some weird things and get angry at you.

"Besides, you promised to tie me to the bed and have your way with me. And, I don't want love to get in the way of that.

"Love,

"Michael."

Michael sent it and remembered it was Friday morning, and he had scheduled an appointment with a doctor Sharon recommended, as he wanted to see if he could get a prescription to help him sleep and figured he would get a physical while he was at it.

Michael would not see his e-mails all afternoon, which meant for once, he would not be sitting and waiting for a response from Steve. He had fasted all day, which was easy since he was not eating much of anything by this time anyway. Michael had entered into a state of depression like none other he had ever experienced, and he wondered if he should have told Steve he was in love with him. He came to the conclusion that was the biggest mistake he made. He should have just disappeared, not contacted Steve, and let this weird relationship fade away. As he walked to the doctor's office, Michael pondered ways he could fix this. *Should I tell Steve I'm really not in love with him? Should I apologize for his weird behavior? Should I buy a Hallmark card? Do they make a Hallmark card for when someone falls in love with a fuck-buddy?*

Michael arrived at the doctor's office ten minutes early, and while he waited, he was still thinking about him. Steve occupied most of his thoughts every day by now, and if it weren't for his work, he would have become *totally* obsessed with the situation.

The nurse called Michael and proceeded to take his blood pressure, temperature and weight. Michael had lost thirty pounds in four weeks. Until that moment, he had not realized how little he was eating. The doctor came in for the examination and asked Michael to strip. He was cute, in a nerdy-Jewish sort of way, totally Michael's type with black, curly hair, dark eyes and features, and a large Semitic nose, so Michael stripped rather quickly, thankful for the diversion. After the usual check for hernias and reflexes, the doctor asked Michael to bend over the table for what he referred to as the "Goldfinger exam," and Michael said, "Do you promise to buy me dinner?" The doctor laughed, and Michael was glad he still had his sense of humor, but the doctor was not as gentle as Michael would have preferred. He had a friend who once told him to worry if the proctologist had both hands on his shoulders during an exam. Of course, with Michael's luck, this would never happen. And, this cute doctor was all business.

The doctor then asked Michael to stand in front of him while he sat on a stool, and he performed the "turn and cough" routine. However, he spent an inordinate amount of time on Michael's testicles. Although he was cute, Michael was getting a little nervous, since he was rolling them around and looking concerned. When he was done, the doctor told Michael to get dressed and meet him in his office. He dressed and sat at the chair across from his desk, wondering what bad news he would deliver.

"Mr. Bern, I'm going to give you a referral for an ultrasound. I found a lump on your left testicle. It may be nothing, considering you are over forty, but I want it checked out anyway," the doctor said as if he were telling Michael the walls were painted blue, while reminding him that he was over forty.

"A lump? What kind of lump?" Michael asked with no emotion. Michael never was a hypochondriac, and since he always took care of himself, on the rare occasion that he was sick, he never panicked either. Anyone else would have been upset, but Michael just thought they would see what it was, remove it and that would be that. Michael was also too depressed at this point to get upset about much of anything.

"It could be a vericocele or a spermatocele. Nothing major, mostly benign and not needing surgery. Have you experienced any pain?" the doctor continued asking calmly.

"Only when they are tugged on too hard," Michael said with a chuckle, trying to infuse some humor into the situation. The doctor smiled.

"I'm also going to order some extra blood tests as you indicated you have lost a great deal of weight in the past month," the doctor said, and Michael did not disclose that he was depressed and simply not eating. "Here's a referral. You can schedule the appointment at your convenience. When you've scheduled it, call here and see us about three days after, so we can talk about the results."

He renewed Michael's prescription for allergy and asthma medication and gave him one for a mild sleeping aid, and Michael went to the pharmacy on the ground floor of the medical building at 1145 Connecticut Avenue. Michael handed the prescriptions to the pharmacist and went into the lobby to call the radiology center to make an appointment. Michael didn't know why he filled the prescriptions. He was so afraid of getting addicted to something that he would not take a pill unless he was in a dire condition. Michael had so many bottles of prescriptions that had never been opened, just in case he needed them some day, yet he would continue to go to a doctor for medication he would never take. His Aunt Flossie had a problem with prescription drugs that landed her in rehab, and Michael remembered what she went through. His father and both Bart Shimmer and his mother's third husband Karl Stein were alcoholics, so he did not want to end up like them either, which was why he rarely drank. *Yes, there are Jewish alcoholics, and Hannah managed to marry three of them.*

Michael called the radiology center from the lobby, which had a bad echo. Every time the radiology center transferred him, Michael had to say, "Left testicle." He must have said, "Left testicle," at least seven times before he was able to get an appointment for the following Friday. People kept looking at Michael when he said, "Left testicle," so to spice things up, he said, "Right breast," once to one of the receptionists, which made a little old lady sitting near him do a double take.

Michael wasn't scared. He was only upset because his left testicle was the one that hung higher, which meant without it, his right testicle would look like a pendulum, and he made a mental note to ask if they made prosthetic nuts.

He then went around the corner to the lab to have blood drawn and give a urine sample. They had no problem finding a vein as his weight loss was making them pop, and the only advantage to his newfound thinness was that he was becoming more defined. Michael arrived home around four, tired and actually hungry and thirsty, too. He made himself a protein shake and turned on his computer. And, he had an e-mail from Steve, which said, "Michael, please don't shut me out. Know that someone cares about you – me."

Against his better judgment, Michael e-mailed him that maybe this wasn't the right time to step back as they just found a lump on his left testicle, going for the sympathy vote.

Michael then called him, and Steve actually answered the phone.

"Hi, big guy," Steve answered.

"Hi, Steve. Did you see my e-mail? They found a lump on my left testicle," Michael said to be sure he knew.

"Don't be so dramatic," he said in response.

Michael knew that was not a Jewish response. A Jewish response would have been first to whisper, "Is it cancer?" then to go into mourning and buy a burial plot after consulting with seven other doctors. *Don't be dramatic? How could he say don't be dramatic?* But did Michael argue? No.

"What are you up to?" Michael asked not pushing the issue.

"Oh, I'm making dinner for a guy I met online. I haven't tried anything like this before, and I want to see how it turns out, you know making dinner on a first date," Steve told him.

Michael's heart sank even further. He had invited someone he just met online over to his home. Any more news such as this, and Michael would be walking on his heart.

"Oh, and I've never seen your place," Michael said, sarcastically. "So, you want to come over and feel my lump?"

"No, it will make me deal with my own mortality," Steve said.

How did he manage to make my lump his issue? It is all about him, Michael thought.

"Listen, there is a knock on my door, so I have to go," Steve said.

"Go, go. Have a good time," Michael said, hoping the guy would give him crabs, and whatever Steve cooked would give them diarrhea.

Michael could not describe how low he felt at that point. "Why was I not asked over for dinner? Why did he never want to date me? I should be knocking on that door. Where the hell *is* that door?" Michael said to himself.

Michael sat on the futon, thinking about all that had happened in D.C., when his cell phone rang. He didn't want to talk to anyone, and he first thought it was Steve calling back. Michael looked at the caller ID and smiled when he saw who it was.

"Hi Sam," Michael said, sounding down.

"Michael, what's wrong? You sound depressed."

"Oh, I don't want to burden you with my problems," Michael said, sounding ever so dramatic.

"Oh, come on, Michael, burden me," Sam said.

He thought about what he should and should not tell Sam. He liked Sam, and he didn't want him to think he was friends with a real nut job who got involved with other nut jobs over and over again.

"Well, I had my annual physical today," Michael said, avoiding the subject of Steve.

"Are you OK?" Sam asked with genuine concern in his voice.

"Well, I've lost thirty pounds in four weeks," Michael said.

"What? Are you sick? What's wrong? That can't be good!" He asked and exclaimed.

"I've lost my appetite. I'm just not eating," Michael said, not telling him he was depressed. "My HIV test was negative as usual, and so far everything looks fine."

"Why aren't you eating? Maybe I should send you a care package," Sam said with a chuckle.

"And, they found a lump on my left testicle," Michael said with no emotion.

"Oh my God! Michael, are you in pain? What do they say it is? Are you nervous?" Sam asked, more worried than Michael.

"No, I'm not nervous. If it's cancer, they'll just remove it. It's very curable. I have an ultrasound scheduled for next Friday," he answered as he got up from the futon and walked outside to have a cigarette.

"Do you want me to fly out there and go with you to the ultrasound? I can be on a plane tonight," Sam said, offering to be at his side.

"Oh no, Sam, that's awfully generous and thoughtful of you, but I'll be fine. Really, they're just taking a picture. It's going to be fine. I really appreciate it," he said, really touched by his offer.

"I'm serious; I can be there by tomorrow morning. It's no problem at all," Sam said insistently.

"Sam, you stay put," Michael said. "I'll call you after the ultrasound. Enough about me, what's going on with you?"

"Me, you want to know about me? You have a lump on your testicle, that's what's important," Sam said.

"Seriously, Sam, tell me what's going on with you," he insisted.

"OK, if you insist," he began, "Sid lined up a couple of auditions for me. I'm filming a commercial for a jock itch product ..."

Michael started laughing, and said, "Now that's ironic."

"Yeah, I get to scratch my nuts for fifty million people," Sam said.

"Sam, I'm glad your career is taking off," Michael said. "And, break a leg with the auditions. Listen, I'm going to go take a nap now, but I'll talk to you on Friday, OK?"

"OK, and if you change your mind, I'll hop on a plane and be out there."

After moving to Washington, Michael found out his father was not his father, he had a half brother, he met a man who ripped out his heart, and now there was a lump on his left testicle. Michael really hated Sharon at this point. That was when he made up his mind he was done with D.C.

Michael wanted to go home and never look back.

Chapter Nine

By the following Monday, Steve left for another work-related trip, and the e-mails became less frequent. The dirty talk had stopped, and Michael had not talked to him on the phone at all. He really thought he had scared him off, yet he knew that he should not have contact with him anyway, but he persisted. The depression was getting worse, and Michael was still not eating, and he had started chain-smoking, up to three packs a day. He decided to try to rectify the situation by sending Steve another e-mail, saying he was really not in love with him and hoping it would put Steve's mind at ease.

It read:

"Dear Steve,

"I have come to realize that I am not in love with you. I thought I was in love with you because I miss you so much and was not sure what we had going on.

"I am just confused because we have this strange intimate connection, and I want everything to fit neatly into a little box.

"I don't want to be your boyfriend or partner, just your friend for life. As we have connected in bed, I feel that I should accept that as some new kind of relationship for me, and I hope I did not frighten you with my declaration of love.

"My only concern was that you would get back together with Tom or some guy you met, and I would not fit in the picture. I need to get over that, and I will.

"You are a great guy, and I want and need you in my life.

"Love,

"Michael."

Michael sent it, and after he did, he realized he had gone completely nuts. He was totally out of control. "What bullshit! I *am* in love with him. I am *deeply* in love with him. What was I thinking?" Michael said out loud after hitting send and regretting it. He was trying to undo what had already been done, and now he had made things worse. If he received something like this, Michael knew he would run for the hills.

He waited and waited for a response, but there was none. He chain-smoked outside and went inside every five minutes to check for an e-mail from Steve. When there was none, he decided to call, but Steve did not answer, so he called and called until Steve finally picked up.

"What?" Steve answered bluntly.

"Hi," Michael said. "Did you get my e-mail?"

"Yeah, listen I'm busy and a guy is picking me up in a few minutes for a date. There's a knock at the door; I have to go."

He hung up.

Michael knew he screwed up.

Steve e-mailed Michael the next morning saying he was thinking of getting a dog. He then e-mailed Michael to tell him how tired he was and tired of traveling and sent two more that were about how he was feeling and whom he was seeing. It was as if nothing had happened. Michael told him with his schedule it would not be a good idea to get a dog. He also e-mailed him about his day, since Steve never asked about it.

That evening, Michael received the following in all caps:

"OK MICHAEL, STOP!!!

"YOU SENT ME SIX EMAILS TODAY. CONSOLIDATE WHILE I AM ON TRAVEL. I RECEIVED 37 EMAILS TODAY, I CANNOT DEAL WITH THIS."

Michael was heartbroken. Four of those e-mails were responses to Steve's e-mails. Michael decided then and there that it was over, but another e-mail came that Michael was cc'd on, and it was to one of Steve's bodybuilder friends in Baltimore.

"Hey sexy! Congrats on the new job in Los Angeles. My dear friend Michael lives out there and perhaps he can help you find an apartment, Love Smithy."

"Hey sexy? I get yelled at, and this guy gets hey sexy?" Michael said out loud as he read and re-read the e-mail. All of his hostility was aimed at Michael, yet Steve called him a dear friend.

Then another e-mail came from Steve with pictures for Michael to see. *What is going on? Just a few minutes ago, I was told to stop e-mailing him, and now I'm receiving another one from Steve with pictures.* One was of Steve leaning against a car, wearing a tight T-shirt and cargo pants; in another, he was standing in a field shirtless; and in another, he was standing in front of a mirror also shirtless. Michael then noticed something disturbing. Steve was so much bigger than the last time he saw him, which had been over a month already. He looked more muscular, if that was possible, and Steve's face looked different, too. *Is he on steroids?* Michael thought as he looked at the other picture, where Steve was standing in a field with his shirt off, and he became absolutely convinced he was on the juice. He then thought about the e-mail Steve sent when he wrote in all caps. He was becoming hostile and unpredictable.

Michael knew people on steroids in Hollywood, and their personalities would change so dramatically, and in his experience, Michael was usually the target of their hostility. They had a guest star on *Los Angeles Live* once, an ex-football player, who threw a chair at Michael when he suggested rewriting a line because the football player could not pronounce one of the words in the dialogue. The guy just snapped with no provocation, and

Michael knew to avoid guys on the juice. For some other reason, pregnant women also took out their hostilities on him, but he was sure Steve wasn't pregnant.

Michael's ultrasound was the next day, but he decided not to remind Steve about it to see if he asked him on his own. Steve never did ask him about his test results or how he was feeling. As Michael lay there on the table while they scanned his testicles, he never felt so alone in his life. He watched on the monitor not knowing what he was seeing. Sharon had offered to drive him and wait, but he insisted it was just a picture they were taking, and he would be fine. However, while lying there exposed, he regretted that decision. Michael didn't know why he always preferred to be alone in these situations.

"Well, Mr. Bern, your testicles are not large," the doctor said.

"I beg your pardon?" Michael responded.

"I mean enlarged," he said.

"That's better," Michael said.

"However, I am concerned about this small mass on your left testicle. Get dressed and come with me to my office."

The doctor immediately scheduled an appointment with an oncologist. Michael told him how his doctor wanted to see him to go over the results, but the doctor said he would call Michael's doctor to discuss the results with him as he wanted him to see an oncologist that afternoon. In a couple of hours, Michael was again standing with his pants down while two doctors examined him. The good news was they were both cute, but Michael was not in the mood.

"Mr. Bern, I think we should remove this testicle. The mass is small, but once we remove it, you should have nothing to worry about," one of the doctors said as the other agreed.

"How long will I be in the hospital?" Michael asked.

"This will be an outpatient procedure. We can schedule you for Friday, May 5," one of the doctors said as if Michael were having a pimple popped, so Michael scheduled the surgery.

Sam called to find out the results, and Michael told him about the surgery. Again, he insisted on flying out, and again, Michael told him to stay put. Sam really cared about him, but he didn't want to be a burden. Michael really could be a Jewish mother sometimes, almost saying, "Never mind, I'll sit in the dark."

He called Sharon, who asked to drive him to the hospital, and this time he took her up on her offer. During this time, Steve and Michael e-mailed sporadically, and the Thursday night before the surgery, Michael decided to call him, and surprisingly, Steve answered.

"What's up?" he said, sounding annoyed at the sound of Michael's voice.

"I just wanted to say hello?" Michael said.

"Listen to this. This guy I had over for dinner just wrote me: 'Dear Steve, I cannot date you as I could easily fall in love with you, and you are going through a break up, and I don't want to be the rebound guy.' Who needs this drama? What the fuck?"

"I can totally see where he's coming from," Michael said, agreeing with the guy he never met.

"I am so lonely and in a funk. And now this shit. I don't get men. Why can't guys just have fun?" Steve asked him as if he would sympathize.

Do I really need to listen to this?

Michael told him to go out and have some fun and didn't tell Steve about his surgery as he did not even ask about the ultrasound. It was all about Steve, and he was beginning to see it would always be all about Steve. He could also detect more changes in his personality as he became more self-centered – if that were even possible.

The following morning, Sharon drove Michael to George Washington University Hospital at six for his nine o'clock surgery. They gave him an epidural, so he could talk to the doctor throughout the surgery. Michael could not believe what Washington had done to him. He arrived a relatively happy man, and he would leave a depressed man with a new brother, an unrequited love, thirty fewer pounds, and one testicle. Michael decided he really needed to schedule his flight home.

"Are you feeling OK, Mr. Bern?" the surgeon asked.

"Yeah, it's been a while since I've had surgery, but I think I'll be OK," he answered wishing he could see what he was doing, but glad he could not feel it.

* * * * *

During the summer of 1983, Michael had sinus surgery to remove a calcium deposit that had made it almost impossible for him to breathe through his nose. He ended up arguing with Hannah about having a private room at Mary Immaculate Hospital because she did not want to spend the money on one. She absolutely would not listen when Michael explained they only had private rooms and that was where Dr. Mirmelstein performed his surgeries. Dr. Martin Mirmelstein was Florence's second husband, whom she married in 1974 and divorced in 1976. It was her only amicable divorce. He was also the doctor who discovered Michael was deaf when he was three years old.

Hannah never worried that Michael stopped talking after the age of two. She probably found it less annoying to have a toddler speaking to her. Michael often wondered if she even noticed. Dr. Mirmelstein stood behind Michael during a physical exam and clapped his hands, and he did not flinch or notice.

"Hannah, he's deaf," Dr. Mirmelstein told her.

"Should I put him in an institution?" she asked, which is how Michael always imagined her response.

"No. We can correct it. He needs both his ear drums reattached as they've ruptured," the doctor said. "It's unusual for this to happen. Has he had a head injury in the last few months?"

"No," Hannah answered, knowing full well she had slapped him repeatedly on the head.

Dr. Mirmelstein reattached his ear drums, and ever since then, whenever Michael had a physical, doctors would ask what happened to his inner ears.

The surgery in 1983 went well, and once out of recovery, Michael was taken back to his room, where his mother and Aunt Flossie were waiting for him.

"Thank you for not costing me a lot of money on this surgery," Hannah said.

"Hannah, what kind of thing is that to say?" Florence asked her as she put her hand on the back of Michael's head and stroked his hair.

"Where are you car keys, Michael?" Hannah asked. "My air conditioning is out, so we came in Florence's car, and I just got my hair done, so I'm taking your car."

"They're in my bag over there," Michael said as he pointed to the table in the room, reluctantly letting Hannah drive the Cadillac Doreen and Sammy had given him.

"Hannah, aren't we going to stay awhile?" Florence asked her.

"You can stay, Florence, I have errands to run," she said as she pulled out Michael's car keys and started to leave the room.

"I'll be back to see you, later," Florence said as she kissed Michael and trailed behind his mother to get his car from the parking lot as he had driven himself to the hospital because Hannah was busy that day.

Fortunately, Florence took Michael home from the hospital the next day because Hannah had to work and refused to take the day off. It was one of the few times, Florence's driving was not scary, or Michael was too heavily medicated!

* * * * *

"Did you feel that?" the surgeon asked as he tugged.

"No, I don't feel anything," Michael said as he stared at the ceiling.

"OK, we have just opened up. And here it is. It looks like a small cyst almost like a pimple. I'm going to laser it off, and you'll smell something burning. Don't worry that's just the laser," the surgeon said, grabbing a large torch-like instrument from one of the nurses.

Michael smelled what seemed like burning skin or flesh for a few minutes.

"OK, got it. It looks like you have a small vericocele on this side, and I can take care of that also," the surgeon said.

"Doc, can I ask you something?" Michael asked, still wondering what exactly he had removed.

"One minute," the surgeon said as he continued to work, and Michael continued to smell burning flesh. "OK, let me sew you up."

It only took twenty minutes. *That was awfully fast for a castration*, Michael thought as he was convinced he was now a gelding or at least half of one.

"OK, what did you want to ask?" the surgeon said as he stood up and looked at Michael.

"Can I take my testicle with me? I want to put in on a shelf and ask people if they want to hold it," Michael asked.

"Oh, no, we didn't have to remove it. It was just a cyst. You have four stitches, and we can remove those in ten days. The nurses are going to take you to recovery, and as soon as the epidural wears off, you can go home," the surgeon said with a smile.

Michael was not leaving his testicle in Washington! However, he knew he would leave his heart there.

Sharon drove Michael home and stayed with him the rest of the afternoon as they went over the final version of *Romancing the Capitol.* She was submitting the final on Monday, and he was happy to know that his work there was done. After a while, Michael told Sharon he was fine, and she went home reluctantly. He then called the airline and made a reservation for June 1 to Los Angeles, and he called the man who rented his house to let him know he would be back on time. The tenant said he would be out of the house on May 31 and thanked Michael. He then debated about calling the garage where his car was in dry storage and asking the owner if his offer to buy it was still valid. After spending time here in D.C., Michael really wanted a break from the past, and driving a car that was identical to one from his childhood was not going to help him do that.

Before he had a chance to call the garage, his cell phone rang, and it was Sam.

"Hello Sam."

"Michael, which apartment is yours?" he asked.

"What?" Michael asked him.

"The cab dropped me off on the corner of Newton and Mount Pleasant Streets, and I cannot figure out which door is yours," he said.

"You're here?" Michael asked. "Oh my God, wait, I'll open the door." He hobbled over to the door as he was starting to feel some pain. He looked outside, and Sam was standing in front but looking down the street, still holding the cell phone to his ear.

"Sam, over here," Michael yelled.

Sam turned around and looked the other way.

"Sam, here turn around," Michael said.

He then turned around, and his eyes lit up. Sam was wearing jeans and a blue T-shirt and looking really fit and happy. He ran up to the door carrying a suitcase, and he walked in, dropped the suitcase and hugged Michael, who was wearing loose fitting sweats, so Sam could not see how thin he was, and Michael didn't let him hug him too tightly.

"Careful," Michael said as he didn't want Sam to bump him too hard.

"Michael, how are you?" Sam asked as Michael led him into the living room.

Michael sat down next to him on the futon and grabbed the ice pack from the end table and placed it on his crotch.

"Seeing me gets you that excited?" he asked.

"Don't make me laugh, it'll hurt. The good news is it was just a cyst, and I got to keep my equipment," Michael replied. "What the hell are you doing here?"

"That's fantastic, Michael, but did you think I was going to let you have surgery and not be here for you? I tried to get an earlier flight, but this was the best I could do," he said almost apologetically.

"Oh, Sam, you are so considerate," Michael said as he reached out to grab his hand. "But, won't you miss your audition?"

"Michael, I got the part, I'm going to Argentina for three weeks to film a small part in a movie," Sam said. "But I wanted to see you first, so I scheduled a flight here, and then I leave from Dulles."

"Argentina, wow. It looks as if Sid really worked his ass off for you. That's great. Will you be in LA when I get back?" Michael asked.

"For a while, then I'm going to Montana for three months, and after that I may be going to Toronto. Things are happening so fast. My head is spinning, and I owe it all to you for showing me how to drive that cool car of yours," Sam said.

That settled it. Michael made up his mind he was not going to sell the Corvair. "Hopefully, you won't forget me when you become Hollywood's hottest sexy screen sensation!" he said, happy for his success and very happy to be talking to him.

"I would never forget you, sexy man. Never! Hey, you can come see me in Montana and Toronto. We can hang out and have a blast!" Sam said, hoping he would visit him.

"Plan on it," Michael said, so happy to be sitting here with him.

"Unfortunately, my flight to Argentina leaves from Dulles in a few hours."

"A few hours?" Michael asked obviously disappointed as he was the one true bright spot in the past couple of months.

"Yeah, but I really wanted to see you. I have a cab picking me up in about ninety minutes," he said again apologetically.

"Well, what can we do?" he asked. "I would seduce you, but I have four stitches on my nut."

"We could do the next best thing and order Chinese take-out?" Sam said.

So, Michael called the Chinese take-out on Mount Pleasant Street and gave him directions to it. He even drew a map, so he wouldn't get lost walking the two blocks to get their food. Sam picked up the food without any problem, and he even picked up chopsticks, even though Michael never asked for them.

As they sat there eating, Michael realized this was the first full meal he had eaten in six weeks. Sam had put him in a great mood, and he wished he could stay longer. Soon after they finished dinner, Sam's cab arrived, and he was off to Argentina. Michael really liked him, and having him here for just a few hours, kept him from thinking about Steve.

Before going to bed, he turned on the computer and checked his e-mails, and there were none from Steve. He had no idea he had just had surgery, and Michael was beginning not to care.

Around 5:00 pm the next day, which was Saturday, Michael did get an e-mail from Steve, which read, "I am in such a funk. I am so depressed. I am going to a Leather-Daddies Weekend banquet, and I have nothing to wear. I feel so bloated."

Michael e-mailed back, "Do you want me to call you?"

"No, I'll be fine. Bye."

Michael asked himself why he asked for permission to call him? Why could he not stop thinking about him? Why did Steve only contact him now when he was depressed or angry?

Then, Sunday afternoon, Michael received the following, "I just got home! What a blast. I made out with three guys! I'm so glad I went! Woof to you!"

Michael was heartsick. He didn't ask Michael how he was doing or what was new. He was glad to be leaving in a few weeks, and he also felt it was time to let Steve know how he felt, but surprisingly, he waited until Monday morning to send the following:

"Dear Steve,

"I am done. I cannot do this anymore. I am holding onto something that only exists in *my* head. Being friends with you is painful, lonely and exhausting. I cannot imagine what it would be like to be in a relationship with you.

"I only hear from you when you are down or angry. I cannot have a friendship solely by e-mail. I need conversation.

"You tell me you are depressed then you come home after an all-nighter telling me you made out with three guys. Do you have no regard for my feelings? I have not seen you in almost seven weeks, and we never talk on the phone.

"You said you trusted me and felt an intimate connection, but how can I trust someone who won't be seen with me in public, screens my calls, and won't tell me where he lives?

"If you think I am being dramatic, whatever!

"Michael."

Michael then left the apartment and walked down to 7-Eleven to get a pack of cigarettes as he had smoked his last one. When he came back, there was a response from Steve, which read:

"Michael

"You know what fine! Fuck you! We are not dating. We are not boyfriends, Christ we are not in a relationship!

"You know my schedule and what I am dealing with. You are a selfish person.

"I thought we had a connection. You are a strange dude and you know what so am I.

"If you don't want to make yourself available to me, fine!

"I think you have major problems with OCD. Shame on you for your words.

Think about what you said. Shame on you.

"Good luck with your life.

"Steve."

Michael couldn't just walk away. He had to have the last word, and this is what he got.

He felt awful and didn't want someone to be mad at him. And, knowing he was acting like an idiot, he still responded:

"Dear Steve,

"Thank you for yelling at me. I needed that. I am so sorry. I have been an asshole throughout all of this. Please forgive me. I cannot say I am sorry enough.

"If you cannot forgive me, I will understand. Please know that I care for you and think you are a wonderful guy.

"Michael."

Michael then called Dr. Mikowsky and left the following message: "I totally screwed up. I am a mess. Please, I need two hours of your time today."

He then smoked a pack of cigarettes in an hour.

Chapter Ten

Dr. Mikowsky called back a half hour later and told Michael he could talk to him at 1:00 pm. He then decided to call Mark Greenberg, whom he had not seen since the wake he held for *Los Angeles Live* a year earlier.

"Michael, I was just getting ready to call you. It's been a year. When are you coming back?" Mark said as he answered his phone.

"I'm flying back June 1," he answered.

"Get this. HTO is really excited about the treatments you sent, and they're leaning toward the one about the gay couple with the kids. And, guess who's going to be your producer?" Mark said.

"Let me see ... you?" Michael said, feigning surprise.

"Like old times, pal," he answered happily. "But, the best part is Peggy Martin wants to direct it."

"Are you serious? She's an Academy Award-winning director, why would she want to direct a TV show?" Michael asked with bewilderment.

"Because you're writing it, dumb ass!" he said as if the answer were obvious.

"Seriously?" Michael continued to doubt what he was hearing.

"Jeez, Michael, get your ass back here. You have no idea how big you are now. *Birthright* has surpassed all predictions at the box office. You're fucking hot. What the hell have you been doing out there? Don't you talk to anyone out here?" Mark asked.

Michael realized he had talked to no one except Sid, and they had not talked in almost six months. He had sent the two treatments to HTO a few weeks earlier and heard nothing. Michael also realized that he had been obsessing so much about the situation with Steve that he had blocked out almost everything else.

"I really am out of the loop," Michael said.

"I'm telling you, dick wad! They're saying your show will be the next hottest thing. What the fuck have you been doing with yourself?" he asked again.

Michael then told Mark about the entire situation with Steve.

"Michael, he's Mr. DC Falcon? I can't believe you are in involved with a leather queen in a sash! Why do you want anything to do with this guy?"

"Because I'm in love with him," Michael said.

"Michael, this is called co-dependency. He used you to fill a void, and when your use was no longer needed, he cut you off. He only contacts you if he is down or needs support. You don't need this. You need to cut him off completely. I know, I've been there," Mark said.

"I know. I know. But it hurts so much. How do I fall out of love with him?" he asked as he stood outside smoking.

"Michael, every time you have an urge to contact him, call me! Call me immediately," he said. "And, I can hear you puffing away there. Put out those goddamn cigarettes!"

"But, he would tell me he missed me and trusted me like no one else," Michael said.

"Michael, do you want me to fly out there and kick your ass? He told you those things to keep you close. If he contacts you, don't respond. Call me!"

"I think he's on steroids, too," Michael blurted out.

"Oh Lord, Michael, run as fast as you can. You cannot get involved with someone on roids. Believe me, I know. Ask Gary. When I was first diagnosed with AIDS, they put me on steroids to help me put on weight. I became a maniac. My personality changed, I felt invincible, and I didn't give a fuck about anyone's feelings but my own. Gary wanted to leave me. Everything you have described about Steve is classic."

"He does seem to take out his hostilities on me," Michael said, knowing Mark was right, but he also knew that not contacting Steve would be next to impossible as he was so much in love with him.

Michael then called Dr. Mikowsky at 1:30 pm and asked if he had enough legal pads. He chuckled, and then Michael told him the entire story of Steve, repeating it for the second time that day – how he was angry at himself for his behavior and how he screwed things up.

"Dr. Mikowsky, I should have given him his space. I bombarded him with e-mails and calls."

"Michael, you sent six e-mails in one day. I have a friend I e-mail twenty times a day. If he didn't want to read them, that was his choice."

"But he was busy with work and other stuff, I should have left him alone," he said.

"You know, Michael, you keep making excuses for him and blaming yourself. Think for a minute; would you want to be in a relationship with him?"

Michael was sitting on the stoop out front at this point, smoking cigarette after cigarette and noticing how his fingers were turning yellow from the tar. He thought for a minute before responding. "No. I know that being in a relationship with him would be exhausting, painful, and lonely," he answered.

"Then, Michael, would you want to be friends with him?"

"I don't know," he answered.

"Think about it. What I need to understand about you is why you gravitate towards these men who do not care about you, use you and mentally abuse you. Did he physically abuse you?"

"No, Dr. Mikowsky, he didn't physically abuse me. I would never be with someone who did. If someone hit me, I would leave in a minute. I saw enough of that growing up."

* * * * *

In August 1968, Michael was playing with his Matchbox cars in the den, when he heard his mother yelling from the kitchen after hanging up the phone.

"Michael, get in the car. We have to go somewhere, NOW!"

He raced upstairs to put on his shoes and was out the door and waiting by his mother's red 1965 Chevrolet Corvair 500 in less than a minute. He knew better than to keep his mother waiting when she was in one of her moods. She walked out the front door carrying her purse and her new Polaroid camera. *Why does she need a camera?* Michael thought. Once in the car, she lit a cigarette and started the engine.

"Where are we going?" Michael asked.

"Shut up with the questions, I am not in the mood for your goddamn questions," she answered.

Michael slumped down and looked at his feet not saying a word. When he did look up, as his mother shifted from second to third, he still wondered where they were going, but dared not say anything. Within a few minutes, he realized they were pulling into Farmington, a new development in Hampton, where Aunt Flossie and Uncle Al had just bought a new house. Hannah pulled up next to Florence's white Camaro with the black vinyl top, but Michael didn't see Al's station wagon. They had sold the Chrysler-Plymouth dealership a couple of years back and now exclusively drove Chevys. Michael was always fascinated with cars and could remember what year and car every one of his mother's friends drove.

Hannah jumped out of the car, purse and camera in hand and ran for the front door, forgetting Michael was behind her. She knocked on the door, and Florence's maid, Katie, answered. They nodded knowingly at each other, and Hannah raced up the stairs to Florence's bedroom. Michael followed her, and when they reached the second floor, he saw Doreen, Rona and Arlene standing at the door to Florence's bedroom crying. When Hannah walked over to the girls, she looked in the bedroom and started crying also.

"Oh God, Florence. Oh my God," Hannah said between sobs.

Michael inched up closer, but his mother spotted him and yelled, "What the hell are you doing? Go downstairs. This does not concern you." The other girls looked in his direction, but quickly looked back into the bedroom.

Michael walked downstairs to the den and saw all of Florence's children watching TV, oblivious to what was unfolding upstairs in their own home. He sat down on one of the orange vinyl couches and said hello, but no one acknowledged him. Michael wanted to ask what was going on, but something told him not to ask. *Is Florence sick? Is she dead? What happened?* Michael was worried as Florence was his favorite of his mother's friends, and he was closer to her than his own mother. Her son, Scott, was his best friend, but Scott did not want to talk either. Scott just sat there staring at the television.

Within fifteen minutes, Hannah came downstairs and called for Michael to get into the car again. They drove home in silence as Hannah chain-smoked. After arriving home, she went into her bedroom and shut the door. An hour passed, and Michael was hungry, so he knocked on the door and asked about dinner.

"Fend for yourself, I cannot deal with you right now," Hannah answered.

Since he had learned to make his own meals by then, Michael went into the kitchen and made a peanut butter sandwich and poured himself a glass of milk. He sat there eating his dinner alone still wondering what was going on. After he finished eating, Michael cleaned up his dishes and went into the den to watch television just when his mother emerged from the bedroom. She sat down on the couch next to him and did not say a word until it was time for him to go to bed.

Later that evening, Michael found it hard to sleep, so he got out of bed and walked downstairs. His mother had fallen asleep in front of the television, still sitting where he had left her hours earlier. He decided not to wake her and walked upstairs to her bedroom, where the light was still on. He looked at the bed and saw some Polaroids sitting on the side of the bed near the telephone. Michael slowly walked over to the pictures, and what he saw frightened him. They were pictures of Florence, lying in her bed. Both her eyes were black and blue, her nose was bruised, and her lip was swollen. Somebody had beaten her up. Michael stared at the pictures for quite some time, then realized he better get back to bed. He put the pictures back exactly as he had found them, walked back to his bedroom, and tried to fall asleep.

But, Michael could not sleep. He could not get the image of Florence with a beaten-up face out of his mind. *Who would hit her? Why would anyone want to hit Aunt Flossie?* Michael thought if anyone needed to be beaten up, it was his mother, not Florence. He also vowed never to tell anyone he had seen the pictures and kept his promise.

Michael did not find out what happened to Florence or who beat her up until he was a teenager and Scott told him that it was an accident. He said Florence went into the bathroom for a tranquilizer, and his father tried to stop her with his arm, accidentally hitting her face in the process. Michael always knew it was a lie. That was a beating. He knew a beating when he saw one. That was no accident.

In 1970, Florence knew Al was having an affair. They both had car phones, and she knew if she called his phone, and he was not in the car, the horn would beep. The car phones looked like regular telephones mounted on the transmission hump in those days, and she kept driving until she heard a horn beeping and located Al's car. Why he did not go out to his car, no one ever figured out. She pulled up to the house and knocked on the door, and he actually answered the door in his underwear and kicked her in the stomach. Soon after, she divorced Al. It was a scandal for any woman with four children to divorce her husband then, but she didn't care. She needed to have her life back. She could never figure out why he answered the door in his underwear, and it became a running joke for years.

* * * * *

"I know Philip mentally abused me when I was with him, but he never hit me. I have never been in a fight. I won't scream at anyone. I grew up in a house with screaming and violence, and I refuse to have a life filled with that," Michael said with confidence.

"Michael, why did you apologize to Steve? You were honest in what you said, and you probably hit a nerve. Why did you say you were sorry?" he asked.

"Because I was mean to him. I didn't want him to hate me," he answered.

"Do you do these things because you want people to like you? Do you allow people to walk all over you, so they will like you?"

"I just try to follow the rules. I want to be known as a nice person. I care about people, and I care about Steve," he said.

"Michael, what happens if you don't follow the rules?"

"Someone will hit you, and you'll get punished," Michael said rather quickly and realized he sounded like a five-year-old. And, a light bulb went on in Michael's head. "Oh my God! I've spent my entire adult life following the rules and never wavering because for some reason I thought I would get hit and punished," he said. "I've somehow known it was the reason *Los Angeles Live* was cancelled. As head writer, I never wanted to push the envelope and always cowered to the network suits. The ratings started to plummet, and the show was done."

"Michael, this is what we call a minor breakthrough," Dr. Mikowsky said.

"What do I do if he responds to my apology?" he asked.

"Michael, what do you think you should do?"

"Not respond and call Mark if I have an urge to respond," he answered.

"Michael, you just answered your own question."

"Thanks, Dr. Mikowsky, I'll put the check in the mail today. When can I call you again?"

"Call me on Wednesday at the same time, Michael."

Later that evening, Steve did respond to Michael's e-mail with, "No worries. We should stay away from each other for awhile. It is for the best."

Steve was still calling the shots. When Michael asked for a break, Steve would not give it to him, but now that he wanted one, Michael was to grant his wish.

Michael did not respond.

For the next week, whenever he had an urge to respond, he called Mark, who talked him out of it. Michael then realized Mark was a real friend, and Steve was not.

Chapter Eleven

On Saturday May 20, Michael was determined not to spend the evening alone, so he went out to dinner with Sharon and Wes, who decided not to go their cabin in West Virginia for a change. He was still thinking about Steve every second but was starting to emerge from the depression over this strangest of strange relationships or situations or whatever the hell it was that he still had not figured out. However, he was still losing weight.

Sharon and Wes dropped Michael off at the apartment after dinner, and once inside, he turned on the computer. He had heard from Steve once when Steve told him he saw his ex with his new boyfriend, and it sent him into a tailspin of depression, which confirmed to Michael that he was still in love with his ex and always hoped they would get back together. Michael could only imagine what his ex went through with him. He did not reply to that e-mail, and he discovered that if he did not e-mail Steve, he didn't fret over a reply or even wait for an e-mail from Steve. Michael was proud of himself for cutting off communication with him, but he still missed him, and he knew he was still in love with him.

The more Michael examined the situation with Steve, the more he reminded him of his mother. The obsession with his appearance, his refusal to answer questions, the way he would tell Michael things with no regard for his feelings, the secrecy, the non-responsiveness, etc. Michael had fallen in love with his mother, and as with his mother, Steve did not love Michael back.

Michael would repeat this mantra daily: "He is not your boyfriend; he does not love you; you are not in a relationship; he is no good for you," and it helped. It didn't make him fall out of love with him, but it helped keep Michael from contacting him.

He stepped outside to have a cigarette, and while he stood under the stars, he had this overwhelming feeling that something was wrong. Michael had this same feeling a few years before, and he called Aunt Flossie immediately only to find out she was in the hospital. Michael could not shake the feeling, so he went inside and sat down at the desk. It was eleven o'clock, and for some unexplainable reason, he e-mailed Steve, "Are you OK?"

Michael was convinced something was wrong with Steve, so he e-mailed him again, "Steve, I am really worried about you. Please call me."

Michael knew Mark and Dr. Mikowsky would be angry with him for breaking a rule, but he had to do it. There was no response, so he went to bed, but he didn't sleep at all. Sunday morning, he got up and went running. Even at his now three packs a day, he was able to run five miles. Michael guessed obsessing over Steve helped him forget how labored his breathing had become. Since getting his stitches out on the Friday before, the doctor said he could resume working out, and Michael who was obsessed with exercising resumed his daily routine within minutes.

When he arrived back at the apartment, he stepped on the scale while he waited for the computer to boot up. He had lost over fifty pounds in the past nine weeks, weighing what he did in high school. Michael always wanted to lose the weight, but not like this. The blood tests and all revealed he was in perfect health, but in a state of ketosis from taking in too few calories. The doctor asked if he was dieting, but Michael told him he just wasn't hungry. The doctor told him to eat more. In forty-three years, Michael never had a doctor tell him to eat more, and when he relayed the news to a couple of the guys he would chat with at Results the Gym, they each asked for the doctor's name, wanting the same advice.

Michael logged on to his e-mail, and there was one from Steve which read, "I am in excruciating pain. I am taking myself to the hospital. No e-mail, call me."

Michael called, but Steve did not answer. He then called every hospital in town to find out if a Steve Smith checked himself in. No one had a Steve Smith, so he started to think his initial instinct was right, and that was not his real name. His phone rang, and it was a number he did not recognize.

"Hello," Michael answered.

"Michael, this is Nathan, Steve's friend from Miami. Steve is in the hospital, and he told me to call you." Michael remembered Steve mentioning Nathan as his Jewish friend in Miami, as if all Jews knew each other like the game of Jewish geography.

"Nathan, what hospital?" Michael asked.

"Washington Medical Center," he said.

"There is no Washington Medical Center. I have to ask you a weird question, Nathan."

"What?" Nathan asked.

"Is that his real name?"

"Steve Allan Dean Smith, yes that is his real name, why do you ask?"

"Because, there is no Steve Smith in any hospital here, and I thought it might be a leather drag name," Michael said.

"Well, he said the hospital was on Irving and North Capitol Street."

"That's Washington Hospital Center," Michael exclaimed, knowing the address from calling them just a few seconds before Nathan called.

"Oh," Nathan responded.

"Thanks, Nathan, I'm going over there now," Michael said and hung up.

He took a quick shower, threw on some jeans and a T-shirt and hailed a cab on 16th Street. When Michael arrived at the Emergency Room, they told him Steve was in Room 8 and he had a visitor, so he had to wait, but they would tell the visitor Michael was there. After a few minutes, a handsome man with a goatee, who was about the same height and weight as Steve walked up to him and said, "You must be Michael. I'm Tom."

Michael finally met the boyfriend, and Tom said Michael could go back to Steve's room in the emergency wing. He walked back, and he opened the curtain, seeing Steve for the first time in almost nine weeks. Steve was sitting up with a tube in his nose, an IV, and a foly catheter. He was also crying and reached for Michael's hand.

"Michael, you are so skinny," Steve said. "I'm so scared. They are going to remove part of my intestines." Steve continued to cry, and Michael pulled a tissue out of his pocket and wiped away the tears.

"Don't be scared, Steve, I'm right here," he said as he held Steve's hand.

"Did Nathan call you?" he asked between sobs.

Michael told him yes, and then he stroked his hair. "You put product in your hair?"

Steve smiled, "Yeah, I wanted to look good when I came in." He continued to cry and said, "Kurt is on his way, too."

"Who's Kurt?" Michael asked.

"Oh, he's this guy I met online, and he's really nice. He's painted my home and put up a ceiling fan. He's so good to me."

Michael's heart sank, and his depression suddenly returned. *This was a mistake. What am I doing here? He already met someone online who was allowed in his home and into his life.* Steve actually sensed Michael's discomfort.

"You'll see my home, you will," Steve said, realizing for the first time he had upset Michael.

Michael looked into his eyes, which were filled with tears and bloodshot, but which still pulled him in, and he said, "It has been over two months since I've seen you. That's too long."

Michael stroked his head one more time and kissed him on the forehead. Steve proceeded to feel Michael up and grabbed his left nipple before he backed away. Michael asked the nurse, who was standing there fiddling with the tubes, what Steve was on, and he said, "Morphine and Adavan."

"No wonder he's being so nice to me," he said directly to the nurse.

He asked Steve in a whisper, "Does the doctor know you're on steroids?" Steve looked at Michael with surprise as if it were a big secret. "I know I can act naïve, Steve, but look at you," Michael said motioning over his shoulders and arms.

"The doctor knows, and he knows about the human growth hormone also," Steve acknowledged. Michael was amazed at what lengths he would go to for the sake of his appearance.

Michael told him he loved him, and Steve said, "I love you, too, mister."

As he walked out, he ran into Tom and said, "He's a mess."

"Yeah," Tom said. "He can be a big baby."

"Who's Kurt?" Michael asked.

"Oh that's his new boyfriend," Tom confirmed with a smirk. Steve was upset when Tom had a new boyfriend, yet he had one all along. "Steve's a selfish prick. If you ask me, I think he's just using this guy to get things done around his condo," Tom added.

Michael did not react, so he would not end up in the middle. He then said his goodbyes and left.

When Michael arrived back at the apartment, he called Mark and told him what he did and how he knew something was wrong. Mark said what Michael did was fine as he is a caring person, but that he need not do anymore. Michael then called Dr. Mikowsky, and he agreed with Mark, yet he warned him not to visit Steve and to move on as he would be drawn in again and revert to his old behaviors.

Michael wished he had listened.

He knew Mark and Dr. Mikowsky advised against it, but Michael decided it was best for him to visit Steve one last time to be sure he was OK. The morning after his emergency surgery, Steve text messaged Michael with, "I love you, mister," but he was sure it was the medication still talking.

On Monday, May 22, Michael again headed over to the hospital. Once inside, Michael got lost as usual. He could drive anywhere without getting lost, but once inside a building, he was always walking in circles. Steve was in room 3F22A. *What kind of number is that?* Michael thought. After getting directions from three orderlies, he located the room. There was a sign that said, knock before entering. Michael didn't knock, thinking, *screw the rules for once.*

Michael stood there for a few seconds taking deep breaths and then entered the room. Steve was lying in the bed, with a tube in his nose, an oxygen tube under that, an IV drip and still connected to a foly catheter. He looked up and said, "Hi, Michael."

Steve's hair was perfect.

There were two other men in the room, and Michael finally met Kurt. Kurt was not as Michael expected. He stood about five-nine with a shaved head and was much older than Steve. He was in his late forties and said he was an emergency room doctor. Kurt was friendly enough, shaking Michael's hand and smiling. There was another guy there around twenty-two years old, who had no personality and looked like a redneck. Michael didn't quite catch his name, thinking it was Matt or Mitch or something like that.

"How are you, Steve?" Michael asked as he approached the bed.

"Oh, he is in a lot of pain," Kurt began. "He can't eat until he passes gas, and we are waiting for his intestines to wake up. He was supposed to go to a job interview this morning at the CIA, but they were rude on the phone, and I talked to them, but it didn't help. I tried to get a refund on his airline ticket for Memorial Day Weekend to Chicago for IML, but they were being dicks about it. He did walk around today. I spent the night last night and pulled the other bed over, so I could be next to him ..."

He continued like this until Michael interrupted and said to Steve, "Wow, you didn't even move your lips."

Kurt smiled and was not even fazed by Michael's remark.

Steve grabbed Michael's hand and looked at him. He bent over to kiss him and asked Kurt, "Is it all right to give him a kiss? I don't know if you're the boyfriend or not."

Kurt said, "I'm not his boyfriend."

Michael kissed Steve on the forehead while holding is left hand and said again, "It's been over two months since I have seen you. I was here yesterday, but you probably don't remember."

"I am in so much pain. I remember you being here. You look so good," Steve finally spoke, weakly though.

As Michael stroked his hair, he noticed it was gelled. "You did your hair again?"

"Oh yeah, I brought some product from the house, and we made sure he looked good," the emergency room doctor Steve met online, who apparently had a lot of time off, said.

"How long are you staying today?" Michael asked the new man in Steve's life.

"We'll stay until his friends get off work around six. I don't want him to be alone," said Kurt, whom Michael was beginning to dislike.

He decided to ignore Kurt as it might be the best way to conduct a conversation with Steve. Besides, a doctor should know that he needed rest and not have a lot of company right after surgery. Michael also noticed a DVD player sitting on the tray with a movie playing on it.

"Is there anything you need? I'll be in town all weekend, so if you need anything, I can come over in a minute," Michael said directly to Steve.

"Oh, he got all his grocery shopping done, and I'll be here," the overly garrulous physician chimed in.

Michael looked at Kurt and said, "Do you and your friend need to go eat lunch or something? I can stay here with Steve for a while if you're worried about him being alone."

"Oh no, we're fine," Kurt said. But Mitch or Marty or whatever his name was looked bored.

Michael didn't really care who the kid was or why he was there with the hyperactive doctor, but he was disappointed he could not have a conversation with Steve, as this would probably be the last time he ever saw him, and Michael had to spend it with his new friend and "vacuous-boy." He also made a mental note of the situation, so he could one day work it into a script. He then told Steve that he would be in D.C. only another week and a half before heading back to LA.

Ignoring Michael, Steve said, "Did you know I will be bachelor of the month in *InsideOut Magazine*?" *Typical Steve*, he thought upon hearing this, *it is all about him and his latest photo op.*

"Yes, I'm a subscriber. The pictures will probably look great as you always photograph beautifully," he told him.

"He even looks good now, don't you think?" Kurt, who could not shut up for one minute, said.

"I cannot work out for two months," Steve told him.

Michael touched his head and said, "Good, you can work on what is up here and not what is below your neck for a change."

Michael saw Steve had a bare foot sticking out of the sheets, and he said as he prepared to leave, "Want me to lick your toes?"

"No, I don't want to get a hard-on with this foly in. I got one this morning, and it hurt, and I had to make it go away," Steve said, not smiling but grimacing in pain.

"Yeah, he was in pain when that happened," Kurt who had to be a part of everything said.

Michael had had enough.

He kissed Steve on the forehead one more time, held his hand and told him to get well soon and call him if he needed anything. He also said to Steve, "I want you to know that I do love you and always will." He then said quick goodbyes to Kurt and the kid, whose name he could not remember and left.

As Michael found out when he called Steve's friend Nathan to give him an update the day before, Steve not only had to have a section of his intestines removed, but also the doctor who performed the liposuction had done something to create a great deal of scar tissue, puncturing his intestines, and causing the blockage. In addition, injecting anabolic steroids three weeks after his liposuction followed by a cycle of human growth hormone only exacerbated the condition.

Michael was convinced Mark and Dr. Mikowsky were wrong. Visiting Steve again was the best thing Michael ever did. It was then he realized that although he was still in love with him, he could never be in a relationship with Steve. He did not want a lover, boyfriend or partner, Steve wanted a mother. Part of

Michael wanted to pull Kurt out into the hall and ask him if he knew what he was doing. Kurt had called Steve's potential employer. Kurt had painted his apartment. Kurt tried to get a refund for his airline tickets. Kurt even did his grocery shopping *before* Steve became ill! Steve needed rest, and this so-called doctor refused to give it to him. "Vaysmir," Michael said out loud as he walked down the hallway.

The scariest thing of all to Michael was that could almost have been he. But after a few moments, Michael knew that would never have happened. Michael knew he had co-dependent tendencies and wanted to take care of people, but he never wanted to be at someone's beck and call twenty-four hours a day. Michael now realized what Steve meant when he said, "If you don't want to make yourself available to me, then fine."

Michael wondered if this "Kurt the Quack" would burn out or just hang on for eternity like some gripper. What was he – the boyfriend, a friend, a severe co-dependent? Michael did know deep down that Kurt was in love with Steve and hoping he could make Steve fall in love with him. "Good luck, Kurt," Michael said as he navigated his way to the Metrobus stop and walked over to the smoking area. As he lit a cigarette, Michael breathed a sigh of relief. Weird as it may sound, he was glad to have met the new man in Steve's life, knowing he, himself, could never be that. As Michael waited for the bus, he also knew that he had come completely out of his depression.

For close to five months, he was sick over a guy he could never have, and as it turned out, did not need, and the more Michael thought about it, never wanted. Michael put out the cigarette and threw the rest of the pack into the trash can.

Life goes on.

Chapter Twelve

On June 1, 2006, Michael arrived in Santa Monica to an empty house. He had left shortly after Aunt Clara died, exactly one year before, and really did not realize how much he still missed her until his first night back home. Michael was very happy to be back in California and looking forward to going back to regular therapy sessions also. Filming for *Romancing the Capitol* would begin in the fall, but Michael made up his mind he was not going back for that. Sharon and he agreed that he could do any re-writes from the West Coast because he was just not psychologically equipped at the moment to handle being there anymore.

However, he was excited and happy for the first time in a long time. He had begun eating again, but he was also determined to keep his weight down enjoying the thin Michael to the not-so-thin Michael as he referred to his yo-yoing weight over the years. He also did something he had not done in almost a decade – went jogging in broad daylight with his shirt off, confident enough to compete with the California pretty boys who were half his age.

HTO called the day after he arrived home and asked Michael about the pilot for the one-camera sitcom they would shoot in Los Angeles. Michael had finished it but told them he would have it on their desks in one week as he wanted to make some minor changes. With *Birthright*'s success, Michael felt he had a secure future, even if the sitcom was not picked up. Sid had secured Michael a short-time writing gig with a highly-rated summer replacement series, and although he enjoyed working regularly with this new writing team, it was not like *Los Angeles Live*. HTO promised Michael that if the pilot was picked up, he would not only be head writer, but also executive producer with Mark Greenberg producing and Peggy Martin directing. With that team, he was sure the show would be a success.

HTO approved the script for the pilot and arranged to film it at the end of the summer, so Michael soon found himself resigning from the summer replacement series as he was now busy with Mark and Peggy, casting the show and putting together a crew.

At the end of July, Sam arrived back in California and called and apologized for not contacting Michael sooner as his cell phone would not work in Argentina, but Michael told him that was all right as he received regular updates on his career from Sid. He wanted to see Michael, so he told Sam to come over that Saturday night, and they would go out to dinner.

Saturday arrived, and Michael was so involved with the pilot and constantly on the phone with Mark and Peggy that he lost track of time and realized Sam would be over in about twenty minutes. He hung up the phone and quickly got undressed to take a shower, when there was a knock on the door. He threw on some shorts and went to the door peeking through the window. It was Sam, and he was early. Michael opened the door, and Sam walked in wearing jeans and a red dress shirt, looking better than the last time he saw him. Sam hugged him tightly, remaining around him for some time as Michael hugged him back. He then stepped back to look at Michael, and he realized that was the first time Sam had seen him with his shirt off. They had made out before but never had sex.

"Damn, Michael, how much weight did you lose, you look so fucking hot!" Sam said, whistling as he stood there embarrassed. "Turn around for me, let me see it all." He turned around, and Sam grabbed his butt and squeezed it and said, "Are you sure you are ten years older than I? You look yummy!"

"Thanks, Sam, you look pretty damn delicious yourself," Michael said, "How did you find time to work out on a movie set? Listen, I lost all track of time. I'm going to hop into the shower, and I'll be ready in five minutes, promise. Make yourself at home. There are sodas in the fridge."

Michael went into the bathroom, took off his shorts, turned on the shower and stepped in. As he lathered up, Sam asked him, "So, are you glad to be home?" Michael realized Sam wasn't speaking from another room in the house, but was standing in the bathroom while he showered. He didn't care, and to be honest, he was glad Sam was so close.

"God yes. Washington had way too much drama for me, more drama than Hollywood. I don't ever want to go back there again. I'll tell you about it over dinner," he answered.

"Good, because I want you here with me," Sam said, as he opened the shower door and stepped in.

"What are you doing?" he asked as Sam stepped closer to Michael and grabbed the bar of soap from Michael's hand.

"Something I have wanted to do since the moment you put your hand on mine to show me how to shift your gears," Sam said as he ran the soap down Michael's torso and proceeded to touch him as he had not been touched in several months. "MMM, how many speeds does this gear shift have," Sam said as he stroked Michael, who laughed at his corny humor.

He grabbed Sam, who was equally excited and said, "I hope as many gears as you have."

Sam leaned in to kiss Michael, and they made out in the steam. They meshed perfectly together, and Michael felt so comfortable in Sam's arms. They continued to stroke each other, never parting lips, and within minutes, they both came.

Afterward, they decided not to go out to dinner and ordered Chinese take-out instead – with chopsticks.

That entire evening Michael wondered if he could fall in love with a guy like Sam. He was a nice Jewish boy, and they would make a great couple. This is the man Michael needed to be with, but he knew that in some weird way he was still in love with Steve. However, he wanted to give Sam a chance. In the back of his mind, Michael worried that if things did not work out with Sam, they would ruin what so far was a wonderful friendship – now with benefits. He also never told Sam about Steve, and he vowed not to until the time was right.

The next Tuesday, Michael arrived at Dr. Mikowsky's office a few minutes early and vowed to insist the doctor let him redecorate the waiting area, which was dominated by depressing tans and blacks. It had been a year since they had seen each other in person.

The door to his office opened, and the doctor motioned for Michael to come in. He sat down on the couch remembering the first time he came to see the doctor right after Florence died, on the recommendation of Dr. Sylvia Rose, and how they worked through Michael's finishing *The Girls* as he told him the story of Hannah, Florence, Rona, Doreen, and Arlene. Although Michael liked him immediately, he didn't want to reveal anything. He had to probe Michael to get him to open up, and it wasn't until a couple of months into therapy that Michael began to tell him things he had told no one.

He sat down opposite Michael, settling in his leather chair and putting his legal pad on the floor, choosing not to take notes right away. "So, Michael, how are you?"

"I'm great, Dr. Mikowsky," Michael said, truly feeling better than he had in weeks.

"You've lost a lot of weight."

"Yeah, you know I didn't eat that entire time I was involved in that weird situation with Steve, and I have decided to work to keep it off."

"Is there anything in particular you want to talk about today?"

"I don't know. Everything seems to be going well. I don't think about Steve so much anymore," Michael said with confidence.

"Have you been dating?" the doctor asked.

Michael then realized he had not told Dr. Mikowsky about Sam Jacobs. "Well, now that you ask, I have met someone. His name is Sam, and he's an actor."

"Where did you meet?"

"He was working as a valet at Sylvia's birthday party, and I showed him how to drive my car, and we had dinner. He was my date for the premiere of *Birthright*, and he visited me right after my surgery. Since I returned home, we've seen each other once."

"Wait a minute. You said he was an actor, then you said he was a valet," the doctor asked obviously confused.

"Well, he was a struggling actor when I met him. He left his headshot in my car that night, so I gave it to Sid, my agent, and asked that he talk to Sam," Michael began.

"That was nice of you, Michael, and you did say he was a valet at Sylvia's party? Was he the cute one with the dark features?"

"You noticed him, too? I'm surprised you remember him," Michael responded.

Dr. Mikowsky smiled. "I don't think anyone with a pulse could forget him ... It's also nice to see you're back to your old self, talking rapidly and jumping around from subject to subject. I just need to readjust."

"Yeah, I feel like my old self, but better," Michael began. "Well, I just wanted to look out for Sam. No one really ever looked out for me when I arrived in town, but I like helping people."

"Michael, why do you look out for people? Do you want them to like you?" Dr. Mikowsky asked again.

Michael thought about this. *Did I do things for people so they will like me or because it is the right thing to do?* He really didn't have an answer. Michael went to visit Steve in the hospital, and what Michael didn't tell anyone was that he had the hospital ombudsman and chaplain look in on Steve to be sure he was being cared for properly, and this was a secret he vowed to keep. Michael enjoyed helping people, and maybe deep down, he hoped they appreciated it.

"I don't know," Michael answered. "But, I did find out something interesting when I visited Newport News last January."

"You visited Newport News last January?"

"I didn't tell you that?" Michel asked, surprised.

"Michael, as long as I have been your therapist, I know there are a great many things you don't tell me."

He didn't want to say it out loud, but he was more like his mother than he wanted to admit. "I guess it was right before I met my real father, and it completely slipped my mind. I was in Richmond for a premiere of *Birthright*, and I decided to visit Aunt Arlene's and Aunt Flossie's graves, and then I visited my mother's grave for the first time, then I went to visit Rona and Doreen ...." Michael began.

"You visited your mother's grave for the first time?" Dr. Mikowsky said, interrupting. "How did that go?"

"Sad. It was strange standing there looking at her marker, which said 'loving mother and wife.' I stood on Karl Stein's marker while I put a stone on hers," Michael said. "But I wasn't angry. I just wanted to know why."

"Why what?" the doctor asked.

"Why she was the way she was. What did her mother do to her that made her that way? I wasn't angry. I think I'm over the anger. It is a waste of energy to be that angry ... and I took a piss on Karl's grave," Michael said.

"Michael, that's good. You can't change the past, only learn from it. So, you said you then visited Doreen and Rona ... wait ... you took a piss on Karl's grave?"

"Yeah, and that felt great ... Rona is living with Doreen while they remodel her new home. They haven't changed a bit, but it was weird sitting there with the two remaining girls. Who would have thought some twenty years ago that they would survive all the others, including their husbands," Michael said.

"Did you feel better after visiting them?"

"I did," Michael said. "They told me something I never knew. The four girls, Rona, Doreen, Arlene and Florence, made a pact when I was born to look after me because they knew what my mother was like. They also told me my mother wanted an abortion."

"And you are not angry that your mother wanted an abortion?"

"No," Michael said. "I wasn't even surprised. But I was touched to know that all those years I thought nobody really understood what I was going through, these four women did and tried their best to look out for me. Maybe that is why I look out for other people. Subconsciously, I must have realized they were looking out for me," Michael continued. "They would always have me over for dinner or take me on vacations with them. Doreen even taught me how to drive, and she and Sammy gave me my first car. They even paid the insurance."

"You never told me that."

"I haven't told you a lot of things," Michael said. The doctor smiled. "So, what I really want to talk about is why I am still in love with Steve, and how I can fall in love with Sam," Michael said, totally changing the subject.

"You are still in love with Steve?" Dr. Mikowsky asked. "I thought you didn't think about him very much."

"I don't think about him as much as I used to, but every day something will trigger a memory, and then I start thinking about him. I don't want to be in love with him. I met a great guy that I love, but I am not *in* love with him. Sam is caring, considerate, nice, thoughtful and handsome. He's the perfect man, and he's Jewish, too," Michael said. "I want to spend the rest of my life with him, but I'm afraid that it wouldn't be fair to him if I'm still in love with someone else," Michael said as he stood up and walked over to the window.

"Why do you think you're still in love with Steve?" Dr. Mikowsky asked, finally picking up his legal pad and taking notes. "What is it about him that you love? Do you want to spend the rest of your life with Steve?"

"No!" Michael said emphatically as he turned around and leaned on the window sill.

"You answered that question very quickly. Do you even like Steve?"

"No. As a matter of fact, I feel like Fanny Brice, who said, 'I loved a man I never liked, and I liked a man I never loved,'" Michael said as he returned to the couch.

"But you just said you love Sam."

"I do love Sam. I would do anything for Sam. I'm just not sure I'm *in love* with Sam," Michael said as he crossed his legs.

"When you are around Sam, are you happy or are you miserable?" Dr. Mikowsky asked as he stopped writing and looked right at Michael.

"Now that is the best question you ever asked me," Michael said, and the doctor smiled. "Most every moment with Steve was miserable," he continued, "but every moment with Sam is happy. I cannot wait to see Sam, but I dread ever seeing Steve again. Whenever I see that I have a new e-mail, my heart skips a beat because I really don't want to hear from Steve. If my cell phone rings, I pray it isn't Steve. I haven't heard from him since mid-May, but I still worry that he will contact me."

"Why?"

"Because if Steve were to come back into my life, I don't know how I would react, and I don't want to become that idiot again who was involved with him," Michael said. "For some reason, he pulls me in."

"He only pulls you in, Michael, because you let him pull you in," Dr. Mikowsky said. "You control yourself, and as much as you think others can control you, they don't. You can't allow others to have that kind of power. They only take advantage of you because *you* let them."

Michael thought about this as he leaned forward and rested his chin on his clasped hands. He apologized to Steve, when Steve should have been the one to apologize to him just as he apologized to Bart when it should have been the other way around. Michael wanted to be liked, and the only way he knew how was to relinquish control.

"Does Sam control you?" Dr. Mikowsky asked. "Or do you control Sam?

"Neither," Michael said as he leaned back again. "He has his life, and I have mine. We're both confident that the other will be there. As a matter of fact, Sam told me he also experienced relationships where he was swallowed up."

"How do you like being in a relationship with equal footing?"

"It's weird because for the first time I'm happy in a relationship. Every time, and I mean every time, I was involved with someone, I was miserable. I was always wondering when he would call, did he like me. I was always walking on eggshells, trying to be perfect," Michael said. "With Sam, I'm myself. We just totally enjoy each other's company. He's getting ready to leave to film a movie for a couple of months, and I'm not miserable because I know if I were to call him, he would answer his phone and be happy to hear from me."

"Michael, that is what a healthy relationship is all about," Dr. Mikowsky said. "This may be the first healthy relationship you've ever had."

"So how do I keep from screwing it up?"

"You keep from screwing it up by not trying to be somebody else. You maintain control over yourself without controlling Sam. You stay on an equal footing. And most of all, you quit worrying and enjoy yourself," Dr. Mikowsky said with a smile. "You're worried that you will eventually end up miserable, so you're not allowing yourself to truly feel for him what you truly feel."

"You're right. I'm worried because this is a happy relationship, and I don't know how to handle a happy relationship," he said. "But the good thing is I think this is a first for him, too."

Dr. Mikowsky sat back and smiled. "And, Michael, I think that given time, you may actually fall in love with Sam, but you need to let go of your insecurities and allow yourself to be happy."

Michael left Dr. Mikowsky's office feeling better than when he arrived.

He and Sam saw each other just about every night for the next few weeks, until Sam had to fly to Montana for a three-month shoot. His career was really taking off, and Michael could not have been happier for him.

He managed to get to Montana for one weekend while Sam was there, and Sam was so excited to see him, showing Michael all over the small town where they were filming. When Michael prepared to leave, Sam grabbed him and hugged him tightly. "Michael, I like you so much," Sam said as he started to cry. "I wish you could stay here and be with me all the time."

Michael didn't know how to react. He also knew that he liked Sam more than any man he ever knew. "Sam, you are so special to me, you know that," Michael said. "I do like you, and I want to make this work, but I need you to be patient with me as this is so new to me, being with someone who cares for me as much as I care for him."

Sam kissed Michael deeply, and when they parted lips, he said, "I know. I'm the same way, always falling for guys who are wrong for me, but when I met you, I knew you were different, and I knew I wanted you in my life."

"Now, I have a plane to catch, and I'm going to miss you like you will not believe," Michael said.

Sam returned from Montana in November, and they continued dating until he left for Toronto in December. Michael did not envy his going to Canada in the middle of winter, and Sam was supposed to be there for three months, possibly four. Michael visited him a couple of times, but as he hated winter weather, he was whiny the entire time, and Sam actually found that endearing and kidded Michael constantly about it, which made Michael whine even more and had them laughing all the time. They talked about where their relationship was headed, and they grew closer with each visit, and just hearing Sam's voice made Michael so happy. Although he hated the cold, Michael hated leaving Sam even more.

Michael was driving down Pico one morning in late December after returning from Toronto, and he spotted Anna's Italian Restaurant where he worked upon arriving in California in 1985, and where he and Sam had their first meal together. He then spotted something he hadn't noticed before. There was a Cadillac dealership on the next block. Michael kept driving then he suddenly made a U-turn at the next light, doubled back and pulled into the lot of Charles Smith Cadillac. A short, young, blond salesman with a tight build came out as Michael exited his car, and the salesman extended his hand to shake Michael's.

"Good afternoon, Sir," he said. "This is a beauty ... '66?"

"No, it's a '65 Corvair 500 with a three speed manual," Michael said as he closed the driver's side door.

"Hi, I'm Paul Tripp, are you looking to trade it in?" the salesman asked.

Michael looked at his gold metallic Corvair. His mother's was red, but the exact same model with the same engine and transmission. Michael once thought about trading it in, but he had other plans for it now.

"No, I'm going to keep her," he said as he patted the roof. "I want to look at a Cadillac Deville or Fleetwood."

"Oh Cadillac doesn't make those anymore, however, we have the DTS, which I think you would like," Paul said as he led Michael into the showroom.

These were not the big land yachts Michael remembered, and he was a little disappointed that they no longer made the Deville, but he saw a white Cadillac DTS with a cashmere colored interior, as the sticker said, although it looked like tan to Michael, that peaked his interest, so he walked over to it, taking in the car's exterior design. The salesman opened the driver's side door for Michael to sit behind the wheel.

"What do you think?" Paul asked as Michael made himself comfortable.

"I like it," Michael said as he stroked the steering wheel and scanned the dash. "How much?"

"Well, this one has the premium luxury package," Paul said as he pointed to the leather seats and other features.

"How much?" Michael asked again as he stroked the dash.

"Well, sir, we have financing available," Paul continued.

"Paul, are you going to tell me how much this car costs?" Michael asked while looking directly at him.

"Well with the dealer incentives, it is $44,700," he said almost apologetically.

"Will you take a check?" Michael asked as he stepped out of the car.

"Excuse me?" Paul questioned as he closed the car door behind Michael.

"I said, Paul, 'Will you take a check?'" he asked with a smile as he turned to face Paul.

"Uh, sure," Paul said, clearing his throat. "Come with me to my office."

Michael sat down in Paul's office and wrote him a check for the Cadillac DTS. Paul looked at the name on the check, and his eyes lit up. Michael then gave Paul his card and asked that they deliver the car to his house as he would be driving his Corvair home. Paul's hands were shaking as he filled out the paperwork since he had just started working at the dealership a few weeks prior, and this was the first time he sold a car in only fifteen minutes – and for cash.

"Mr. Bern, do you always do things so quickly?" Paul asked as he had Michael sign the bill of sale.

"Frankly, Paul," he said, "I usually over-think everything. But, today I wanted a Cadillac, and when I saw your dealership, I decided I better do this now before I change my mind."

Paul gave him a copy of the receipt. "Mr. Bern, if you're ever in the market for another Cadillac, please give me a call."

"Thank you, Paul, but the last time I made a decision this impulsively was December 1985, twenty-one years ago, so I hope you're still selling cars in 2027," Michael said with a wink as he went outside and sat down behind the wheel of his Corvair. He patted the dash and said, "Don't worry, girl, you'll always be my baby."

Paul waved to Michael, and when he re-entered the showroom, his boss rushed over to him with an angry look on his face.

"Tripp, if you let one more customer go that quickly ..." Paul's boss began.

"He bought a car," Paul said, as he watched Michael back out of his parking space.

"What?" his boss asked with incredulity.

"He paid cash. He saw the car he wanted, asked how much, wrote a check and asked us to deliver it to his house this afternoon," Paul said as he watched Michael pull up to Pico, waiting for a break in traffic.

"What? You took a check from some guy who drives an old Chevy. Did you run it through the VeriCheck machine?" his boss asked, still not believing his youngest salesman.

Paul watched as Michael pulled onto Pico and drove off, then he turned to his boss and said, "The check cleared, and that's not some old Chevy. That is a 1965 Corvair 500 ... Oh, and Mr. Gasthalter, the gentleman who just paid cash for that Cadillac was none other than Michael Bern."

"Who the hell is Michael Bern?"

"There's a copy of *Variety* in Pam's office. Check out Page Three," Paul began as he walked toward his office, leaving his boss in the middle of the showroom, then yelled over his shoulder, "Michael Bern is only the hottest screenwriter in town, but if you want me to return his check and cancel the sale ..."

"Oh, that Michael Bern," Mr. Gasthalter said as he walked to his own office. "Good work, Tripp."

"Thank you, sir," Paul said as he smiled and arranged to have the hottest screenwriter in Hollywood's car delivered that afternoon.

The Cadillac was delivered on time, and Michael took it out for a long drive, enjoying the feel of a luxury car he could call his own again. When he arrived back home, he parked the Corvair in the garage and left the Cadillac in the driveway, so Helen Epstein would have a reason to call Sid.

For once, Michael enjoyed treating himself well.

Chapter Thirteen

In January 2007, they announced the Oscar nominations, and *Birthright* was nominated for four Academy Awards – Best Picture, Best Director, Best Actress and Best Original Screenplay. When Michael called Sam to tell him, he had just heard it on the news and dialed Michael simultaneously. It was so good to have someone who was so happy for him and aware of what he was doing in his life as Michael was about his. Things were starting to look good elsewhere in his career as HTO picked up the pilot, and filming would begin in spring 2007. As promised, they also made Michael executive producer. Michael also decided to write most of the episodes himself, with Sharon pitching in when she had time. Michael wanted as much control as possible. Peggy and Mark wanted Sam to play one of the leads, but Sam said if he and Michael worked together it would ruin everything and remind them of Lucy and Desi and Sonny and Cher, but then Michael reminded him of Steve and Eydie.

Michael respected Sam's wishes when he promised to do a guest spot or two, and he visited Sam a few more times in Toronto, whining as usual about the weather and endearing himself to Sam and vice versa along the way.

The night of the Oscars, Michael debated whether to order a limo or just drive himself in his Cadillac, but Sid said that as a nominee, he should treat himself. Sam tried to fly in for the telecast, but filming had run over schedule by another month, and he was so upset he could not be there for Michael that he cried over the phone. Michael, although a little disappointed, told him it was OK.

As Michael dressed for the telecast, there was a knock on the door. He finished tying his tie and walked to the front door and peaked through the window. He smiled as he saw who it was and swung the door open. Sam came in carrying a suitcase and a garment bag, dropped them both and hugged and kissed Michael, who started to tear up.

"I thought you couldn't make it," Michael said as they parted lips, realizing it had been over three months since Sam had been home.

"I pulled some strings, and I borrowed a tux from wardrobe," Sam said as he pointed to the garment bag. "I thought my plane would be late. How much time do I have?"

Michael was already dressed and told him he had about fifteen minutes. Sam ran into the bathroom, stripped, and jumped into the shower. He yelled from the shower, "When did you buy a Cadillac?"

"In December," Michael said as he stood at the bathroom door.

"It's about time you treated yourself," Sam said as he finished showering, stepped out and dried himself off. "Did you sell the Corvair?"

"No, it's in the garage," he answered as he stepped aside, so Sam could exit the bathroom and change.

"I just thought of something," Sam said, as he put on the tux that although was not a perfect fit, looked fabulous on him anyway. "Do you have a date for tonight?"

Michael looked at him as if he just asked if he was pregnant and said, "Yeah, I'm going with this hot actor, who really knows how to treat a man."

Sam looked down, and Michael realized he believed him. "Jeez, Sam, did you leave your sense of humor in Toronto? I don't have a date. I didn't even give away my other ticket. I wouldn't go with any man but you, silly boy."

Sam grinned from ear to ear and blushed with embarrassment. Right then, the chauffeur pulled up in the limousine and beeped his horn. He opened the door, and as Sam stepped out, Michael slapped his behind. He was flying on Cloud Nine, knowing Sam would be there with him. Michael then directed the limo driver to go to the Beverly Hilton as they had two more people to pick up.

"Who else is going with us?" Sam asked.

"Two people I have wanted you to meet for a long time," Michael said and left it at that.

They pulled up in front of the Beverly Hilton, and Michael stepped out of the limousine with Sam following. He walked up to his other two guests, who were already standing outside waiting.

Dressed in a peach sequined gown, with diamonds dripping from her ears, neck and fingers, Doreen could not have looked happier. And, dressed in an orange sequined dress, with a low v-neck, and wearing her amber jewelry and smiling literally from ear to ear with her wide mouth and large teeth, Rona was equally as excited.

"Aunt Rona, Aunt Doreen, there has been a slight change in plans," Michael said. "I can't be your dates for tonight as this wonderful man just flew in from Toronto to be at my side." Michael motioned for Sam to come closer. As he walked up, both of them smiled with approval.

"Sam Jacobs, I want you to meet two very special people," Michael said as Sam went to shake their hands, "Aunt Doreen and Aunt Rona."

"What is this shaking of hands?" Rona asked as she grabbed him and kissed him on the cheek. "And, such a handsome young man."

"And a nice Jewish boy," Doreen said as she grabbed him for a kiss. "Michael thinks the world of you.

He has talked about you the whole time we've been here."

Sam looked over at Michael with a pleasantly surprised look on his face and said, "You talk about me?"

"A little," Michael said sarcastically with a smile. "Listen, Aunt Rona, Aunt Doreen, Sam is my date, so you two have to be each other's dates tonight. You make a nice couple anyway."

"Come on, Honey," Doreen said as she put her arm in Rona's.

"Yeah, yeah," Rona said, "and if anyone asks, I'm the top."

They all looked at Rona and laughed. Then they stepped into the limo and headed for the Oscars.

As they alighted from the limousine, photographers immediately started taking their pictures as Sam and Michael walked up the red carpet holding hands. Sam was so comfortable with himself, and for the first time in a long while, Michael smiled for the photographers as they said, "Look over here," and he was getting dizzy from spinning in this direction and that direction. They were the only couple entering the Dorothy Chandler Pavilion without an entourage of PR people and the like, except for Doreen and Rona, who were close behind them. Michael spotted Joan Rogers' booth and whispered in Sam's ear, "Let's see if she'll talk to us."

They managed to get over to her booth, and she had just finished interviewing one of the nominees for Best Actor when she saw Michael. He had known Joan for years as she had done a couple of guest hosting spots on *Los Angeles Live*. She waved them up to her makeshift stage, and she didn't talk directly to them, as she apparently was talking to her daughter who was on the other side of the red carpet, saying, "Mindy, I have Michael Bern here, we'll switch to you in a minute." Then, she turned to Sam and Michael and kissed Michael on the cheek.

"Michael Bern has been nominated for Best Original Screenplay for *Birthright,* which has been a huge hit. Michael, how does it feel to be nominated for an Oscar?"

"I have never been happier," Michael said. "This is the highlight of my career, and even more exciting is that Sam was able to get away from filming in Toronto to be my date tonight. Have you met Sam Jacobs?"

"I know Sam, he plays the sexy delivery guy on *Working for a Living,* right?" she asked Sam.

"And, he'll be in *Montana Round-up,* which opens in the fall and *Melvin and Sandra,* which will be released next year," Michael said, beaming proudly for Sam.

"Please, Michael, this is your night. Joan, ask him a question?" Sam said, proud of Michael's achievements.

"How long have you two been together?" she asked Michael, who froze. They had been dating, but was he ready to call Sam his boyfriend? Were they together? They had been apart more than they were actually together.

"We met almost two years ago, when I parked his car," Sam said, recovering for Michael.

"Tell me, Michael, who are you wearing?" Joan asked.

He was wearing a black suit with a black shirt and a gray tie, and he wasn't sure who designed it, so he said, "Something I picked up at Loeman's on sale."

Joan and Sam laughed.

Then, Sam said, "I picked up mine in wardrobe, yesterday," referring to his ill-fitting tuxedo.

"Oh, who cares? You two are so handsome you could be in jeans and still look fabulous," Joan said. "So Michael, what is your next project?"

"I'm producing and writing a sitcom for HTO, called *Mickey's Life.* We begin filming in a month," Michael told her.

"I know it'll be a hit," she said.

"And, Joan, I want you to meet Aunt Rona and Aunt Doreen who flew in from Williamsburg, Virginia, to be with me tonight," as he motioned for Doreen and Rona to step up to the makeshift stage.

"How long have you two been together?" Joan asked.

"Fifty-six years," Rona said.

"Liar," Doreen said, "it's been fifty-four years."

"Well, it feels like seventy," Rona said.

"However many years it is, you both look fantastic," Joan said. "Good luck tonight, Michael. And, Sam, hold on to this one, he's a catch." She kissed both of them, and they stepped down.

As a nominee, Michael had an aisle seat eight rows from the front, and Sam and he sat down and looked around at all the stars and other celebrities in attendance. Doreen and Rona sat directly behind them and bickered the entire time about everything from the program to the seats to who this was and who that was, not knowing any of the actors' names. Michael had to shush them a couple of times, but they would just smile and resume their banter. He also knew Sam was having the time of his life. Michael, however, was a nervous wreck. He had not prepared a speech as he always found that to be pretentious and did not expect to win.

As with any award show, the festivities dragged on longer than necessary, and Michael just wanted it to end. His category came up during the third hour of the broadcast, and as his name was read out loud, Sam squeezed his hand. Michael could swear Sam was more excited than he was.

"And the Oscar goes to ... Michael Bern for *Birthright.*"

There was applause, and Michael sat there in shock. He didn't know what to do. Sam leaned over and kissed him and said, "Get up. You won! Go!"

Michael stood up, turned around to kiss Doreen and Rona, and Stanley King also stood to hug Michael on his way to the podium. Michael thought he was going to trip, but he managed to walk up to the podium without making a complete fool of himself. They handed him the Oscar, which would not be his, as they would have to engrave it then send him the real one by the end of the week. Michael had won enough Emmys to know that routine, but for the sake of the audience, he looked at it as if his name were on it. He stood in front of the podium and could feel his heart beating through his suit, knowing everyone at home could, too. Michael looked down at Sam, who had a big smile on his face and tears in his eyes as well as Rona and Doreen, who pulled tissues from their sleeves.

"Wow, I didn't expect this," Michael began. "Thank you. I thank my agent, Sid Goldman, the entire cast and crew of *Birthright*, and everyone over at HTO. I also thank four women who watched over me as a child, Rona Sapperstein and Doreen Weiner Eidleman, who are alive and well and sitting in the audience tonight, and Arlene Feld and my godmother, Florence Kennof, whom I wish could be here to see me holding an Oscar." As he mentioned Florence and Arlene, Rona and Doreen held each other's hands as they continued dabbing their eyes. Michael also started to choke up a bit. "I also thank my therapist, Dr. Andrew Mikowsky." The audience laughed. "But, most of all, I thank Sam Jacobs, who borrowed a tux from wardrobe and flew in from Toronto just to be my date for the evening, and who has shown me that there still are caring, considerate and wonderful men in the world. I love you. Thank you, so much." Michael looked right at Sam, who was crying, and held up the Oscar and turned around.

Michael was led off the stage by the Oscar models to the press room, where they peppered him with questions about his career and what he was doing. Surprisingly, no one asked him about Sam. So, he said to one reporter, "Don't you have any questions about Sam Jacobs, my date?"

"Yes," he said. "How long have you two been together?"

"Sam and I met almost two years ago," Michael said. "Remember his name, Sam Jacobs. He's a great actor and a terrific guy."

With that, Michael excused myself, handed the pseudo Oscar to one of the stage hands and returned to his seat. Sam hugged him before he sat down, then he whispered in Michael's ear, "Thank for what you said about me. And for the record, you are also a caring, considerate, and wonderful man." Michael smiled at him, still reeling in the excitement of winning an Oscar.

His was the only win for *Birthright*.

The four of them went to Spago for the after-Oscar party, then they made the rounds to all the other Oscar parties, ending up at Stanley King's house, where Michael received thunderous applause when he arrived with Sam by his side and Doreen and Rona in tow. He was the belle of the ball. Sam and Michael both only had the occasional sip of champagne all night as they both discovered that neither liked bubbly. At around 1:00 am, Doreen and Rona were exhausted, so Michael sent them back to the hotel in the limo, which returned to pick up Sam and Michael. By 3:00 am, they finally arrived home, still sober, and they wondered how many others in Hollywood were sober that night. Michael tipped the chauffeur, and he was on his way.

They were still full of energy from the evening, so Michael and Sam decided to sit out on the deck and enjoy some alone time, as they had not been able to talk since he arrived at what seemed a day earlier, but was really only a short time ago.

As Sam went out to the deck, Michael reached into the refrigerator and found a bottle of Manischewitz

Blackberry Wine, which he kept for no particular reason. He unscrewed the top and poured two glasses.

Before he carried them out to the deck, Michael went into the bedroom, took off his jacket and tie and found a small box he had kept in the drawer of his nightstand, and he put the box in his pocket. He then went back into the kitchen, picked up the two glasses of wine, walked out to the deck, and sat next to Sam.

"Here, some Jewish bubbly for you," Michael said, handing him one of the glasses.

"Oh boy, Concorde grape?" Sam asked.

"No, Manischewitz Blackberry," Michael answered with a smile as he raised his glass.

They clinked glasses and sipped the wine.

"Mmmm, I love this stuff, but I should be careful. I get drunk on one glass," Sam said, winking at Michael.

"Me, too," Michael said as they laughed.

"Michael," Sam began as he put his glass down on the table. "I have something to tell you."

Michael's heart stopped. This was such a great night that he didn't want anything to ruin it. "If it is bad news, don't tell me tonight," he said.

"It isn't bad news, I promise," he began. "I just have to return to Toronto in the morning. My flight leaves at seven," he said.

"That's in less than four hours," Michael said, disappointed that he was leaving so soon after arriving. "At least I got this small amount of time with you."

Sam looked at Michael and smiled. "But I do have good news. We should wrap up in the next two weeks. I'll be coming back then to stay. Sid lined up an audition for a new police drama," he said, reassuring Michael he would see him again.

"Then we can be together more often and take this relationship to the next level," Michael said with a wink. But, Sam remained quiet and stared into the darkness.

"You do want to continue seeing me, don't you?" Sam took a sip of his wine, put the glass down, then took a deep breath. "Oh, no," Michael said, "I know that look."

Sam looked at Michael, and he had tears in his eyes. He then looked down before beginning to speak.

"There is something I've been meaning to talk to you about for some time ... and I don't know exactly how to tell you this ..."

"You're seeing someone else," Michael said.

Sam looked up at him, surprised.

"I've been around the block a few times," Michael continued.

"We met a year ago, and I wouldn't call it serious, and he knows about you, but I swore a long time ago I would never fall in love again, so I told him, I could not be in a relationship unless we were able to see other people, and I know you are perfect for me, but if I saw you exclusively, I would fall in love with you, and I can't risk that," he said without taking a breath.

"What?" Michael asked. "I'm perfect for you, but you can't risk falling in love with me because you swore you'd never fall in love again? What kind of weird bullshit is that ... and where the fuck is this coming from?"

"I know it sounds crazy," Sam said. "I don't understand it myself. I want to continue seeing you, but I can't see you exclusively because ..."

"You'll fall in love with me, I heard you," Michael said as he shook his head. "Well, I'm not ready to expend my energies on a relationship that is doomed from the start as you have no intention of falling in love with me and will do anything to keep that from happening ... Is there anything else I need to know, or is this your only surprise tonight?"

Sam looked out into the darkness again and took another sip of the sweet wine. He put the glass down and looked at Michael. "Sam Jacobs is not my real name."

"What?"

"I'm not Jewish, either."

Michael was in shock. He stood up and paced the deck before stopping and looking at Sam's back.

"Who the fuck pretends to be Jewish? Are you also straight?"

Sam looked back at Michael and said, "I'm gay ... by my career was going nowhere, and I figured I was just another WASPy actor, so I changed my name to give me some ethnicity. I know it sounds backwards, but I needed a boost, and if you knew I wasn't Jewish, would you have called me?"

Michael sat down and looked at Sam. "I guess we'll never know, will we. So, what is your real name, and how did you come about looking so Jewish?"

"Bob Essex ... and I had a nose job to give me a more ethnic look, and I dye my hair and eyebrows one shade darker. It's amazing what a difference the slightest change can make," Sam answered with an attempt at a smile.

Michael looked right at him and said very calmly, "Get the fuck out of my house. Leave ... now."

"But, Michael ..." Sam pleaded.

"Leave before I call the police and have you forced off my property, Bob Essex. Don't say another word unless you want me to call Sid right now and tell him everything you just told me," Michael said without looking at him or raising his voice.

Sam stood up and grabbed his jacket, "How can I get a cab this time of day?"

"I don't give a shit ... walk," Michael said.

Sam hesitated then opened the back door and walked through the house, and when Michael heard the front door close behind Sam, he put his head in his hands and cried.

After a few minutes, he sat up, wiped his eyes and looked out into the yard. He reached into his pocket and pulled out the box he intended to give Sam. He rolled it around in his palm before opening it. Once he opened it, he pulled the gift out and held it in front of his face. It was a key ring with the keys to his house and the Corvair on it.

"What an asshole," Michael said as he returned the key ring to the box, stood up, and walked into the house shutting the back door behind him.

Chapter Fourteen

On a Friday night in May 2007, Michael came home around 1:00 am from a day of taping *Mickey's Life.* He had forgotten about the long days taping a one-camera show. The show was about a mixed-race gay couple, one a writer and the other a former actor, who adopt three kids and live in Los Angeles, so they filmed a lot of exterior shots into the night.

He took a shower and climbed into bed, hoping to get a few hours sleep since he would not have to be at work until Monday morning.

Around 7:00 am, there was a knock on the door. Michael opened his eyes and saw the time. He thought it must be a delivery or something, but he quickly realized it was Saturday. Michael jumped out of bed and didn't even bother putting anything on figuring his white briefs were enough of a cover up. He looked through the window in the front door, and he could not believe who was standing on his porch. Michael opened the door and stood there with his mouth wide open.

"Michael, I can't believe I actually found your house," Steve said as he walked in. He gave Michael's crotch a quick squeeze as he passed by him. Steve was wearing jeans and a green T-shirt, and Michael thought he looked sexier than ever. Michael closed the door and walked back to the bedroom without saying a word. He grabbed a pair of sweat pants and a T-shirt and, after slipping them on, returned to the living room.

"Can I get you some coffee?" Michael asked as he walked back to the kitchen.

"You know I don't do caffeine," Steve yelled from the living room.

Steve walked into the kitchen as Michael prepared the coffee, and he hugged Michael from behind and pressed his head on his back.

"I've missed you, big guy," Steve said. Michael didn't say anything just focusing on his task of making coffee. "What's the matter? Aren't you glad to see me?"

After plugging in and turning on the coffee maker, while Steve continued to clutch him, Michael shook him off and turned around.

"I haven't heard a word from you since I visited you in the hospital," Michael said.

Steve hugged him again and pressed his head on Michael's chest.

"I'm sorry, so sorry," Steve said as he began to cry. "I've been a bad friend. I know. I didn't mean to shut you out."

Michael pushed him away and walked over to the refrigerator. He reached into the cabinet above it and pulled out a pack of Salem Lights.

"You smoke?" he asked.

"I started smoking when I moved to Washington, and I quit the day after your surgery," Michael answered.

"When did you start again?"

"What time is it?" Michael asked.

"A little after seven."

"That is when I started again," Michael replied as he sat at the kitchen table.

Steve grabbed the cigarette from Michael's hand and then the pack. He then placed a hand under Michael's chin. "Don't do this to yourself," he said. "It will kill you."

"So will steroids and human growth hormone," Michael replied.

Steve sat down opposite Michael at the kitchenette. He looked into Steve's gray eyes remembering the first time they met. He was so sexy, so beautiful, so into himself.

"I've been through a lot this past year and have worked on a lot of issues," Steve said as he stared at him.

Michael continued to stare at him and picked up the pack as Steve had laid it on the table. He pulled out a cigarette and lit it. It had been over a year since he had one, and the first few drags made him dizzy.

"Michael, I miss you so much. You mean so much to me," Steve continued.

Here we go again, Michael thought. *What timing.*

"We had a connection, and well, you kinda weirded out on me, and I kind of weirded out on you," Steve continued.

Michael continued to stare at him puffing away on the cigarette. Part of Michael wanted to fuck him right there on the table, and part of Michael wanted to throw him out of his house, realizing how dangerous it was for his mental health to even be in the same room with Steve.

"Michael, say something," Steve pleaded as he got misty-eyed again.

"What do you want me to say? You don't call or write and then you show up at my door at seven in the morning, three thousand miles from your home. I'm in shock more than anything else," Michael said.

Steve grabbed a napkin to dab his eyes. Michael hated seeing him cry. Steve was such a little boy when he cried. This hulk of a man with his tough leather persona was the most vulnerable person Michael knew. If only he had let him into his world, he would understand what made Steve this way. *Why was he so unhappy? What did he want?*

"How is Kurt?" was all Michael could think to ask.

"Oh my God!" Steve began. "He was so full of drama." There was that word. Drama. Steve, the most dramatic guy Michael knew, always accusing everyone else of being full of drama. "He wanted to be my husband. He told me he was in love with me and couldn't live without me. He wouldn't leave me alone. He was always at my house. Always wanting to do everything for me. I couldn't be alone. I told him I needed my space, and he wouldn't give it to me. He tried to cut me off from all my friends," Steve said between sobs. "I had to get a restraining order once he started threatening me. How can a thirty-nine-year-old doctor be so fucked up?"

"The same way a thirty-two-year-old leather queen or, for that matter, a forty-four-year-old Oscar nominee could," Michael answered. "And, he was only thirty-nine? He looked much older."

"You were nominated?" Steve asked.

"I won," Michael answered offering no further explanation as to the category. He got up to pour himself a cup of coffee. "Are you sure you don't want anything? I have juice. I could make you breakfast," Michael asked against his better judgment.

"That would be nice," Steve said.

Michael pulled out a frying pan and began making breakfast while Steve talked.

"So, how are the boys out here? Have you met anyone? Having any fun lately?" Steve asked.

Michael remained silent, figuring Steve never answered his questions, so why should he all of a sudden answer Steve's. "My, my, with all the questions," Michael finally said reversing their roles for the first time. "Not even a how are you?"

"You're right, Michael, I'm sorry. How are you? Have you been well?"

Michael proceeded to fix six eggs and put four pieces of bread into the toaster, figuring he would join him. He decided to say nothing until the breakfast was ready. He placed a plate of eggs over easy in front of Steve, then grabbed some silverware and poured him a glass of orange juice.

"Oh, could I just have water. The acid really irritates my stomach," Steve said as he pulled up his shirt to show him the scar. So much for liposuction, the scar went from three inches below his navel all the way up to his sternum. Steve had also put on a little weight, returning to the man Michael first met in October 2005, almost two years earlier.

Michael poured him a glass of water and sat down at the table, but he wasn't really hungry, so he pretty much pushed his eggs around the plate. He never seemed to have an appetite when he was around him. Steve, on the other hand, ate as if he had not seen food in a week, and Michael realized this was the first meal they had ever eaten together.

"Steve, why are you here?"

"To see you," Steve answered between bites. Then he smiled with those perfect white teeth, although there was a piece of toast stuck in between two of them.

"You flew all this way to see me?" Michael asked.

"No, I live here now," Steve answered.

"Since when?" Michael asked, his heart skipping a beat.

"About two weeks ago," Steve said and looked up at Michael waiting for a reaction.

"Great, now I have to move," Michael said. They both laughed at the comment. "Where are you working?"

"I'm working as a consultant and a writer for a new TV show about the CIA," Steve answered. He must have sensed the surprised look on Michael's face, especially after he almost choked on his coffee. "Yeah, I was actually contacted by a head hunter, who asked if I could write also," he said as he continued to eat.

"What studio?" Michael asked.

"HTO," he answered.

Michael could not believe it. He had moved out here, and now they were going to work in the same building.

"Now, I definitely have to move," Michael said seriously.

"Why?"

"Because I work for HTO. They produced my picture. I'm now the executive producer and writer of a sitcom I created for them."

"Oh my God. We can be lunch buddies," Steve said with a smile.

"You had no idea I worked for HTO?" Michael asked.

"No, seriously, I didn't," he answered even though Michael could have sworn he told him about his association with HTO when they first met.

He sopped up the rest of the eggs on his plate with the toast as Michael watched him. Michael realized then he knew so little about him, nor the other way around.

"All this time, and you never knew where I worked. Steve, we never knew each other at all did we?" Michael asked.

He finished chewing and looked right at him, stunned as Michael was at that comment. "We never did get a chance to know each other," Steve said.

"Correction, you never gave us a chance to get to know each other," Michael said as he looked at him.

"Do we have to travel down that road again?" he asked as he sipped his water.

Michael sat back and lit another cigarette, giving up on his breakfast. Steve looked at Michael's plate, and without even asking, Michael placed it in front of him. He then proceeded to finish Michael's breakfast as well. He wondered what it was that made him fall in love with Steve. Was it purely physical? They talked, but it was mostly about Steve. Michael was never the subject of their conversations. He worshipped him, fed his ego, and gave him what he wanted and needed, but he never became Steve's caregiver. He refused to become Steve's mother. Yet, here they were after all this time, sitting across from each other – practical strangers. Steve ate in silence for a minute then looked up at Michael again.

"What are you thinking?" Steve asked.

Michael took a puff and answered, "Why I fell in love with you."

Steve stopped eating and put his fork down. He rested his elbows on the table and his head in his hands. "I was thinking the same thing," he said.

Michael furrowed his brow and asked, "Why I fell in love with you?"

"No," he answered, "Why I fell in love with you."

Steve fell in love with Michael? Michael knew that was impossible. Guys like Steve never fell in love with anyone except themselves.

"Michael," he began, "I'm still in love with you." Michael was silent and stared at him. "Did you hear me?"

"I heard you, but I'm not sure this is all happening. This is my imagination right? I was up filming into the wee hours of the night," Michael answered.

Steve laughed at him, finished his breakfast and sat back in his chair.

"All this time, I thought you were not in love with me. I wanted to retreat because I knew I had to get over you. I tried like hell to get over you, and I did. I truly came to terms with the fact that we would never be together, maybe never see each other again. Yet, here you are, telling me you were and still are in love with me. I'm at a loss. I don't want to say anything stupid, yet I don't want ... I really don't know what to say," he answered, more confused than he had been in a long time.

"Don't say anything," Steve said. "I understand. You really opened yourself up to me back then and although I said I would stick around, I shut you out. I was scared. I didn't know what I wanted. I was going through a bad breakup then I met you. Then you freaked out on me. Then I met Kurt. He freaked out on me. Now, I'm here telling you all this and expecting you to be happy about it, but I guess it all may be too little, too late."

Michael got up from the table and walked out the back door, taking his coffee with him. Steve got up from the table and poured himself another glass of water. He sat in one of his deck chairs and placed his coffee on the table next to the ash tray, which sat there waiting to be filled ever since he returned to Hollywood a year earlier. Steve put his glass next to Michael's coffee cup and sat in the chair next to him. They did not talk at first. He placed his hand on Michael's leg. He then worked his way up Michael's thigh, but he stopped Steve just short of the prize. Michael grabbed his hand and looked at him then he removed it from his thigh.

"This is what screwed us up in the first place. You cannot separate friendship from sex, and I can't separate sex from love," Michael said.

"So, if we were to have some fun, you would fall in love with me again?" Steve asked.

Michael looked right at him and said, "We don't have to have 'fun' for me to fall in love with you again."

"Really?" he asked almost excitedly.

Michael placed his hand on the back of Steve's head and stroked it a few times. "I told you at the hospital, 'I do and will always love you.' Remember that?" Michael asked. Steve nodded yes. "That should give you your answer," he said. "But, Steve, I don't want that. I have been really happy this past year without you in my life. So, I think it would be a good idea if you leave."

Steve stood up and put his hand on Michael's shoulder. "I don't get you, Michael. Isn't this what you always wanted?" he asked, looking down at him.

Michael looked up at him and smiled. "It was what I wanted ... but it is no longer what I want."

Steve didn't say another word and just walked back through the house.

As he heard the front door close, Michael looked toward his yard and said to himself, "I think it's time I got another dog. Who needs the drama of a boyfriend when you can have a dog?"

The End

Milton Stern resides in Washington, D.C., with his toy parti-poodle, Serena Rose Elizabeth Montgomery, where he works as a writer and editor and volunteers for a gay antique car club. He is the author of four books and numerous short stories.

* 9 7 8 1 9 3 4 1 8 7 4 6 3 *